Ghost of Dark Harbor

***Other Five Star Titles
by Clarissa Ross:***

Secret of the Pale Lover
A Hearse for Dark Harbor

Clarissa Ross

Ghost of Dark Harbor

Dark Harbor Series
#1

Five Star
Unity, Maine

Five Star Romance Series.

Published in 2000 in conjunction with the
Maureen Moran Agency.

Set in 11 pt. Plantin by Al Chase.

Printed in the United States on permanent paper.

Library of Congress Cataloging-in-Publication Data

Ross, Clarissa, 1912–
    Ghost of Dark Harbor / Clarissa Ross.
      p.   cm. — (Dark Harbor series ; bk. 1)
    ISBN 0-7862-2941-1 (hc : alk. paper)
    I. Title.
PR9199.3.R5996 G47 2000
  813'.54—dc21   00-062270

To my friends Basil and Jamesie Stead.

CHAPTER ONE

The steady throb of the ferry's engines was creating a terrible pattern in her mind! The heavy pounding, magnified in her brain, filled her with panic. She was standing alone in the bow of the ferry as it drew nearer to Pirate Island, grasping the iron railing with hands clammy from fear.

Joyce Mills knew she mustn't allow the throb of the engines to dominate her thinking this way. If she allowed the pattern to remain foremost in her thoughts she would soon break into hysteria. It had happened before and she knew exactly how it began. The repeated sound of a foghorn, the too-loud blare of a rock band, the clamor of hundreds of car horns in jammed traffic—all had served at one time or another to send her into a fit of screaming and uncontrollable sobs!

Her husband, Derek, did not like her having these spells, and Derek was not far away from her now. He'd gone to the stern of the ferry to speak to a neighbor about the next town meeting. Derek, like all his family, played an active role in the affairs of Pirate Island and especially of its principal town, Dark Harbor.

She lifted her eyes from the hypnotic view of the waves parted by the bow to stare ahead, hoping it would make it easier to push the throbbing from her mind. There was a slight fog over the water despite it being a fine summer afternoon and the island could still not be seen. She wished fervently that Derek would finish his conversation and return to her. She needed him so at this minute! Panic surged up in her and she looked back to catch a glimpse of him. Fear had glazed her eyes so that she could not make him out among the many passengers gathered there talking.

The throbbing engines continued their malevolent pattern. They were pounding at her because they knew she was weak, that she could only stand so much pressure before her nerves would give way. And they were heartlessly bringing her to that point unless something happened. Something like Derek's returning with his calm voice and pleasant smile to reassure her and get her mind off that dreadful pattern of sound!

The light fog seemed to have become a little thicker and she felt encompassed and shut in by its moist veil. A deep sigh of anxiety rose from her slim, young body and she raised her head high, closed her eyes, forced her chin up.

"Chin up! You mustn't give in, you know," the hearty voice with the British accent rang out in her mind. Dr. Beckett, ruddy and rotund, always seeming to be on his way to or coming from the golf course.

"I'm so frightened!" she'd sobbed.

"Fear like yours isn't rational, dear girl! Your fear is natural instinct magnified into a neurotic horror! You're afraid of things that don't exist, of happenings that will never take place! Do you play golf?"

"I used to, but what has that to do with it?" she'd demanded almost tearfully.

In his jolliest fashion, he'd replied, "Excellent! You and I shall take a try at it one day soon! We have a fine course here at the hospital! Many of my patients enjoy the game! Some of them much more ill than you are!"

The wash of the waves against the bow of the ferry brought her thoughts back to the present again. The fog remained fairly thick and she continued to grip the railing to steady herself against the throbbing engines. Soon they must reach the wharf at Dark Harbor!

She'd been all right until they came aboard the ferry almost an hour ago. Then she'd felt the familiar symptoms, had known she was going to become nervous. Was it the thought of returning to the island and Dark Harbor that had brought on her tension? Perhaps in part. She'd been so ill on the island and at the time of her leaving it so it would always remain a nightmare period in her life.

And now she was returning to Dark Harbor and the ancestral home of Derek, supposedly cured. They described her at the hospital as in the final stages of convalescence. Not quite herself but well enough to go home. That was what Dr. Beckett had said but she'd not felt by any means so sure. She'd wanted to protest and ask that she be allowed to remain at the hospital but Derek was there and she knew he wanted her to leave.

So she allowed them to discharge her. Because she wanted to please Derek. She had let him down so badly thus far in their marriage! That was what had seared her mind and started it all in the first place. Her brooding knowledge that she had failed this man who loved her!

"I've failed him so!" she'd told Dr. Beckett brokenly during one of the many therapy sessions with him.

The ruddy-faced doctor had chuckled at this. "I wish I had a wife as lovely as you. You know you've got a Mona Lisa face with large gray eyes that truly mirror your thoughts. That's how I can tell when you're afraid. Those eyes telegraph the message to me. Your hair is silky, pitch black, and falls to your shoulders. Find me a man who wouldn't approve of that! I'd say you should be a true inspiration to your husband. You would be to me!"

"I'm not talking about what I look like," she said. "I'm talking about the kind of person I am! What is wrong with me!"

"I see nothing wrong with you but nerves," Dr. Beckett said. "You seem charming to me!"

Joyce had given him an entreating look. "Please listen to me! It began so many years ago. Before I ever met Derek at college and fell in love with him. It began with my father's death. You remember. My mother had died in my first year of high school. From then on my father came to mean everything to me. Then he went to Korea and was killed over there. That was when I had my first breakdown and hospitalization for it.

"I was in the hospital then for nearly a half-year. Then my aunt took me out and she was so kind to me I began to feel I had a reason to get better. And I did seemingly get well."

Dr. Beckett nodded. "You jolly well did! You returned to perfect mental health. So why labor it?"

"No!" Joyce had protested in a pathetic manner. "I wasn't all that well. I was still terribly lonely and unsure of myself. When I met Derek at college he seemed to offer me the kind of love and security I needed. He proposed and we were married right after graduation."

Dr. Beckett glanced out the window impatiently. "It looks cloudy. It may rain. We should be out there playing golf now. But you insist on dwelling on every minute tragic experience in your life. The past is over. There is no reason to dwell on it or be frightened by it. Live for the present moment!"

"How can I live happily in the present when the past has poisoned everything for me?" she asked the doctor. "I wanted to like Dark Harbor. I've always disliked islands. But I fought it and I really do think the old town is fascinating. And the house Derek's family lived in is called the castle by the local people. I seemed to be entering on the kind of life I always dreamed about."

"Well, there you are!" Dr. Beckett sighed. "You're never satisfied, are you? Perfect setting and a fine husband and yet you aren't happy. Out there the golf course awaits us and you won't go out! You're a difficult young woman, Mrs. Mills. You must fight against it!"

"There is more to life than golf!" she'd chided him.

"I sometimes rather doubt that," the British doctor had replied.

"I knew Derek's family were against me almost from the start," she'd lamented. "His mother is proud and aloof. And there is that adopted sister, Mona. She let me know right away she considered herself more attractive than I was and more suited as a wife for Derek. She hated me on sight!"

"Now you are exhibiting unfortunate signs of paranoia," Dr. Beckett said sadly. "A companion of mine missed a hole-in-one the other day and blamed it on my blowing my nose just as he was about to play. Another clear case of incipient paranoia, I fear!"

Joyce had gazed at his ruddy face with a hint of reproach in her lovely gray eyes. "You know what brought me here to you as I am? I thought when our child was born Derek and I could battle off all the unpleasantness and build a happy life at Dark Harbor. Even after the doctor told me I could never have another child. Things did go fairly well for a very short while. I built all my hopes on Lucie. Then came that horrible day when she ran from me and before I could stop her she'd toppled over the cliff to her death. I wasn't able to do anything to save her! My three-year-old!" Her voice rose to a wail as she ended and she bent with her face buried in her hands. It was all familiar; she'd done it so many times before. And always she ended up blankly before this wall of hopelessness.

Dr. Beckett said, "So you were not to blame. It was the child's act which cost her life, not yours!"

"I should have been able to save her!"

"No!"

11

"Derek told me that with his eyes the night it happened. And even now his eyes give me the same message. I know that he despises me and my weakness. His lips may form a smile, his words be sympathetic, but his eyes remain cold and unforgiving."

"Purely your imagination, dear girl. Your husband is most desirous of your recovery. He wants to take you back to his island. He's been very lonely without you!"

"He hates me!" she insisted. "He hates me because when I married him I concealed that I was not really normal mentally. And he hates me for giving him only one child and allowing her to be lost. And most of all he hates me for going mad again and being a nuisance to him. Derek doesn't like nuisances of any sort!"

Dr. Beckett had risen hastily. "I'll tell you the end of your story. We're going straight out to the first green now to tee off. Your husband is coming for you next week and he's taking you home with my blessing. You're cured. And you're also playing a fine game of golf!"

"No!" she'd protested, hoping he would listen to her.

But it had done no good. The hearty Dr. Beckett had kept her busy and refused to listen to her pleas. She had gone out with him and played golf and when her husband came to get her the doctor used her golf game to illustrate that she was nearly normal once more.

"I shall hate to lose her as a partner," Dr. Beckett said sadly. "But there it is! You do your job and the patient goes home!"

The throbbing engines seemed to be slowing now. And she peered into the fog ahead to try and make out the familiar outline of Dark Harbor. How many times had she approached its wharf? How many times had she glimpsed its rocky shoreline with the town huddled on a hill leading down to the wharf and the great houses on the high land above it. A gull came flying by close to her head and crying out its hoarse, melancholy call.

It made her start and let go the rail with one hand. She watched as it passed and then circled back again to follow the ferry. They were the scavengers of the sea, gulls. Captain Zachary Miller had told her that. And the lively old octogenarian should know. He's been the skipper of an iron-clad freighter for most of his life and now lived in his old mansion on the street behind Dark Harbor's main street.

The harsh cry of the gull brought back memory of another harsh voice. That of Mrs. Allain, another of the patients. An older woman whose alcoholism had brought about her mental breakdown. She was now somewhat better but not ready to leave the hospital. Many said she never would leave it, that she didn't want to. She was a bitter, cruel woman who seemed to delight in hurting others.

And on this very morning she'd come into Joyce's room as she had been packing to leave. She'd smiled coldly at Joyce and said, "You'll be back!"

Joyce had paused in her packing to gaze at her in fear. "Why do you say that?" she asked tautly.

"Because I know."

"How can you know?"

Mrs. Allain's sallow face took on a mocking smile. "Because you haven't forgiven yourself. You'll admit that, won't you?"

Credit one for the opposition, Joyce thought grimly. Of course it was true. "Suppose I haven't?" she asked.

"There's an answer to that. You'll have another breakdown. You may hold out for a week or a month or even six months, but then one day you'll think about it all and you'll break!"

"Thanks for your good wishes," Joyce said ruefully.

"I'll be here to greet you," Mrs. Allain promised. "Though I doubt if that will make you hurry back."

"You're quite right," she said. "It won't!"

The older woman gave her a jeering appraisal. "Trying to make yourself pretty for your husband? You are still attractive. But you know what he'll see, don't you?"

"What?" she asked, though she didn't really want to hear. But this vicious woman fascinated her and almost made her believe that she could see things clearly.

Mrs. Allain said, "He'll see the pretty vacuum head who allowed his child to die needlessly. That's all he'll think about. And that's what you both have to live with. So I know you'll be back!"

"You're cruel and hateful!" Joyce hurled hack at her, tears brimming in her eyes.

"I'm mad," the older woman said calmly. "Why don't you say it?"

"Get out! Get out before I call Dr. Beckett," she'd said in despair.

"I've had my say and I'm going," Mrs. Allain had replied. "And I'll be the first to visit you when they bring you back whimpering and trembling." And having delivered herself of this baleful prediction the older woman had left her.

She'd returned to her packing even more upset than when she'd begun. She debated telling Dr. Beckett about it but she knew that would mean discussing it in Derek's presence and she couldn't do that. It would be embarrassing for both of them and she'd already embarrassed her husband far too much.

In the beginning no two people had ever had a happier existence. The island thirty miles south of Cape Cod had seemed a retreat. And although she'd never cared for islands—and Pirate Island was only fourteen miles long and three miles wide at its widest point—she'd been quite content there. There was a ferry service each way once a day and in the summer when many vacationers came to the island there was also a return plane service daily.

The town of Dark Harbor had interested her from the beginning. Legend had it that it had gotten its name because the Puritan families who'd left Provincetown to found it had been under suspicion of being in league with the Devil. They were said to have left the mainland so they might better practice witchcraft. The town's main street rose up the hill from the wharf where whaling ships had once tied up. The cobblestones with which the street was paved arrived as ballast aboard some of the trading vessels. And rumor was that on foggy nights when the town was deep in sleep the ghosts of long-dead sailors made their way up the hill with loud oaths and laughter in search of taverns that had vanished over a century ago.

Derek's home had particularly fascinated her. It had been built by an ancestor of his who was a whaling captain as an exact replica of a castle he'd seen and admired in Scotland. It was large and rambling with several turrets and one large central tower. The captain had also been religious and he'd built his own chapel of the same gray stone as the castle on the grounds near the castle. The chapel had a high belfry tower that was now a tourist attraction since it commanded a wide view of the island and the surrounding ocean.

The chapel was no longer in use, but Derek, his adopted sister Mona, his mother, and his uncle, continued to live in the castle. Derek had predicted that Joyce and Mona would get along very well but he couldn't have been more wrong. He hadn't realized that Mona was in love with him and would be bound to hate anyone he married. And even after Joyce's advent at Mills Castle the wily redhead had covered her feelings so well that Derek had not become aware of them. Whenever Joyce accused her of jealousy Derek scoffed at the notion.

In spite of her happiness with Derek she'd always felt like an outsider at Mills Castle. Independently wealthy, Derek gave all his energies to the betterment of the island. He was the full-time director of the island's historical museum and dedicated to the job. So much so that there were days when she hardly saw him.

With the coming of her child Joyce had felt things would be better. She'd feel more a member of the tight family group. But it hadn't turned out that way. She'd had a painful and near-disastrous pregnancy although her little girl, Lucie, had been born healthy enough. Yet her doctor had advised Joyce she could not have another child.

Joyce had always felt it was the discovery of her earlier illness which had confirmed the doctor in his opinion. She'd been able to conceal her initial breakdown until her pregnancy. Thinking she had been completely cured she saw no point in worrying Derek by telling him about it. But soon after she became pregnant she began having odd nervous spells. They continued and worried her so that she'd confessed, first to Derek and then to the doctor.

From then on it had been difficult. Regina Mills, Derek's haughty mother, had showed concern over the Mills strain being weakened. Mona had made a number of cutting remarks about her mental state. Only old Henry Mills, Derek's uncle and a confirmed alcoholic, had shown real sympathy. Derek had been understanding but at the same time coldly reserved.

Shortly after her baby was born, her obstetrician, Dr. Baines, had a long chat with her. He was blunt. "Because of the physical hazards involved and because of your mental state I advise you to have no more children."

She'd stared at him. "You mean that seriously, Doctor?"

He had frowned. "I'd hardly mention the matter if I weren't serious," he said.

Her eyes had questioned him. "Is it my history of mental illness or my physical condition which weighs more in your decision?"

Dr. Baines sighed. "I'd say it was about fifty-fifty. You could have another mental breakdown if you went through another pregnancy. And there are many known cases where these breakdowns then become permanent. I'd say the risk was great."

She'd smiled wanly. "At least I'll have Lucie."

"And she's a fine, healthy little girl," the doctor had agreed.

Perhaps some of the happiness had gone out of her marriage at that time. Certainly Mona and Derek's mother seemed to delight in making things more difficult for her. But when she'd pointed this out to him he'd scoffed at the idea and claimed that this was all in her mind, a result of the mental illness which had returned to her in her pregnancy. It was a hard argument for her to fight.

But her baby gave her a compensating joy and kept her interested and busy. And Derek showed a great pleasure in the lovely little girl they'd named Lucie. So, though things had not been as good as before, they were somehow bearable. Three years went by swiftly and once again Joyce was positive she'd never have another bout of mental illness.

Then had come the most shattering experience of any she'd ever known. Lucie's death by accident. It had happened on a sunny afternoon with her standing by helplessly. Lucie had been racing after a large black cat, Timmy, which was a favorite with them all. Timmy had skirted the edge of the cliff. Joyce vainly cried out to her baby not to follow the cat. But it was too late! Laughing happily and following the cat, the three-year-old had gone too near the edge of the cliff and fallen down the one hundred foot drop to the rocks below.

Joyce had somehow quickly clambered down the steep cliff to reach her. And that was where they had found her. Seated on a boulder with the battered and bloodied body of her dead child in her arms, singing softly to it as she often did when the child found it hard to sleep. It wasn't until they'd tried to pry the body from her arms that she'd become violent.

She made a partial recovery but later had to be sent to the hospital where she'd just ended a year's sojourn. And it seemed she was returning to a world in which everything had changed, including her husband's attitude towards her. She could only wonder if Mona or some other woman hadn't won his love during her year in hospital. He remained kind to her but it was a polite, preoccupied kindness compared to his former warmth. It made her feel he was playing some kind of game, pretending to still love her when he no longer did.

But was she being fair? Wasn't it more likely that the loss of their child and her illness had brought him a maturity that she'd not seen in him earlier? Life would certainly be more sober for him now. His wealth and family position had saved him from any early difficult experiences. Suddenly he'd undergone a quick process of growing up. That could be the explanation for the grim look his handsome face now showed in repose and the coldness which she noticed had come to his eyes.

Dr. Beckett had discharged her and now she was aboard the car ferry on her way to Dark Harbor. And she knew she wasn't really out of trouble and that it would not take much to set her off once more. During her minor breakdown when she was pregnant she'd suffered from unexpected weeping spells and hysteria. And towards the end she'd imagined seeing ghostly figures about the castle.

Mills Castle, like many old houses on Pirate Island, had a ghost story attached to it. One of Derek's ancestors, a ship captain, named Peter Mills, who was rumored to have made a fortune in the slave trade, had returned to the castle after a voyage to find his beloved young wife romantically involved with a neighbor. Insanely jealous, he killed his wife in a quarrel. Afterward he hung himself in the cellar. Legend had it that ever since his phantom, a ghostly figure in the captain's cap and uniform of a century earlier, had stalked the castle. It had been one of Joyce's delusions that she'd several times seen the phantom of Captain Mills.

The fog ahead lifted a little and she was able to see the island. Within ten minutes they would be safely wharfed at Dark Harbor and the ordeal she was experiencing from the engines would be at an end. She knew it was ridiculous of her to allow them to cause this turmoil in her mind, but knowing wasn't enough. Her nerves were still so bad that she had no proper control over them.

She leaned against the railing again, trying to ignore the tormenting throbbing. Gradually the outline of the island coast became clearer. She could see the cove and the cluster of houses that marked the town of Dark Harbor. Far to the right on the distant cliffs was the castle and just beyond it the chapel with its tall belfry tower.

"You're looking very serious!" Derek commented as he returned to her side.

She turned to look up into his sober, tanned face. "I'm glad you've come back. I was getting a little jumpy."

The keen brown eyes in his handsome face showed surprise and concern. "But I only left you for a few minutes!"

"I know."

"And I wasn't more than twenty feet away from you. You could have called to me if you'd wished!" His curly brown hair was blowing in the wind.

"I didn't want to do that."

His arm went around her. "Were you really nervous?" His tone was too carefully controlled to hide his obvious fear.

She nodded. "I'm afraid so. You know how it is with any kind of pounding noise. Just now it's the ship's engines I felt I couldn't bear!"

He frowned at this. "The thing I never will know is why you allow sounds like the engine throbbing to bother you when you realize that they are just that, an annoyance. Why do you let them send you off?"

"You're ignoring the entire problem of nervous illness," she said. "Knowing what drives me to spells doesn't help me from taking them. It is my sickness which lets me down, not my knowing that I am ill. I know I have this weakness and I can't help it!"

Derek looked unhappy. "I'm afraid that's too involved for me."

"You've never known anyone ill in this way before," she pointed out. "So it's all new to you."

"Yes, I agree with you there. None of my family have ever shown the slightest mental instability." He hesitated. "Unless you consider Uncle Henry's alcoholism a mental illness."

"Dr. Beckett would consider it so. And most authorities would agree," she said. "I think you're far too quick to claim you have no mental illness in your family. I think you could well have without really knowing. What about that ancestor of yours who killed his wife and hung himself?"

Her husband smiled grimly. "Captain Mills! But then he is your ghost. You are the one who claimed to have seen him before you went to the hospital."

Joyce gave him a reproving look. "Sorry. It has no humor for me."

Derek at once showed himself penitent. "That was stupid of me," he said. "Forgive me!"

She turned to glance at the shore and saw they were nearing the wharves of Dark Harbor. Since it was mid-July the water was full of pleasure craft of all kinds and sizes. The colorful boats had sails and flags of almost every color. She'd often used to watch them from the grounds of the castle. Now they were leaving a wide path for the big car ferry as it slowly headed for its own wharf.

There were lots of cars and people around the docks and the main street seemed busy enough. The fog had vanished and it was a warm, pleasant day with the sun turning the waves to silver. The throb of the engines slackened as the ferry slowly coasted in.

Derek asked her, "Is that better?"

"Much," she said. "I've only just thought of it. But I've kept you from the museum and your work during the busiest part of the summer."

"Only for a couple of days," he said casually. "We are busy because we're trying to catalogue our book collection and registry of Pirate Island shipping at the very season when we have the most visitors."

"I'm sure you must have more work than you can do," she said, studying him sympathetically.

He smiled in the manner of a father tolerating his child's comments. "I have Brook Patterson as my assistant and he's a hard worker and able to take over when I'm away."

She recalled the slight, balding man with a rather ineffectual manner who had married into one of the island's wealthy families. People wondered what his wife, Faith, a volatile blonde, had ever found in the young man to attract her. Her family had found him a position in the island museum and he'd shown an aptitude for the work until now he was second only to Derek.

She said, "Brook is very dependable."

Derek smiled. "True. And I'll surprise you. Knowing we are short of help for the cataloguing, his wife, Faith, has come down to work with us for the summer."

"It's usually nothing but tennis and the beach for her all summer long!" Joyce said in surprise. "That's an impressive change of heart."

"I agree," he said. "Still, I'm grateful to her. Of course she may tire of it before the summer is over. Just now it's a novelty for her."

Joyce said, "Any other changes in the staff?"

"No. But we have a young man doing a series of sketches of early sailing vessels for us. He's a specialist in marine paintings and is living on the island for the summer. So we've hired him part time to do the paintings and help in the mounting of them for a permanent show."

"Sounds like an important project," she said.

"It is."

"What's his name?"

"David Chase, he hails from Boston," her husband said. "You'll meet him as he's living at the castle. I persuaded mother to let him have a room. He also has a shack down the beach and once in a while on fine nights he stays down there. He often works there in the day time because it's quiet. But most of the time he's at the castle."

"I'm surprised your mother would consent to have a paying guest in the house," she said.

Derek laughed. "I got around her by having him pay her board and then having her turn it over to her favorite island charity."

"A marvelous diplomatic triumph!"

"I think so. You'll like Chase. He's a quiet sort of fellow yet friendly when you get to know him. He's not one to talk much about himself and his past work but he comes to us well recommended."

"He sounds pleasant."

"He is," Derek agreed as they neared the wharf and the ferry bumped against the pilings with their smell of sour, salt water. He said, "We must be ready to get the car now."

"I know," she said, bothered by the sound and action around her. She clung close to Derek and tried not to pay to much attention to it.

The ferry docked and they walked ashore and waited for the cars to be run up a ramp from the lower part of the ship. Members of the crew, specially trained for the job, brought the cars off. They waited rather impatiently for perhaps ten minutes and then Derek's green hardtop came shooting up the ramp and over to where the line of cars were located. Derek gave the crewman a tip and then opened the car door for her. She got in rather gratefully, somehow feeling more protected.

Derek took his place at the wheel and started the car. They drove slowly until they had left the confusion of people and cars gathered on the wharf behind them. He headed up the main street with its clutter of weathered gray one story buildings. An occasional neon sign showed but the island's council had discouraged too many of the gaudy electric signs.

She stared out at the buildings and the people on the sidewalk. The car rolled on up the cobblestone street. She said, "Nothing seems to have changed a great deal."

"We're having a healthy crop of tourists this year," her

husband said as he drove on.

They passed the lane which led from the main street to the quiet street beyond where Captain Zachary Miller lived. She said, "How is Captain Miller?"

"He must be all right," Derek said. "I've seen him in the museum once or twice in the last month."

Now they drove by one of the few buildings with a neon sign. It housed an ancient tavern and inn and was known as the Gray Heron. She recalled that a dour, elderly man by the name of Matthew Kimble owned and operated it. His great-grandfather had suddenly appeared on the island one day and gone straight to the single island bank. He let the manager know he'd made a fortune in the California gold fields after deserting the whaler of which he'd been a crew member. And he'd announced his wish to settle down and open an inn and tavern there.

He'd done so and his descendants had continued to operate it. Matthew Kimble himself had an evil reputation. When his parents were alive and managing the tavern he went to live and work on the mainland. While he was gone his father died. He committed some crime there for which he spent several years in prison. Some time later he returned one stormy night and immediately stepped behind the bar to serve drinks to the amazement of the few gathered there. It was his signal that he'd come back to his birthright. He remained and took over full control of the inn from his ailing mother.

She asked, "What about Matthew Kimble?"

"Almost lost his license for selling after closing time," Derek said. "The case wasn't proven so he got off. But they warned him."

"So he hasn't changed," she said.

"No."

This at once made her think of the other rebel on the island. A wealthy playboy who had a mansion in what had once been a monastery that took care of lepers. A ship had been wrecked off the coast of the island in the early days and a number of the crew who escaped drowning were found to be afflicted with leprosy. The dread disease was passed on to many of the villagers and made dreadful inroads in that section of the island. A religious order had offered to build a monastery and care for the lepers and for years it remained an active institution. Then, as the original patient died, the monks had disposed of the building. It was later converted into a luxurious home by one of the early, marauding railroad barons.

The mansion was said to be both haunted and cursed. But the latest owner, a New York playboy, enjoyed the reputation of the place. He dabbled in Satanism and lived there with a group of hippie type devotees, including a circle of lovely young girls. Dark Harbor had lately been stirred by tales of strange rituals and drug orgies taking place there. But the island's single police constable, Titus Frink, had always insisted these reports were exaggerated.

She immediately asked Derek, "What's happening up at the monastery?" Everyone still referred to the mansion as the monastery.

He shook his head grimly. "There have been a strange crew going and coming from there all summer. I wish that fellow would sell out and get off the island. The council have made an offer for the place for a second historical museum but he doesn't seem interested."

Now they left the village and drove along the dirt road that would eventually lead them to the castle. As she began this last lap of her journey she felt the familiar panic surge up in her once again.

In a voice more taut than before, she asked, "What about things at the house? Are they the same?"

Derek kept his eyes on the road. "I told you about the artist, David Chase, who is living there."

"Yes."

"Mona is working on a new romance," he went on. "Her last book had an excellent sale and her publisher is interested in more."

"I'm glad," she quietly.

He gave her a rather urgent glance. "I hope you honestly mean that. I think one of the first signs of your mental illness was when you began suspecting Mona of all sorts of evil."

"I don't remember," she said.

"I'm afraid I do," her husband replied bitterly. "Mona is a very decent person. You shouldn't feel any animosity towards her."

She glanced at his handsome profile, grim as he concentrated on the wheel. "How does she feel about me?"

He glanced at her quickly. "I'm sure she is sorry for you."

"Oh, that's it," she said. "She is sorry for me. I would have hoped that she might like me."

"I take that for granted," her young husband said impatiently.

"Can you?"

He frowned. "I'm not sure I like this line of conversation. I hope you're not going to be difficult."

"You and Dr. Beckett are the ones who decided I was better," she said with grim humor.

"And so you are," he replied at once. "Just don't start brooding about Mona."

"I promise you I shan't," she said, glancing out at the ocean as they drove along the cliffs.

"Mother talked to me about you last night," Derek went on.

"Did she?"

"Yes. She wanted to be sure that you were really well and I went all out in promising that you were. So you mustn't let me down. I'm depending on you."

"Very well, Derek," she said meekly.

"Because Mother is a strong woman she can't understand weakness in anyone else," he pointed out.

"And I am weak in her eyes."

Derek looked pained. "You must make allowances for Mother," he said.

"Yes. I must," she said with a sigh. She was trembling again. This conversation was not good for her.

"Uncle Henry putters with his stamp collection, does a little boating and still drinks as much as ever," Derek said. "But you and he always seemed to get along well. You got along with him better than anyone else in the house."

She smiled wanly. "A case of two weak vessels meeting."

"Don't!" Derek begged her as he turned the car off the main road to the long private roadway that led to the castle and the chapel. It was marked for the benefit of tourists who came during the day to visit the belfry.

Joyce closed her eyes and clenched her teeth so they ground together. Once again she worried whether she could make it or not. The first few minutes were bound to be an ordeal. If she could only manage them perhaps the rest would be better.

She opened her eyes as the car came to a halt before the front entrance. Derek came around to open her door and help her out.

"Welcome home," he said, with a nervous smile.

"Thank you." She tried to match his smile with one of her own and was only moderately successful.

"I'll get your things from the trunk," he said. And he left her to go and unlock the car trunk.

She stood there taking in all the atmosphere of the place. The towering graystone mansion, the broad front lawn reaching to the cliff, and the ocean beyond. It was so familiar, yet she didn't feel at ease there. Not any more than she ever had.

But there was no one around and that was helpful. If she just could get into the house without meeting anyone she would be all right. Then she could lie down and rest a little and take one of her tablets. By the time she made the mandatory appearance at dinner that Regina Mills would surely insist upon she might be able to control herself.

These thoughts were running through her mind when she suddenly felt something brush against her ankle. She glanced down and then in spite of all her good resolutions she screamed loudly.

CHAPTER TWO

It was Timmy.

Timmy, the huge black cat, who had played such a major role in the tragic accident which had caused her child's death. Since the death of Lucie she'd not been able to bear having the cat near her. Now it pressed against her legs as she screamed and stepped back quickly.

The cat took alarm and ran off as Derek came to her with an almost angry look. "What was that all about?" he demanded.

She pointed where the cat had vanished around the building. "It was Timmy! Rubbing against me!"

"You screamed like that because of Timmy?"

"I couldn't help it," she said, unhappily. "I can't bear to even look at that cat!"

He frowned. "You can't blame a dumb animal for Lucie's death. If you hadn't let her go free of her harness she wouldn't have been able to follow it to the cliff's edge!"

"I know!" she gasped, her eyes blurring with tears.

He grasped her arm at once, apologetic as he said, "I didn't mean to say that. It came out in anger. I feel as badly about what happened to Lucie as you do but I can't allow myself to go mad over it. Nor can I put the blame on a poor, simple cat!"

She bowed her head. "Yes. It was stupid of me! But the cat startled me and I reacted automatically!"

He gave her a stony look. "Your usual way of reacting it seems."

"I'm sorry."

"It's all right," he said. "I'll tell the cook to keep Timmy around the kitchen and the rear of the house as much as possible."

She gave her husband a pleading look. "Could you possibly find a good home for him somewhere else?"

Derek's face had become stony. He said. "You must know that is out of the question. Timmy is Mother's cat."

"I'd forgotten. You think she would mind?"

"I'm certain of it," was his reply. He left her to get her baggage from the rear of the car and then returned to her with a suitcase in each hand.

They started up the steps to the front door. But as they did the door opened and a tall, arrogant-looking woman with hair dyed in the blue shade affected by some older women faced them. Her eyes were almost the same shade as her hair and the liveliest feature of her narrow face.

"Did I hear a scream out here?" she asked haughtily in a Boston accent.

Derek spoke up quickly, "Yes. I'm afraid Joyce had a scare."

"A scare?" Regina Mills lifted her eyebrows.

"Yes. Timmy came up to her," he said.

His mother looked perplexed. "My Timmy? I don't understand. Why should he make her scream like that?"

From somewhere within her desperation Joyce found the strength to reply. She said, "I felt the cat at my ankle. He startled me. I've been afraid of him for some time."

The older woman's eyes flashed their annoyance. "Afraid of poor Timmy?"

Standing with the bags still in his hands Derek said unhappily, "You must know the reason, Mother!"

Regina Mills adamantly blocked their way by remaining in the doorway. "I can't pretend that I do. But then I suppose I am not as sensitive as either of you."

Trembling, Joyce said, "It's Lucie! I always feel the cat led Lucie to her death! I know it's silly but I can't help it!"

Her mother-in-law eyed her with distaste. "At least you admit your attitude is silly and I must say that I couldn't agree with you more. You screamed in that wild fashion because of such feelings!"

Derek took a step forward. "We must go inside. Joyce is tired. This has been a difficult trip for her. She needs rest."

Regina stepped back to make way for them. And as Joyce passed her, she said. "I must say the hospital agreed with you. You look much better than when you left."

"Thank you," she said weakly, continuing on to the stairs and up them.

From behind her she heard her husband telling his mother, "You have to have some consideration for Joyce! She's not fully recovered yet. She'll need help!"

Regina Mills replied grimly and loud enough for her to hear. "I know that. The girl was mad long before she met and married you!"

Joyce rushed to the room she shared with Derek, not wanting to hear anything else her mother-in-law might have to say. She was terrified that she'd break down again at once. That she wouldn't be able to remain in the castle. She reached the door of their room and tried the handle. It wouldn't turn. The door was locked.

She couldn't understand it! She stood there in the shadowed hall leaning weakly against the door. The whole thing had begun in the worst possible way. She'd demeaned herself once again before her arrogant mother-in-law. And now she couldn't even get the door to her own room open. Would she be able to cope on the outside at all? Had Mrs. Allain at the hospital been right? Would she have to return there?

Derek's footsteps sounded on the hardwood of the corridor floor and she could tell he was hurrying to join her. When he caught up with her she saw the embarrassed expression on his tanned face.

"Sorry I fell behind," he said.

"I understand why."

He sighed. "Joyce, I see you've come to the wrong door."

"Wrong door?"

He looked apologetic. "I know that was our room but I feel we'd be better off somewhere else. Somewhere with less memories and where you'll have a better chance to rest."

She was staring at him. "Go on."

"Don't try to make everything difficult," he groaned. "Mother has arranged new quarters for us farther down the hall. The rooms are a little smaller but we'll have two of them. And I'm sure you'll be happier there."

"Do I have any choice?"

He looked dismal. "We have moved everything down there and cleared our old room of furniture and locked it. It seemed a good way to turn a key on the past."

Joyce listened to all this with growing disbelief. "Is that what we are going to do?"

"Joyce! It's for your good!"

She arched an eyebrow. "Oh, you didn't tell me."

"Joyce!" he implored her.

"Well," she said, "since you and your mother have it all so nicely planned it would be mean of me to do anything to upset it. Let us go on to our new rooms."

"Now you're behaving more like yourself," he said with obvious relief. "I'll lead the way."

She followed him down a few doors to what she remembered as being guest rooms. They were small as she recalled, but they did have a view of the ocean.

Derek put down the suitcase in his right hand as he reached the door of one of them and opened it. He picked up the suitcase and went in. "This will be your room," he told her. "All your things are in here. I spent a lot of time placing them in the dresser drawers and the closets."

She followed him in. "My room?" she questioned him.

He had put down the baggage and now his face crimsoned. He said, "Of course I have the adjoining room so we will essentially be together." He went to the connecting door between the rooms and opened it for her to see that it was unlocked.

"Essentially," she said in a quiet voice. "But actually we are each going to have our own rooms."

"I thought after being on your own at the hospital you'd appreciate it," he said, looking unhappy.

She nodded. "I can think of nights at the hospital when I actually dreamt of our old room and that wonderful big bed. Knowing I had only to reach out and you'd be there. I'm sure that after Lucie's death I would have collapsed long before I did if it hadn't been for the closeness between us."

Derek came to her earnestly and took her by the arms. "Joyce, you know I've done this only because I wanted to help you!"

"Was it your idea?"

He hesitated. "Yes. Oh, I did discuss it with Mother and she felt it the proper thing, but I'd already considered it."

"I see," she said with a sigh.

"Joyce!" his tone was again plaintive and he drew her to him for a long moment and kissed her tenderly on the lips.

She returned the kiss, knowing that basically Derek loved her. It was a combination of his bewilderment at her illness and the pressures from the others in the family that had made him seemingly let her down. She would have to be forgiving and patient and perhaps even this could be worked out.

When he released her, she said, "Well, I guess we can manage this way for a while. But I do look forward to having our old room again."

He stared at her worriedly. "There'll be no problem. Though I do wonder whether this house is going to be good for you. There are so many memories and many of them bad ones."

Joyce gave him a very direct look. "You're thinking about Lucie and our losing her here. Dr. Beckett had long discussions with me about that. His view is that the loss would be as hard to bear anywhere else as here where it happened. And that the good memories here might actually sustain us until time has passed and our first grief is blunted. That's another lesson he drilled into me. Hold on long enough and time does dull the edge of pain."

Derek nodded. "I actually know very little of the treatment you were given. His opinions sound practical, I must say."

She offered him a bitter smile. "Being in the looney bin does have some advantages."

Derek's sensitive face showed distress. "Don't talk that way. Especially not before the family. We want to forget all that."

"I'll behave," she promised.

"You won't remember," he said. "But things were pretty bad before you left here. You were seeing ghosts and at times you were brutally frank in what you said to some of the others. So you may find them a little stand-offish until you've won their confidence again."

Joyce gave her husband a mocking glance. "Do you think I'll ever manage to do that?"

"Of course," he said, but there was a lamentable lack of

conviction in his tone. "By the way. I don't know whether you've noticed it or not, but there is a new swimming pool at the garden end of the house. I hope you enjoy it."

"It sounds wonderful," she said. "It's quite a walk to the ocean and the beach isn't all that good."

"Exactly my own feelings," he said. "I'll go now and give you a chance to quietly settle in."

"When should I come down?" she asked.

"Any time you like," he said. "Dinner isn't until seven. But we'll be having cocktails on the patio around six-thirty."

She glanced at her wristwatch. "That gives me about an hour," she said.

Derek bent close and chastely kissed her on the cheek once again. "I'll see you downstairs," he said and left.

Joyce had the impression that she made him uneasy and that he'd been anxious to get away from her. It wasn't a flattering situation but she supposed it was one she could expect. The stigma of being in a mental hospital was still very real even in these modern times. With another weary little sigh she went about the rest of her unpacking.

She put on a trim white linen dress and carefully completed her make-up and hairdo before going down to face the family. It was a difficult hurdle for her and she once again experienced a series of nervous fears. The old mansion seemed terribly large and dated after her sojourn in Dr. Beckett's modern hospital.

Making her way down the winding stairway to the foyer she glanced at the familiar portraits of Mills ancestors on the walls and wondered if the ghostly Captain Peter might have had his likeness included in the group. She'd never questioned Derek about it.

As she reached the ground floor a young man could be seen standing in the living room. He was someone she'd never seen before and so she guessed that he must be the artist, David Chase. She went into the living room and smiled at him.

She said, "My husband told me about you. I think you must be David Chase. I'm Joyce Mills." And she offered him her hand.

He shook hands with her rather awkwardly. "Of course," he said. "You came over from the mainland today."

"Yes," she said. She could tell by his embarrassed expression that he knew she'd been in a private mental hospital.

"Well," he said, "welcome back."

"Thank you. My husband says you're doing some work for the museum."

"Some ship paintings. It's fascinating. I have to dig up the data on the ships and try to find old prints. Then I set to work."

"I believe the paintings you are doing are to form a permanent collection for the museum," she said. She was taken by his clean-cut appearance. He had straw-colored hair and friendly blue eyes set in a rather square, even-featured face. He was slim in build and not much taller than she was. In a fawn jacket and dark trousers and shirt with dotted brown cravat at the neck he looked extremely smart.

He smiled. "I came to Pirate Island to do some work of my own. But Derek heard I was here and insisted I do this project for the museum."

"At budget rates I'm sure," she said. "Derek is very dedicated to improving the museum and getting it operating on a solid basis."

The young man said, "And may I say he appears to be doing an excellent job."

"Thank you." She accepted the compliment for Derek. "He is very good at all he does."

David Chase gestured at the magnificent room in which they were standing. "This living room is really something. The castle must be the most impressive house on the island."

"There are a few other large mansions on the fringe of Dark Harbor," she said. "When they were built they were well outside the town. But it has grown over the years, though slowly."

The young man said, "It had its big growth in the whaling days from what I've been able to discover. And then there was another resurgence when fishing in a general way began after the First World War. But that has eased off because of a lack of fish and so tourists offer a main source of revenue for the island now."

"You have it very clearly," she agreed. "That is why Derek is so interested in the museum. He feels that it is one of the main attractions for tourists."

"He's probably right," the young man agreed. "You aren't from an island family?"

"No," she said with a faint smile. "I'm a mainlander."

"I suppose that does make a difference."

"One doesn't get accepted too quickly," she told him. "But after five or ten years you're almost one of them. I haven't been here long enough myself."

His gaze was an interested one. "Do you like the island?"

"I think so," she said. "I didn't at first. I felt very shut in. I've gotten over that."

He nodded. "I think I know what you mean."

As he finished speaking, a young woman in a long flowing dress came in through the French doors to join them. It was Mona, looking chic in a new short haircut. The red-haired girl gave them both a cool smile of greeting. She was attractive and would have been a beauty except that her face was a trifle too long.

Addressing herself to Joyce, she said. "Hello! You're looking very well! Last time I saw you before you left you were pale as a ghost!"

"Thank you," Joyce said evenly. "I feel better."

"Derek said you'd made wonderful progress," Mona told her. "Do you think it was wise to come back here?"

"Yes," she said.

Mona's look was mocking. "I hope you've gotten over your psychic period. It was very trying on all of us to have you seeing phantoms around the place."

Joyce knew the red-haired girl well enough to have expected some comment like this. She said, "I'm no longer hallucinating."

"That's a relief!" Mona replied. "We're having cocktails on the patio tonight."

Joyce asked, "Is Derek out there?"

"Yes," the redhead said. "We were just having a talk." She always adopted an air of having a special understanding with Derek. And she offered a warm smile to David Chase.

Joyce glanced at the artist and saw that he was showing an uneasy, disapproving expression at Mona's remarks. It was evident that he did not find the breezy redhead's comments amusing. He gave no hint of noticing the smile and stood there saying nothing.

Joyce addressed him directly, "Probably we should go outside," she said.

"Very well," he agreed in a warm manner that made it clear he felt sympathy for her.

Joyce had no idea how much the others had discussed her with him. But there could be no question that he knew she'd been mentally ill. And Mona had tried to make it seem as ugly as possible.

Mona now quickly said, "You must join the others, both

of you! Mother is terribly interested in what you're doing David and wants to ask you some questions about those old sailing ships you're painting for the museum."

"I'm not really an authority, you know," the young man protested as he moved to the French doors with Joyce and Mona.

Outside it was warm and pleasant. There was a bar set up on one of the tables and Derek was behind it. He gave Joyce a special nod of greeting and asked them all what they would like to drink. David Chase had a martini and so did Mona, then they went across to the ocean end of the patio to talk with Derek's mother who had taken a seat there.

She found herself standing alone with Derek. She said, "Your artist seems very nice."

"Yes," Derek said. "David is a fine fellow and he has lots of talent as well." He hesitated. "How about a drink?"

"Do you mean is it allowed?"

"Yes," he said awkwardly.

She smiled. "It's quite all right. Dr. Beckett had cocktail parties at the hospital regularly for his more trustworthy patients. Especially those who had distinguished themselves at golf."

"I'm sorry," her husband said. "I didn't know. It's something I forgot to ask him."

"I'll have a Manhattan," she said. "That's what I've been drinking."

"Sure," Derek said. And he quickly went to work preparing the cocktail. His jumpiness and uneasy reaction to whatever minor problem came up did not speak well for their future, she thought.

As Derek made her drink another member of the family came up to join her. It was Henry Mills, Derek's father's younger brother whom everyone called Uncle Henry. He was a man in his late fifties with thick white hair and a bronzed, lined face which would have been handsome had it not been burnt out with too much drinking. He had the bloodshot eyes and shaky hands of an alcoholic along with a too ready smile which he could turn on at will. He had no money of his own and lived on his sister-in-law's charity.

Uncle Henry came straight to her and took her in his arms. "How good to have you back," he said.

"Thank you," she said, kissing him on the cheek. He had always been more friendly to her than anyone else in Derek's family.

"You look wonderful," he said with a smile as he released her. "Your time in hospital really did you good."

"That was the general idea," she said.

Henry told Derek, "I'll also have a Manhattan." Then he turned to glance down the patio where Regina Mills, Mona and David were gathered. With a wry expression he said, "I see your mother is holding court again, Derek. She really makes her house guests toe the line."

Derek glanced up from the bar and told his uncle, "You ought to know, you're the record-holder as far as staying here is concerned."

His Uncle Henry did not lose his smile. "Very sharp, Derek. You are right. I have enjoyed your mother's hospitality for some time. But then she received all my brother's money and I feel some of it was rightfully mine. I'm merely trying to collect."

"I wondered," Derek said as he handed Joyce her drink.

She accepted the Manhattan and turned away to stand alone a distance apart from the two men. The continual bickering that went on among the Mills family had always embarrassed her although they seemed to actually enjoy it. And now that she was in such a tense state she was not ready for the

40

acid talk which was the norm at the castle.

She was still standing there studying the distant Bald Mountain, which was the highest point on the island, when Uncle Henry came up by her again.

This time he looked contrite. "Sorry to have had that exchange in front of you, Joyce," he said. "I know how you feel about that kind of thing."

She glanced at him. "Just now my nerves aren't up to it."

"I know. I should have realized."

"So should Derek," she said. "But it's over. So it really doesn't matter. Are you keeping busy?"

Henry Mills smiled. "I'm still acting as rent collector and general real estate agent for the properties Regina has been quietly buying on the island. For which she pays me a pittance."

"Why has she bought so much property?"

"I'm not sure," he replied. "I think she wants to try to make her own kind of development on a lot of the island. Keep it unspoiled. She's setting up all sorts of rules for those hiring the properties from her and she has the town council considering a plan to beautify the wharves. Privately I think such a scheme would ruin their authenticity."

"You're probably right," she agreed.

He took a sip of his drink. "But Regina loves to steam-roll over everything. You know what she's like."

"Yes," she said with meaning. "I do know."

He stared at her. "I think you've changed."

"How?"

"I don't know," he said. "There is something different about you. A quality I've never seen in you before."

She raised her eyebrows. "Is that a nice way of saying I seem demented?"

"Not at all," he protested. "It's that you seem to have

more character. I imagine you had plenty of time to think in that place."

"You're right. But I don't think my character is any stronger for it. I never felt more shaky and unsure of myself than at this moment."

"I wouldn't guess it," was the older man's reply. "A lot of things have been happening on the island since you've been away. We must have a good talk."

"We must," she agreed. "A year is a long time."

Henry Mills stared at her over his drink again. "You were a very sick girl when Derek took you off the island. I wondered if you'd ever recover. To see you like this is great!"

She smiled ruefully. "What if I should begin all over again? Timmy, the cat, greeted me by brushing against my ankles. I tried not to react but I couldn't help it. I began screaming as I remembered that day and what happened!"

"You'll have to fight," Henry Mills advised her. "Fight hard."

At this point Derek came to join them. He said, "You two seem to be having a very serious talk."

"Not really," his uncle said. "Just going over old times. Joyce and I have always been friends."

"That's right," Derek said, though his tone and expression indicated no great pleasure at the idea.

"Well, I must go and pay my respects to the others," Henry said with another of his smiles. "I'll see you later, Joyce." And he moved off to the ocean end of the patio.

Derek gave a sigh of relief as he stood beside her with his drink in hand. "I'm glad he had enough sense to leave us alone. We haven't had much time to ourselves and dinner is coming up shortly."

She studied his serious face. "I suppose you'll be spending long hours at the museum every day."

"And some evenings as well," he told her. "You have no idea the amount of work we have to do and how far behind we've gotten."

"That means I'll be on my own a lot."

"You'll have the rest of the family for company."

"I'll still be on my own," she said pointedly.

Derek frowned. "You really must make some effort to get along with my mother and Mona. It could make living here much easier for you."

"Do you think it's possible for your mother and sister to get along with me?"

"I'm sure of it. And it's a sign you're not completely cured that you should doubt it," he said unhappily.

"You think so?"

"I have to," he said. "They have plenty of friends so it can't be their fault. You're neurotic and everything becomes exaggerated in your mind because of that."

Joyce stared at him hard. "I know what you're thinking. What you've been thinking ever since I became ill during my pregnancy. You think that I cheated you into marrying me by not telling you about my neurosis and my breakdown."

"Let's not go over all that again!" he objected.

"You've not forgiven me, Derek."

"I have," he said earnestly. "I give you my word that I have."

"You're ready to accept me as a normal person?"

"Of course!"

Her eyes bore directly into his. "I have an idea of something that might be helpful to me. But I don't think you'll ever agree to it."

Her husband said, "If it will help you I'll certainly agree. What have you in mind?"

Keeping her eyes fixed on him, she said, "I'd like to adopt a child," she said quietly.

It seemed to shatter him. He almost dropped his drink as he stared at her and said, "Adopt a child!"

"Yes. Preferably one about three years old and a little girl. It would make up for Lucie in a small way. And I'm sure it would be good for us."

Derek continued to look shocked. "You don't know what you're saying."

"I do."

"It's not a practical idea," he protested. "And even if I agreed with you I'm almost positive that authorities would refuse to let us have a child to adopt."

"Why?"

Looking embarrassed, he said, "Do you really have to ask me that?"

Her eyes were solemn. "Because of me?"

"Yes, if I have to say it!"

"Dr. Beckett promised to help me if I decided I wanted to adopt a little girl. There are agencies he knows that would accept his word that I'm completely responsible."

Derek's handsome face was crimson now. "I couldn't allow it! Not at this point!"

"What do you mean?"

"I don't think you're ready," he told her. "Nor am I. Let's wait and see how you make out here."

"How long?"

"I don't know."

"You could make my trial period last forever," she pointed out. "I could wind up an old woman with still no baby."

"I'm far from convinced the idea is good," he told her. "I think a child would be too much for you to look after in your present state."

"It might help me," she pleaded.

He shook his head. "It's nothing to discuss at this

moment. Let us see you quietly settled in your place back here first. Then we can talk about going on to other things."

She gave him a bitter look. "You've abandoned the idea already. Without even considering it. You still think I'm a little mad!"

"Joyce!" he pleaded.

"It's true," she said. "And if you go on this way and refuse to give me consideration I may lose my mind again."

Derek showed anger on his handsome face. "Is that a threat?"

"I'm simply telling you the truth," she insisted.

"Let it drop," was his weary reply.

Derek's mother came up from the other end of the patio with the others trailing along with her. She entered the living room through the French doors and there could be no question but that this was the signal for dinner. Joyce and Derek followed the others in to the panelled dinning room, where Derek's mother presided at the table in her usual haughty fashion.

Joyce remembered little about that first dinner except that the talk kept flying past her. She didn't seem able to take in most that was being said. And she didn't really care about their conversation. She saw the cold face of Regina as she made her pronouncements and the smirking features of Mona who invariably agreed with the older woman. She fumbled at her food with her knife and fork and hoped no one noticed her condition.

Somehow she got through the dinner. Almost as soon as they left the dining room a phone call came for Derek. She went on out onto a porch off the music room. It was halfmoon in shape and in the winter glass windows were installed all around it to convert it into a Florida room. Just now only screens were in place and it was airy and refreshing there. She felt better once away from the barrage of conversation at the dinner table.

She was standing there when she heard a footstep behind her and turned to see the artist, David Chase. The young man looked apologetic.

"Will you forgive my intruding?" he asked.

She smiled thinly. "As long as there is just one of you. The conversation at the dinner table was too much for me."

"I noticed that," he said.

Fright shadowed her lovely face. "I hope none of the others did. That it wasn't all that obvious!"

The blond man said, "It wasn't obvious. But I could tell."

"How? You don't know me."

He said, "I know you better than you may guess. You see, I have shared your problem."

She frowned. "Shared my problem?"

"Yes," he said in his quiet way. "Some years ago I also had a nervous breakdown."

"Really?"

"Yes," he said with a wry smile. "Of course I don't brag about it. But I wanted to let you know. So you'd realize that I am aware of your problems and can sympathize with you."

"I find it hard to believe."

"That I was once mentally ill?" the young man said.

"Yes. You seem so normal. So well!"

"I'm cured," he said with a smile of reassurance. "I came out of it well. But it has been valuable in that I now have a true insight into mental illness and what it means."

"You would be bound to."

He looked at her sympathetically. "I think that sister-in-law of yours is a very sour young woman. I didn't approve of her light humor about your mental state."

"Thank you. I'm sure she was trying to make an impression on you at my expense."

David Chase looked grim. "She made the impression all right. But it was a bad one."

"Mona is a strange girl. She's my husband's adopted sister not his blood one."

"But she's enough like her foster mother to be her real daughter," was David's opinion. "Your mother-in-law is also a very arrogant person. Neither of those two women are fair to you!"

She smiled bitterly. "I wish, when the opportunity presents itself, you'd tell my husband that."

"I shall the first chance I get," he said. "I think you're some kind of heroine to come back here and put up with what you have."

"My only fear is that I may not be equal to it," she said.

"Do you have to remain here?" David Chase asked.

She lifted her hand in a futile gesture. "If I left I would be almost sure to lose Derek. And in spite of everything I love my husband."

David Chase gave her a solemn appraisal. "Yes. I believe you do."

"My only hope of solving our personal problems and saving our marriage is my staying here," she said.

"And that is what you want?"

"Yes."

He said, "Then I hope that is how it works out. I'd like to be your friend while I'm here."

"Thank you," she said gratefully. "I could do with a friend."

The young artist said, "I've heard about your illness from Mona, of course. She takes a delight in denigrating you. She dotes on the fact that in your worst stage of illness you claimed you were haunted by the castle ghost."

"Captain Peter Mills? Yes. I thought I saw him."

David's face showed a scowl. "She tries to make it sound very demeaning. But I can understand that in your condition a truly sensitive person like yourself could have believed you were seeing the materialization of a legend told you."

"It was very vivid," she recalled. "He wore the captain's cap of a hundred years ago and a long jacket. He was very real to me."

The artist nodded. "I had some visions of my own. They were real at the time. I know them now for the phantoms that they had to be. You'll come to the same realization in time."

She gave him a strange look. Twilight had settled as they stood there and now the porch was cloaked in shadows. She said, "I'm not all that sure I didn't see a ghost. It was after my little girl's death. And somehow I think she may have acted as a go-between to allow me to see people from the other side. This house surely is filled with phantoms and I may have become sensitive to them."

"Joyce!" Derek called to her from the music room.

"I'm out here," she answered.

David told her, "I'll go. But we'll talk again."

Derek and he passed and exchanged greetings as Derek came out onto the shadowed porch and David went back into the house. Her husband asked her, "What were you two doing out here?"

"It was no rendezvous," she said. "We just happened to meet. So we talked a little."

Derek said, "I didn't mean to infer there was anything wrong about it. I came to explain that telephone call. It was from the museum. There is some fellow down there who wants to see me. He's on the island only for the night and his family here goes back for generations. He asked if I'd look up some records and I hated to refuse him."

"You're going to the museum now? Leaving me on my first night here?"

He looked unhappy. "I feel it's something I should do. And I'll get back as soon as possible. You need the rest so you don't have to wait up for me. You can go straight to bed."

"Yes," she said, "I can. And I do have my own room, don't I? That makes it easy."

"Please let's not have a scene about it!" He bent to her and kissed her on the forehead. "I'll see you when I get back if you're still awake."

"All right," she said in a small voice. She knew there was no point in further argument. He'd made up his mind and nothing would change it.

He left her alone on the porch and she remained standing there. The twilight was turning into darkness. From deep within the house she heard the echo of distant voices. Feeling desolate and on edge she decided she would go straight to her room and to bed. Her fear and disappointment at his deserting her in this fashion on her first night back at the castle had to be borne. But it was not easy, not easy at all.

She was about to turn and leave the porch when she all at once saw a movement in the shadows of the lawn just outside. She froze with fear and fixed her eyes on the spot only to see a figure materialize and lift a hand and wave to her! It was century-dead Captain Peter Mills in the familiar cap and long coat!

49

CHAPTER THREE

The scream of fear that sprang from Joyce was purely automatic. And so was her gesture immediately following when she pressed her hand over her mouth to prevent crying out again. At the same time the phantom figure on the lawn vanished. She stood there still staring out into the near darkness, her entire body seized with a wave of trembling.

There were hurried footsteps from the music room behind her and then Regina Mills stepped out onto the porch to join her. Her mother-in-law had an annoyed expression on her patrician face as she demanded, "Was that you who screamed just now?"

Weakly she turned to her. "Yes."

"What on earth about?"

"I thought I saw something."

"What?"

"Someone out on the lawn. But he is not there now," Joyce replied in a voice with a tremor in it.

The arrogant Regina gasped. "Really! Was that any reason for your behaving that way? Your scream sounded absolutely tortured!"

"I was frightened."

"By a shadow on the lawn," the older woman said with grim disapproval. "We can't have you behaving in that manner. What will the servants think?"

Joyce was still trembling and the attitude of her mother-in-law wasn't helping. She said, "I didn't do it purposely. I did see something. If I could have stopped myself from crying out I would have."

Regina looked at her hand. "I thought Derek said you were better."

"I am," Joyce said.

"It doesn't seem like it," the older woman said spitefully. "If I remember correctly that is how it all began before, with your seeing things that weren't there!"

Joyce turned to her in the near darkness. "I said I was sorry. It's not apt to happen again. And I did see something out there whatever you choose to think!"

Having said that she hurriedly left the porch and went through the music room and the hallway beyond it to the stairs. She lost no time in reaching her room. Once there she closed the door and stretched out on the bed. Now that she was alone and away from everyone else in the house she allowed her emotions free rein. Pressing her face into the pillow she sobbed out her fear.

Her slim body was racked by her sobbing for a short time and then the frenzy of panic passed. She was in reasonable control of herself once again. She didn't think anyone but Derek's mother had heard her scream out downstairs. It was unfortunate that Regina had heard her since she would certainly make the most of it. Joyce didn't dare think how much her mother-in-law would exaggerate the incident for Derek's benefit. It had been a bad lapse on her part. And she knew that she couldn't afford the luxury of many such mistakes. Regina was ready to talk Derek into returning her to the private mental hospital. And it would not be nearly so easy to get out of it another time. Indeed her own will might be broken to the extent that she wouldn't want to leave. She would turn into another Mrs. Allain, content to escape from a world in which she found it too difficult to cope.

She went to the open window of her room and stared out

into the darkness. She was filled with a feeling of desolation. Derek seemed so different from the man she'd known before her year in that mental hospital. Not in any obvious way, he was still kind and considerate of her. But there was an under-current of nervousness and lack of confidence where she was concerned which frightened her.

The wash of the waves on the distant beach came to her clearly. From her window she had a view of the chapel with its high belfry. Had she made a mistake in coming back to this scene of tragedy? She hoped not. One of the things she most wanted to do was conquer her feelings about the past. Dr. Beckett had assured her that was the only way she could save her marriage and her sanity.

What had she seen on the lawn? To her it had been the ghost of Captain Peter Mills. But suppose it had been merely a shadow? An illusion caused by the approaching darkness. That was what Regina had insisted it had been. But Regina could be wrong. It was a troubling question. What would she say to Derek if he asked her about it?

She'd have to tell him the truth. And he would of course join his mother in dismissing the phantom as a product of her imagination. She knew that beforehand. All she could do was stick to her story and let him prove her wrong. That would be better than trying to make him believe what she'd seen. She moved from the window and slowly began to take off her clothes in preparation for bed. It was hard to tell when her husband would return and in any case he had his own room and bed so it was unlikely that he'd bother her. It was a much different homecoming than she'd expected.

She slept lightly, troubled by dreams. And in all her dreams the arrogant Regina Mills played a prominent part. Joyce had nightmare arguments with her and then there were moments of physical fear when she fled from the evil Regina into the darkness. In one of the nightmares she ran along an endless, dark cave to finally come out into a larger underground chamber that was walled with mirrors.

In racing to escape from her mother-in-law she arrived in the mirrored dungeon and suddenly saw a maddened Regina threatening her from every direction in each of the mirrors. Trapped she gave a loud scream of fear. And since the scream was real she woke herself up.

And standing above her in the near darkness of her bedroom was Derek. He stood there gazing down at her with an odd expression on his handsome face. He seemed caught up in some sort of spell since he didn't speak to her.

Lifting herself on an elbow, she said, "Derek, how long have you been here?"

At the sound of her voice he showed a more animated, normal expression. He said, "I've only been here a few minutes. You were dreaming and talking in your sleep."

"What did I say?"

He shrugged. "Nothing important. I could hear hardly any of it. Just jumbled talk!"

"I see," she said, thinking that he wouldn't tell her even if he had heard her clearly. There was no longer that sort of trust between them.

She said, "Are you just going to bed?"

"Yes."

"What time is it?"

"Near midnight."

She said, "You were kept late at the museum, weren't you?"

"Later than I expected."

It was amazing, she thought. They were talking like strangers there in the darkness. She stared up at him. "Did you talk to your mother when you came in?"

"Yes." There was a strained note in his reply.

"I might have expected she'd wait up to see you."

"Why?"

Joyce said, "I think you know. She told you, didn't she?" She tried to study his face in the shadows but it was difficult.

He hesitated awkwardly. "We talked for a moment. We always do."

"But she doesn't always have the interesting news she had for you tonight," she told her husband bitterly. "She did let you know how I disgraced myself, didn't she?"

"Joyce!" he protested wearily.

"Didn't she?"

He sighed. "She said something about you being alone on the porch and suddenly screaming."

"I knew it!"

Derek said, "Well, was there anything wrong in her mentioning it to me?"

"Not from her point of view. She'd be delighted."

"It did happen, didn't it?"

"Yes. I thought I saw a ghost again! Did she also tell you that?"

Derek looked upset. "It did happen, didn't it?"

"Yes! It happened!" she said bitterly. "And I can promise you it really pleased your mother."

"Be fair! Why blame it on her? You did the screaming."

Joyce said, "Now that you have heard the story what do you want to make of it?"

"Nothing. I had no intention of discussing it tonight," her husband said. "I just came in to make sure you were all right before I went to bed."

"I see," she said.

He bent down and kissed her. "Go to sleep," he said, sounding weary again.

She held onto one of his hands to keep him there. "Derek," she asked softly, "do you still love me?"

"Of course. What makes you ask a silly question like that?"

"I can't help wondering," she said, still holding his hand. "You seem very different. And then these separate rooms and everything."

Her husband sighed. "I've only been trying to be considerate of you."

"Derek!"

"Yes?"

"I did see something. It was the ghost of Captain Peter Mills. I'm certain of it!"

"It's too late to talk about it now!"

"You'll never want to talk about it," she accused him.

"Goodnight, Joyce," he said firmly and he pulled his hand away abruptly and freed himself. In another moment he had gone into the adjoining room and closed the door behind him.

It was a long while before she slept again. She listened to the wash of the waves on the beach, heard the wild cry of some night bird, and thought of all that had happened since she'd arrived at the castle. She remembered her last conversation with Dr. Beckett.

"You won't find it easy, you know," he told her.

"I don't think I can face going back there at all," she'd admitted in a panic.

"Nonsense," the doctor had told her. "When you get there stay outdoors. Take plenty of exercise. Do they have a decent golf course?"

She had smiled faintly. "I think so. I don't know. What does that matter?"

"It would matter a lot to me if I were going to have to live on that island," he said. "You've played a very good game here. Find yourself a partner and try and play every day."

"My problem isn't my golf game," she'd told him impatiently, "it's a lot of the past I can't forget."

"Golf will help you forget," the British doctor assured her. "You mustn't allow yourself to mope and be morbid. There is nothing you can do about what happened. But you can control your future. I want you to remember that. Your future is in your hands!"

She slept and when she came awake she again thought of what the doctor had said. He wasn't as unthinking and wrapped up in his golf game as he pretended. There was generally a good bit of wisdom in what he said. But she wasn't by any means sure she could put his advice to good use. She had severe doubts about her future being in her hands.

The first thing she did when she got up was to check Derek's room. He was not there. He'd managed to get up and dress without her hearing him. She supposed that he'd already had breakfast and had gone to the museum. She washed and dressed and went down and had breakfast alone. It was a fine, sunny day and after breakfast she went outside for a stroll.

She was sensitive about what happened the night before. Most likely Regina had spread it among the others. There seemed little doubt that her mother-in-law would be delighted to have her sent back to the mental hospital. Joyce strolled across the lawn and in the direction of the swimming pool. As she neared it she heard a splash and saw that David Chase was already there swimming.

Reaching the poolside she waved to him. He was floating in the middle of the pool. He called back to her and at once swam over to where she was standing and scrambled out. Joyce noticed he looked well-muscled and very tan in his dark crimson suit. He said, "You must come in. The water is great today."

"I will later," she said.

The artist laughed. "I'll be working later. I'm not able to give all my time to swimming."

"I thought you worked on your own time," she said.

"In theory," he agreed. "But I have a certain amount to get done every day and so I have to plan to work a minimum amount of hours."

"The pool is new," she said, giving her attention to it. "I haven't seen it before."

"It's a good one," David Chase said. "I've enjoyed it since I've been here."

She was taking in the details of the kidney-shaped turquoise pool with its white border. A patio and cabana had been built at one end of it. She knew that Derek had planned the pool for some time but she'd talked him out of it. Her argument had been that it would present an extra hazard for Lucie. She'd urged him to wait and build it later when their child was old enough to enjoy it.

A hazard to Lucie! She stared at the pool grimly. It was ironic in view of what had happened. They might well have gone ahead with the project when Derek had first suggested it. He'd probably felt so too and had ordered the installation after she'd gone to the hospital.

David's voice came through to her in the dark maze of her thoughts. He was asking her, "What's the matter?"

She turned to him rather dazed. "The matter?"

His face wore a troubled expression. "Yes. We were talking quite normally and all at once I lost you. You were staring at the pool and in a world of your own."

"I'm sorry."

"You needn't apologize. I'm concerned for you," he said.

"I could see you slipping away. The shadow crossing your face."

She stared at the pool's sparkling surface again, avoiding his eyes. In a low voice, she said, "I had a bitter memory."

"About what?"

"It doesn't matter."

"Please tell me," he said.

She didn't feel she ought to. And at the same time she felt it might help her if she did. Surely the young artist was her friend and understood. He had confessed to having been in a mental hospital himself.

She said, "I was thinking of my little girl. I didn't want Derek to build a pool because I was afraid it might be dangerous for her."

"And she died anyway."

"It was even more stupid than a pool accident," she said bitterly.

"I know. I've heard about it."

She gave him a troubled look. "From Regina?"

He nodded. "Yes."

"Did she tell you that I was responsible? That it was my neglect?"

"No."

"She usually does."

"Regina bothers you a lot, doesn't she?"

"In a way. But I suppose I don't really care anymore."

"I think you do," he said. "And I'm upset for you. I know all you've been through. I went through something like it myself."

She gave him a glance of apology. "Forgive me for spoiling your morning with my troubles."

"Not at all," he said. "I want to hear them. A father confessor often helps. You must have found that out at the hospital."

She looked at the swimming pool again. "I begin to think I should never have left there."

"That's wrong!" he warned her.

"I can't help it!" She walked away from him and went over to sit on one of the new white wooden benches Derek had placed beside the pool.

The young artist came after her and sat on the bench beside her. He said, "Are you worried about last night?"

"So you've heard about that, too?" she said, looking at him again.

He nodded. "Your mother-in-law was pretty concerned."

Joyce said, "I knew she'd make the most of it."

"In fairness I heard the scream as well," he said. "And asked her about it."

"I can't explain it," she told him. "Even if I tried to you wouldn't believe me."

"It's all right," he said. "I can tell you're still in bad shape. Did your husband put any pressure on the hospital to let you go?"

She stared at him. "Why do you ask that?"

"I wondered if he might have. Relatives often do. My parents did the same thing with me. I was released before I should have been and as a result I had to go back again."

"Derek really didn't influence Dr. Beckett," she said. "At least I don't think so. The doctor thought I shouldn't stay in there too long. That I should get out and face reality."

David Chase pulled a wry face. "Yes. I've heard that story."

"So here I am. Facing it none too well."

"It is bound to be difficult. Especially when you have a sister-in-law like Mona and a mother-in-law like Regina," the young man sympathized.

"Where is Mona?"

He said, "She left early to play golf."

Joyce gave a rueful laugh. "I might have guessed!"

"Why do you say that?"

"My doctor advised me to play golf. He suggested that I find a partner. I was thinking what a congenial partner Mona would be. How she would encourage me!"

The artist looked at her seriously. "I don't know how you feel about Mona but I wouldn't trust her if I were you. When your husband announced you were coming home she made a nasty scene."

"That doesn't surprise me."

David Chase hesitated. "What I have to say now, may. I have an idea she is in love with your husband."

"I'm not all that surprised," Joyce said. "And you're probably right. I suspected it soon after we were married."

His eyebrows raised. "And you put up with it? Stayed on here?"

"Yes," she said. "I felt Derek wasn't aware of her interest in him or that he had any interest in her."

"And now?"

"I'm not sure."

The young man gave a deep sigh. "Well, at least you know the danger and who to watch. If you can control your nerves you should be all right."

"They've poisoned Derek against me. He sees me only as a mad person. Everything else is forgotten. I can't bear the way he looks at me now."

David smiled grimly again. "That's another thing I'm familiar with."

She found herself studying him with a strong feeling of curiosity. Before she could stop herself, she said, "About you?"

His expression was quizzical. "You mean my case?"

She blushed. "I'm sorry. I have no right to ask you. I didn't mean to. It just happened."

He smiled. "I don't mind."

"It's none of my business," she protested.

"I'd like to tell you."

"Please."

"It's not a secret," he said. "I killed a girl."

She couldn't find any answer for a moment. Then she managed a weak, "Oh?"

He went on quite casually. "It's not all that unusual. It was a young woman I was engaged to. We had a quarrel. I was drinking and driving. I wrecked the car and she was killed."

"That's rather different from what you said."

"No. It's exactly what I said. I killed her. She would be alive today if I had driven carefully."

"I'm sure there were mitigating circumstances."

"I can't think of any," the young artist said. "I smashed myself up badly. I still have a metal plate in my head as a result. And when I found out what I'd done I had a nervous breakdown. I spent almost two years in hospitals."

"You had treatment longer than I," she said in wonder.

"Right," he agreed. "So don't feel so special. There are a lot like us and we have this in common. We enjoy blaming ourselves for what happened."

"You have strong guilt feelings?"

"Yes," he said. "That's one thing that hasn't changed."

"Coming here has made it worse for me," she said. "I had hoped it wouldn't but now I realize that it has."

"It's understandable," he agreed.

A new thought struck her. "Do the others know about you?"

"That I was in a mental hospital?"

"Yes."

He shook his head. "No. You're the only one I've told. I've had enough of that special look and treatment business when people do know."

"Of course," she said, feeling for him. "You don't have to worry. I won't tell."

"You can if you like."

"No," she said. "But I think there is a humorous side to it. Mona making all those sarcastic remarks to me in front of you and you being in the same fix as me."

He smiled ruefully. "I wonder how she'd feel if she knew."

"She won't know," Joyce was quick to say. "If they ever found out they'd practice their venom on you as well. That's the nice thing about so-called normal people."

David Chase said, "At least we understand them." He stood up. "I must change. I've got to start some work."

She said, "And I've taken all your free time!"

"I enjoyed it," he said.

"And don't worry," she told him. "I'm erasing what you said from my mind."

The young artist picked up his towel and robe and went on into the castle. She remained by the swimming pool and thought over all he'd said. It had come as a surprise to her to learn that he'd also had a breakdown and treatment. But it was also somewhat comforting to have another person around who had gone through the same ordeal as herself.

She strolled alongside the pool and thought of all the different bits of advice Dr. Beckett had given her. She needed to call on all her resources now to meet this situation. David Chase had confirmed what she already knew, that her mother-in-law and Mona were her enemies. And they were doing all they could to turn Derek against her.

They had made good headway during the year she'd been in hospital. But she felt that Derek did have strong feelings of loyalty and would not desert her. They had been very much in love when they were first married and not all of this had been lost despite the tragic experiences they'd shared.

So she must try to fight the battle. But what about the other battle, the one within herself? Was she still mentally unbalanced? Had she seen a ghost last night or had it only been a phantom figure in her mind? She could not be sure. She could only hope that the experience would not be repeated.

While she was musing over these things a car drove up the circular driveway before the castle. She looked up to see that a man and woman were getting out of it. They had seen her and were coming over to greet her. As they drew nearer she saw that it was Brook Patterson, the ineffectual, balding man who worked under Derek at the museum with his attractive blonde-haired wife, Faith. She knew them both well and hadn't seen them since she left for the hospital.

Faith reached her first. She threw her arms around Joyce and kissed her on the cheek.

"I'd forgotten!" she said. "Derek told me he was bringing you home but it completely slipped my mind!"

Joyce smiled. "My return isn't all that important."

"I disagree," the blonde Faith said. "You look so well!"

Brook Patterson had joined them and now he held out his hand to Joyce, saying, "We've missed you."

"Thank you," she said, shaking hands with him. The bald, quiet Brook had always been something of an enigma to her. He was pleasant but one felt that his withdrawn manner might conceal a more complex character than could be guessed.

Brook's thin face radiated good will. "It will be a great load off Derek's mind to have you back and well," he said.

"I hope so," Joyce said.

Faith smiled at her. "I suppose you wonder what I'm doing here. I've been working at the museum but David Chase is doing a portrait of me and I come here almost every morning for an hour. My car is in for repairs this morning so Brook brought me over. And the garage is sending my car here so I can drive back to the museum myself."

Joyce was surprised and interested. "David just left the pool to get dressed. I understand he's a very good artist."

Faith's oval face took on a demure look of approval. "I'm completely sold on him. It was Brook who suggested that he do me."

"That's so," the balding young man agreed. "The way I see it we might not have an artist of David's ability here on the island for years again. Best to take advantage of him while he's here."

"You're probably right," Joyce agreed. But knowing Faith's reputation on the island for being a flirt she wondered if there might not be more to it than just having her portrait painted. David Chase was a most attractive man and Faith was bound not to have missed that. Working at the museum she would see a lot of him. Perhaps that was the reason she'd suddenly decided to take a job there.

Faith glanced towards the castle. "I'll go in after a moment. Give him a chance to get ready for me first."

Brook Patterson said, "I may as well drive back to the museum." And he told his wife, "If your car doesn't get here when it is supposed to let me know and I'll come back for you."

"Don't worry," Faith assured him, "I'll get back one way or another. David may be returning to the museum when he finishes with me."

Her husband nodded and turned to Joyce again. "I hope we'll see something of you now that you're back."

"Yes," she said. "I'm going to take it slowly at first. I need to adjust. My nerves are still not what they should be."

"You seem just fine," was Brook's opinion. "We must arrange a get-together one of these evenings." And with a nod of farewell he turned and headed back to his car.

Faith's pert oval face seemed to take on an expression of

relief as her husband walked away from them. She turned to Joyce and said, "Poor Brook! He's so deadly serious about everything. I should be ashamed to admit it but he's so attentive it gets on my nerves. I like a certain amount of freedom."

"I understand," she said. And she did. She knew that Faith's idea of wifely freedom went a good bit beyond the usual concept. And she again wondered if there might be a summer romance going on between David Chase and the pretty subject of his portrait.

Faith gave her a knowing look. "I wondered if you would come back here. I heard rumors that you'd refused to return to the island."

"They weren't true."

"That doesn't surprise me. You know what the gossips are like here."

"Too well," Joyce said ruefully.

"Believe me I've had my fill of them!" Faith told her. "I know some of the things they've said about me. It's worth your reputation to be seen talking to a man of your own age here. Brook and I had an understanding long ago that neither of us would pay any attention to the local gossips."

Joyce said, "That was probably wise." She thought it especially so since Faith had more than once behaved in a manner to invite gossip. She asked, "How do you like working?"

"I enjoy it," Faith said, smiling. "I'm a kind of an assistant to Derek. That was one of my conditions in going to work. That I wouldn't have to be in Brook's department. That would be too much of a good thing."

"I can see that," Joyce agreed.

"Derek and I have always gotten along well and he's very easy to work with," Faith said happily. "So I'm enjoying the experience."

"Good."

Faith glanced at her watch. "I think David must be ready for me now. I'd better go in. If my car comes and you're still out here just tell them to leave it."

"I will."

Faith went into the castle by the side entrance leaving Joyce alone on the lawn once more. She supposed that David must be using his room for a studio and that Faith was going up there for the sitting. Again she pondered on what the relationship between the two could be. There had been a certain tension in Faith's manner which made her wonder about what the attractive blonde might be up to.

Joyce strolled across the lawn to the garden area. There were large beds of flowers at this end of the house along with shoulder-high decorative hedges that divided the garden into a maze of private areas. She walked along one of the gravel paths that led through the garden. As she rounded one of the hedges she came upon Henry Mills seated on a marble bench with the Boston paper in his hands.

He glanced up at her from his paper and smiled. "Getting some morning air?" he asked.

"Yes. It's so good to be able to walk around this way!"

He folded the paper and lifted his eyebrows in inquiry. "Weren't you allowed any freedom in that place?"

"Of course!" she said quickly. "We had a rather nice garden there." She paused for a moment and her lovely face went in shadow. "But there were always the walls. Tall brick walls with barbed wire at the top of them!"

"You couldn't ignore them," Uncle Henry agreed dryly. "Sort of robbed any air of freedom from the spot."

She nodded and twisted her hands which she held clasped before her. "You always knew that you were contained."

"Well, that's over," the old man said.

"I hope so."

Henry Mills stood up beside her with a concerned look on his alcohol-ravaged face. "Don't let Regina or that Mona upset you!"

She said, "I'm trying not to."

"They will if they can," the old man warned her. "Neither of them ever wanted Derek to marry."

"I've suspected that."

"It's true," he said grimly, shoving his rolled newspaper under his arm. "They enjoyed it when you had your break-down and they weren't overjoyed when they heard you were coming back."

"I'm certain they weren't," she said.

Henry scowled. "Regina is already going around talking behind your back. She's making a big thing of the way you re-acted to Timmy and then your screaming on the porch last night."

Joyce was mildly surprised. "She spoke to you about that?"

"Yes. Said you were probably seeing things again and that you shouldn't have been brought back. That you still needed treatment."

"I see."

The old man said, "I told her to mind her own business. Not that she will! And I told Mona the same thing!" He gave her a troubled glance. "You'd better be careful. What did make you scream last night?"

She hesitated. "I thought I saw something."

"Oh?"

"It was probably just the shadows. I'm still very nervous."

Uncle Henry sighed. "Don't give them any cause to talk if you can help it. And be careful as far as Derek is concerned too. I think they've talked to him plenty."

"I'm sure of it."

"Derek always listened to his mother too much," the old man said darkly.

"I'm aware of that."

"Just don't forget it."

Joyce said, "It's a wonder that Mona hasn't tried to win some attention from David Chase."

Henry looked disgusted. "That would be too sensible of her! She's still showing calf's eyes for Derek!"

"I think Faith Patterson is moving in on David," Joyce said. "I talked to her just a few minutes ago. She's been coming here every morning for a sitting for a portrait of her David is painting."

The old man nodded his white head. "Yes. I know all about that. And of course Faith likes to play around. Why that husband of hers puts up with it is more than I know."

"He seems very devoted to her. Maybe he understands her better than we do," Joyce suggested.

Henry Mills looked grim. "She has the money. Brook knew what he'd have to put up with when he married her. Her family owns almost as much of Dark Harbor as Regina does. But don't be fooled. I don't think it's David Chase that Faith has got her eye on this summer. It's someone else."

Her eyebrows raised. "Really?"

"You bet," the old man said sourly. "I don't like to say this but I think you ought to know. It's your Derek that Faith has been playing fast and loose with. That's why she took that job at the museum to be with him."

Joyce gasped. "Derek!"

"Take it from me! They've been together a lot all the time you were away. Mona complained to his mother about it. I heard them but they didn't know I was around. I hear plenty but I don't say anything."

She was listening to him in stunned surprise. It hadn't occurred to her that it might be Derek whom Faith had latched on to. But now she realized that it could be. Only a few minutes ago Faith had been jubilant to her about enjoying working with Derek!

She stared at the lined, serious face of Derek's uncle. "Do you think it's really so?"

"You want the truth?"

"I do."

"Yes."

"I see," she said tautly.

"It'll likely all blow over now that you're back," the old man went on. "But that's the way it has been. Maybe she will turn to that artist now. Seems like having a husband isn't enough for her, she always has to be fooling around with some other man!"

"Yes. That does seem so," she agreed faintly.

"Don't worry about it," Derek's uncle said. "But keep an eye on those two." And with that he walked away in the direction of the house.

She stood alone in the warm sunshine of the garden. Her heart was pounding as she thought about what she'd just heard. She knew that Derek's uncle had told her about the affair between her husband and Faith to help her. He's wanted to warn her. But it had also added to her generally nervous state. This was trouble from a direction entirely unexpected. And for the moment she didn't know how she could cope with it!

It seemed there was just too much to battle against! She'd known there was a distinct change in Derek's attitude towards her but had blamed it on her illness and the malicious talk of his mother and adopted sister. But now she was faced with still another element of danger. The frivolous Faith had turned her attention toward Derek.

Slowly she turned and began walking back to the castle with her mind in a turmoil. Should she tell Derek what she'd learned and challenge him about it? Or would this only enrage him and turn him against her? Perhaps she should fight her feelings and try and handle it in a more sophisticated manner but was that possible? Was she too nervous to manage such an approach?

All these thoughts were rushing through her troubled mind when she became suddenly aware that there was someone standing in her path. Someone blocking her way and staring at her with intense anger and hatred. She halted and saw that it was her mother-in-law, Regina.

The older woman hissed, "Murderess!"

CHAPTER FOUR

Joyce stared at her mother-in-law. "What are you talking about?" she asked.

The older woman continued to stand there glaring at her. "How can you pretend you don't know?"

"Because I don't!" she said despairingly.

"I knew you were capable of a lot," Regina Mills went on with rage in her voice, "but I scarcely believed you would stoop to such a thing as this!"

"Explain yourself!" Joyce demanded.

"Need I?" the older woman wanted to know.

"Look!" Joyce declared. "I have no idea what you're making all this fuss about! I promise you I don't!"

"So you say!"

"It's true!"

Her mother-in-law regarded her with hatred plain on her aristocratic face. "I might have expected you to deny it!"

"Deny what?"

Regina stared at her in frigid silence for at least a moment. Then she said, "Follow me."

"Very well," Joyce said.

The older woman led her down the garden and across the lawn to a row of bushes at a distance from the house. The bushes served as a sort of barrier between the lawn and the uncultivated area beyond them. When they reached the bushes Regina Mills halted and pointed a forefinger to the ground.

"There!" she said harshly.

A dazed Joyce stared at the spot and to her horror saw the still remains of the black cat, Timmy. Tied tightly around the animal's neck was a vividly patterned scarf that she immediately recognized as her own.

"No!" she cried.

"What do you say now?" her mother-in-law demanded icily.

Joyce looked up at her in dismay. "I don't understand it! I can't imagine who would do such a thing!"

"The scarf around its neck is yours!"

"I can't help that!"

"I've seen you wear it many times," Regina went on. "And it bears your initials!"

Joyce was near a state of panic. "You can't believe that I did this terrible thing? Someone must have stolen the scarf from my room!"

"A likely story!" the older woman said derisively.

"You know I wouldn't do such a thing," Joyce said with tears in her eyes as she turned away from the stiff black remains of Timmy.

Regina's eyes were bright with rage. "You hated Timmy!"

"Seeing him upset me! I didn't hate him!"

"You blamed that cat for Lucie's death! For your negligence!"

"Not in the way you mean!" she said brokenly.

"And you could not bear to have it around as a reminder of your guilt!" her mother-in-law raged.

"No!"

"So you somehow got hold of the poor animal in the night and deliberately strangled it with that scarf!"

"I tell you someone else must have done it!"

Regina sneered, "Who else would be mad enough to do such a thing but you? Who else would have a motive?"

"I don't know!"

"Why don't you at least have the decency to confess?" the older woman raged.

"I will not confess to something I didn't do! Never!" Joyce sobbed. And at the same time she turned from her mother-in-law and started hurrying back across the lawn towards the house. Her progress was uneven as she stumbled several times along the way, blinded by her tears. When she reached the castle she hurried up the stairs and sought refuge in her own room.

She remained there all afternoon. Lunchtime came and went. No one came to her room. She sobbed out her misery and then as she regained control of herself she began trying to sort it all out. It seemed to help her to pace slowly back and forth as she mulled over what had happened. Occasionally she would sit in the easy chair by the window and stare out at the ocean.

A cool breeze coming in through the screen made the room comfortable. She was still so shaken by the scene with Regina that she felt no hunger pangs. What horrified her, and caused her the most tormenting doubts, was the question of who had murdered the unfortunate Timmy and made it appear that she was guilty!

It meant there was someone in the castle who wanted to destroy her. Someone who was trying to send her back to the mental hospital she'd just left. Who? That was the question. She could not believe that Regina would, herself, murder her beloved cat, to put her in a shadow. It had to be someone else. Mona? Or perhaps even Derek if he were in love with someone else and wished to rid himself of her. His uncle had openly stated that Derek and Faith were having an affair. Yet Derek had pretended to be happy that she'd been released from the sanitarium. Maybe someone else was to blame, some unknown person mad enough to do such a vicious thing!

Exhausted by her tantalizing doubts she stretched out on her bed and slept for a little. She was awakened by the door of her room opening and closing. Startled she raised herself up on an elbow and saw a grim-faced Derek standing by the foot of her bed.

In a relieved voice, she said, "You woke me up! I didn't know who it might be!"

"I see," he said dryly.

She said, "Aren't you home early?"

"No."

Joyce glanced at her wristwatch and saw that it was almost six. She said, "You're right. I must have slept longer than I realized."

"You must have."

She could not ignore his strange, tense manner any longer. She said, "You're behaving very oddly."

"That's amusing, coming from you," her handsome husband said bitterly.

She stood up. "I suppose your mother has been telling you about Timmy."

His expression tragic, he nodded. "That's right! Good God, Joyce, what a thing to do!"

"I didn't do it!" she declared, able to protest without the lack of control she'd shown when arguing this with his mother. The time lapse had allowed her to face the situation with more calm.

Derek looked at her with disbelief. "Who else would do it?"

"That's what I intend to find out!"

He hesitated. "It was your scarf."

"I can't help that," she told him. "Anyone here could have taken it from my room."

He turned away from her and went over to the window and

gazed out, his handsome face distorted by sorrow. In a taut voice, he said, "I know you've been ill. And the sight of that cat did upset you. It is possible that you couldn't help yourself. That you did it without having any control over your actions. If that is so you ought to admit it to me and I will try and understand."

Joyce shook her head. "Derek, I'm not mad!"

He looked at her now with pain showing in his eyes. "There has to be some explanation."

"I agree."

"Well, then?"

She said, "The explanation doesn't have to concern me. I'm convinced that someone else took that scarf and throttled that poor cat with it to make me seem still mad."

Derek listened to her with obvious uncertainty. "I want to believe you," he said. "But I find it very difficult."

"Should you?" she challenged him.

He looked surprised. "Should I what?"

"Find it so hard to believe me. Don't I deserve your trust?"

Derek hesitated. "In ordinary circumstances, if you hadn't been ill, I might be willing to listen to your theories. But it seems more likely that you killed Timmy than anyone else."

"You still think so?"

He gave a despairing wave of his hand. "Perhaps you don't even remember it. You might have done it in a kind of trance."

"No, Derek. No. Nothing like that."

"How can you be sure?" There was anguish in his voice.

"Don't ask me that," she said. "I just know."

Derek sighed. "Mother is in a dreadful state about it. She adored that cat."

"I'm sorry for her," she said. "But I can't let her accuse me of killing it."

"She's convinced that you did."

"If it gives her any small satisfaction let her think so. But I can't admit to it. I'm innocent and I expect you to defend me to her not side with her."

Derek began to pace slowly back and forth. "Who else would do such a dreadful thing?"

"There may be someone else here as insane as I was when you took me to the hospital," she said. "I can only tell you that I'm perfectly rational now and I had nothing to do with it."

He glanced at her. "Your scarf! It was your scarf!"

"I don't know why it was used other than to make it appear I did it," she admitted. "The motive and the culprit will have to be discovered."

"Who could hate you so?" Derek demanded.

She shrugged. "Your mother, though I rule her out as a suspect. And Mona."

"Mona wouldn't do such a thing!"

Joyce asked him, "How can you be certain?"

He spread his hands despairingly as he searched for a likely answer. "It isn't like her," he finally said.

"But you can picture me doing it?"

"Not normally! But—" his voice trailed off and he turned away from her again.

She studied him sorrowfully. "You still think I'm mad, don't you?"

"Not really," he protested. "I simply have the feeling that you may have lost control for a moment. I remember how you cried out when you first saw the cat. And then you screamed about nothing last night!"

"You've been convinced of my guilt by your mother!"

"Not altogether! I can think for myself!" was his reply.

"I don't think you have," she said. "You may be interested

76

to know I also hear accusations against you."

He frowned at her. "Accusations? What sort of accusations?"

She smiled bitterly. "Now it's a different story. I have heard that you and Faith Patterson are having an affair!"

Derek's face crimsoned. "Faith and I!"

"That's right!"

"Who told you that lie?"

Joyce said, "I'm sorry. I can't tell you. How do you feel being accused?"

"You're making it up! You must be mad!" he replied angrily.

"I can promise you I'm not making it up," she said. "I thought it strange that Faith had so suddenly become work-conscious. That she was enjoying her work with you at the museum so much."

"There's nothing to it!"

"I see," she said. "And you ask me to believe you?"

"Yes."

"Though you refuse to listen to my explanations."

"That's different."

"Not as I see it," she said, surprised at the calm control she'd managed so far.

Her husband faced her angrily. "We're getting nowhere going on this way!"

"So?"

"Let's drop all this talk," he went on. "I don't want to quarrel with you. Dr. Beckett said you were not to be put under any strain."

Her smile was rueful. "I wonder what he would say about the discussion we've just had?"

Derek waved this aside. "Something unpleasant caused this row between us. I'll try to forget it. But if anything more happens I don't know what I'll do."

She said, "Is that a threat?"

"It wasn't meant to be," her husband said unhappily. "I'm saying that I've come to the end of my resources. I don't know how to cope with what is going on here."

"I see," she said quietly.

He gave a deep sigh. "Are you coming down to dinner?"

"No," she said. "I don't feel like facing your mother and the others tonight. You can have something sent up to me if you will."

Derek showed reluctance at her suggestion. "Not appearing will only make you seem more guilty."

"Then that's a risk I'll have to take," she said.

"You don't care what the others think?"

"If you want to put it that way," she said. "No. I don't care."

He moved to the door to leave. "Why must you always do the wrong thing?" he asked with despairing resignation.

"I wasn't aware that I did," she said.

"Do what you like," he told her. "I'll have the kitchen send you up a tray." And he left.

As soon as Derek went she slumped down in the easy chair and gazed after him in bleak despair. It had been a battle in which she'd barely held her own. She'd put up a bold front but now that she was alone a good deal of her forced confidence left her. She felt a nagging doubt surge up in her.

Suppose he was right? Suppose that in a moment of madness she'd blanked out and throttled Timmy without having any memory of doing so? When she'd first been mentally ill she'd had short blackouts and they'd terrified her! She would be in a certain place doing something only to come alert again in an entirely different spot doing some very different thing. It had frightened her more than anything else. Not being able to remember what she'd done in the blackout!

But those spells had ended. She'd not had a blackout for months. Dr. Beckett had commended her on this point. The old doctor had chuckled and said, "Golf and good fresh air have swept the cobwebs from your brain! That's the answer, my girl!"

Yet what was the answer now? Had she suffered a relapse? Had those spells come back to torment her? Was she indeed still mad? It was a shocking question and she didn't know the answer! There was one thing: she could not picture herself being cruel to an animal whatever her mental state might be. She was not capable of that kind of cruelty!

After a little one of the maids came with a tray of food which she left. In the privacy of her bedroom Joyce managed to eat a little. But she was still in a mood of fear and uncertainty. Derek's behavior had not been encouraging.

Now she became restless and decided to go down to the beach for a stroll. Dr. Beckett had strongly advised exercise and fresh air to overcome mental uncertainty. And she had never known herself to feel so uncertain except in those first desperate days before and after her sojourn in the sanitarium. Things seemed quiet in the house as she left her room and made her way down the hall and stairway.

She reached the freedom of the lawn without meeting anyone. As she strolled towards the cliff she could hear her mother-in-law's voice as she talked to someone on the patio. The autocratic woman was talking emphatically about something, she could tell by the tone of her voice although she could not make out the words. It could be she was discussing her. At this moment Joyce didn't care! She merely wanted to escape!

Escape from the frightening atmosphere of the old house and its people! She even felt like a stranger with Derek. She reached the cliff and then followed a path that led to a flight of wooden steps down to the beach. The wooden steps went down in three stages so that they were not all that steep.

A light breeze swept through her long black hair. The breaking of the waves on the beach became a loud barrier between her and any other sounds. She marched on down the steps until she reached the level of the sand. Then she halted with a deep sigh.

She had escaped from the house without being seen. It was extremely unlikely that she'd be followed. She could walk along the beach and give herself to her thoughts. She breathed deeply of the fresh, salt air and her head seemed better at once. She began to stroll along slowly lost in her thoughts.

Surely Derek had behaved guiltily at her accusation of his having an affair with Faith. It seemed all too likely that his uncle had told her the truth. But what was she to do about it? Had it been one of those unhappy romances which sometimes occur between two people with temporary problems that appear overwhelming to them?

Had Derek turned to Faith through mere unhappiness? Unhappiness caused by her own breakdown? Joyce hesitated to condemn the husband she loved knowing that this could happen. What excuse could Faith use to justify her role in the affair? Likely her sick, warped nature. It could be that she was unable to help herself from having a succession of affairs that brought her ultimately nothing but misery.

Joyce knew that she was trying to deal with all these problems while her own reason was still in a state of precarious balance. It would not take much to topple her and send her into a state of madness once again. This she feared above all. But she knew if she fled from Dark Harbor at this point nothing would be solved. She would be haunted by the macabre events which had taken place there for the balance of her life.

She would lose her husband. If she left the island there would be no reconciliation. Derek would regard her running away as an admission of guilt and defeat. Their love had to be reconstructed carefully and leaving him would doom any hope of this. So if she wanted to save her marriage she must remain! But what of the ghost that haunted her? And of the evil person lurking somewhere in the background who appeared intent on bringing her to a swift madness? Could the phantom be responsible for the throttling of the cat? It seemed much more likely it was someone among the living. Mona?

She had suddenly come upon a barrier of huge boulders. And all at once she realized that dusk had settled while she'd been strolling along lost in her thoughts. It was uncertain whether she'd make the return journey along the beach and up the wooden steps to the lawn before it was really dark. The knowledge of this sent a thrill of fear through her body.

Turning she began to rapidly retrace her steps along the beach. Far out in the ocean tiny lights marking buoys and pleasure craft were beginning to show. And the lighthouse on a distant reef far ahead was casting its beam of light in a slow revolving motion. Her terror began to mount.

Because of all that had happened it needed only the darkness to heighten her fears. The terror she barely suppressed during the daylight hours now bubbled over and left her trembling and panicky.

She was within a few feet of the wooden steps and it was almost dark. The beam from the lighthouse touched on the beach before her for a short instant. And in its brief, weak beam she saw outlined the phantom of Captain Peter Mills! There was no mistaking the cap with its gold braid and the long coat with its brass buttons in two rows down the front.

The ghostly figure raised a hand to hail her and then the beam of light moved on and the darkness closed in around the ghost again. She screamed in fear and made a mad dash for the wooden steps. As she started up them she heard footsteps below and then someone following her up the steps. Someone breathing hard and close behind her!

She exerted her last ounce of strength to mount the several flights of wooden steps at a madcap pace. And when she reached the lawn she ran wildly ahead in the darkness. All the while she heard the phantom close on her heels!

She saw the outline of a building ahead and too late knew that she'd run in the wrong direction. Instead of heading towards the castle she'd gone in the direction of the chapel. She was almost at its open door now. What to do?

It was a hopeless situation! The phantom was going to trap her in the chapel! Gasping for breath she tottered towards the doorway with its several steps leading up to it. She let out a cry that was something between a harsh sob and a scream. Then she literally fell up the stairs and crawled inside the chapel. She was trying to shut the heavy door behind her when the phantom came in pursuit and seized her by the throat before she could help herself.

She could not see his face but she felt the mad strength of his cruel fingers. As her breathing came to a gasping end she sank into a coma in which she speculated on why the ghost should be throttling her when he'd stabbed his wife in that long ago murder. Why hadn't he repeated his crime and stabbed her with a ghostly dagger? Committed this murder as he had the one a century earlier?

"Joyce!" It was her name being anxiously spoken and someone was shaking her. Trying to rouse her.

She opened her eyes to darkness and felt her throat ache.

Was she dead? Was this how one awoke to the other side? She stared nervously into the shadows knowing she was still not entirely conscious.

"Joyce!" Her name was repeated again and she thought the voice was somehow familiar.

"Who are you?" she asked in a hoarse whisper, aware of the pain in her throat once again.

"Henry! It's Uncle Henry! What in the world happened to you? And what brought you here?"

"Uncle Henry?" She could not believe it.

"Yes."

"Then I'm not dead!"

"Not that I know of," the old man said with some disgust. "I was out for a walk in the garden and I saw you racing across the lawn towards the chapel. Then you screamed and seemed to fall. I followed as quickly as I could and found you stretched out on the floor just where you still are. You were unconscious!"

She raised herself up with an effort. "He was chasing me!"

"Who?" Uncle Henry was only a shadow in the darkness.

"The phantom!"

"The phantom?"

"Yes. Didn't you see him?" Her voice was more her own now and her throat pained a little less.

"I saw no one but you," the old man told her irritably.

She began to struggle to her feet and he helped her. Still weak and dizzy, she said, "I was on the beach. It grew dark before I knew it. Then the lighthouse beam touched the beach in front of me and I saw him!" She shuddered at the very memory of it.

"Who did you see?"

"The ghost of Captain Peter Mills."

"Now you know no one will ever believe that," the old

man said somewhat peevishly.

"I'm telling you exactly what happened. The phantom came after me and chased me up the steps and across the lawn and caught me here and began to throttle me. I lost consciousness until I heard you calling my name."

"You were here alone when I found you," Uncle Henry said.

"You didn't see him, either chasing me across the lawn or trying to murder me here?"

"No. I just saw you."

She stared at him standing beside her in the darkness and in a taut voice said, "There can be just one explanation. The phantom must reveal himself only to me."

The old man standing by her groaned. "I hate to hear you say such things," he said. "You know what Regina will say and make all the others think?"

"That I had another crazy spell?" she asked bitterly.

"Close enough," the old man said with a sigh.

She looked out the chapel door and saw the distant lighted windows of the old house. She said, "I meant to run towards the house. I don't know why I didn't. I somehow became confused."

Uncle Henry said, "I don't know what to make of all this. Come on into the chapel."

"It's pitch dark in there," she objected.

"I know," he said with some annoyance. "But there are candles on the altar. Part of the show for the tourists. And I have some matches. We can light the candles and talk here for a few minutes longer."

"I didn't understand," she admitted, following close after him as he walked down to the front of the chapel in the darkness.

He grumbled aloud to himself as he reached the altar and

lit a match and groped for the candles. He found one and lighted it and then its two companions in the candelabra.

He stood at the altar with the candlelight showing off his grim, lined face. He looked like some dour Old Testament prophet with his mane of white hair. She stepped up to the altar with him.

He asked her, "Are you going to tell Derek about this?"

She frowned. "You think I shouldn't?"

"Definitely," was his reply. "If you go to him with this story now it will be received as just another wild tale."

"I suppose so."

"I know it," the old man said worriedly. "Even I find your story hard to credit and I'm on your side."

She looked into his rheumy, troubled eyes and said, "I know I saw the Phantom on the beach and it did follow me and attack me. Haven't you ever seen the ghost?"

Henry Mills said, "If I admitted it they'd say it was a drunken man's wild talk. You know their opinion of me."

"You haven't answered my question," was her reply. "You haven't told me whether you've seen the ghost or not?"

The old man hesitated, his ravaged face highlighted in the glow of the candelabra, as they stood there on the altar in the ancient chapel.

At last he said, "There have been times I thought I've seen something. But nothing so definite as you've described nor have I been attacked."

Joyce said, "Perhaps you are not as attuned to the supernatural as I am. I think I became more sensitive to the other side following Lucie's death and after my period of insanity."

The old man eyed her nervously. "That kind of talk won't do you any good either."

"So what does that leave me?" she inquired wearily.

"You are in a most difficult position," he agreed. "I don't

know what to advise. Perhaps you should leave the island."

"And lose Derek? I still love him."

Henry sighed. "In that case you can't leave. There is that business between him and Faith Patterson."

"I know," she agreed. "If I leave now it will mean the end of my marriage."

"And if you remain here it might mean your life? Have you thought about that?"

"Yes."

Old Henry Mills studied her closely. "Derek is that important to you?"

"So it seems," she said in a taut voice.

The old man shrugged. "I suppose that's why I'm a bachelor. I can't picture myself willing to make that kind of a sacrifice for anyone. Derek is a lucky young man though I'm not sure he deserves your love."

"I'm willing to give him the benefit of the doubt," she said. "At least for the present."

"How is your throat?"

"Much better. You must have frightened whoever it was off before any real harm was done me."

"You were unconscious."

"Part of that is due to fear," she said.

The old man studied her worriedly. "Are you sure it all wasn't due to fear? I still wish that I had seen someone following you and I didn't."

"Probably because it was a ghost after me."

"We always seem to come back to that," the old man said grimly.

"Perhaps because it is the truth."

"Perhaps," he admitted grudgingly. "I find it difficult enough to cope with humans, I have no suggestions to offer where ghosts are concerned."

"I know. It is baffling," she agreed.

"And why should this ghost show hostility towards you?" the old man asked.

She gazed down into the shadows of the chapel below them. "I don't know. Perhaps he identifies me with the wife who was unfaithful to him and whom he murdered."

"I wonder," the old man said.

"In any event I intend to remain here and try and find out what it means."

"Regina will do her best to get rid of you," the old man warned her. "Now she's blaming you for killing Timmy."

"I've been through all that with her."

"She claims you're still not in your right mind and if you repeat this story of the ghost chasing you the others are apt to side with her."

"I appreciate your advice," she told him. "I won't say anything."

Henry sighed. "Well, now we should go back. The others will miss us and start wondering. You make your way to the door before I put out the candles."

She did as he instructed her. When she was safely at the door of the old chapel he put out the altar lights and followed her down.

He told her, "We'll walk back to the castle together. As far as the others are concerned we've been strolling in each other's company."

"Very well," she said.

"Remember if you have any serious problems I want you to come to me," the old man warned her as they went down the chapel steps and began making their way across the lawn.

When they entered the foyer of the old mansion a nervous Derek was waiting there to greet them. He gave her a strange, questioning look.

"I thought you were determined to remain in your room," he said.

She met his glance with a defiant one of her own. "I decided to take a walk," she said. "And your uncle was kind enough to join me."

Uncle Henry took up the cue. "Nothing like the night air," he said.

Derek eyed him stolidly. "I wasn't aware that it had any special therapeutic value."

"I've always enjoyed it," the old man said. And with a parting nod he left them and entered the elegant living room.

Derek stood there in awkward silence for a moment. Then he said, "You're feeling better?"

"Yes."

"Good. Would you like to come into the living room? Mother and Mona are in there chatting by the fireplace."

"Oh!"

Hastily, he said, "But we don't have to join them. The room is large enough for us to find a corner of our own."

Deciding that she must make at least an effort to show courage and not be completely cowed by her domineering mother-in-law, she quietly said, "Very well."

Derek escorted her into the living room and they took a stand just inside the door of the room and to the left of it. There was a large mirror on the wall across from them, a priceless antique of an earlier era. It was at least eight or ten feet wide and flawless.

She had heard that it was brought to the island from Boston. When a famed old hotel there had been torn down one of the Mills family had placed a bid on this mirror which had once graced the finest suite. It was said that Charles Dickens, William Thackeray, Oliver Wendell Holmes and Ellen Terry were among the many famous persons who had at one time or another seen their reflections in the huge mirror.

The mirror reflected the entrance to the living room and the shadowed foyer beyond it. She saw that Regina and Mona, who were seated by the fireplace at the other end of the room, had noted the arrival of herself and Derek. Her mother-in-law gave her a cold, angry glance, leaned over and said something to Mona in a low voice.

Resolutely Joyce turned her back on the two and gave her full attention to her husband. She said, "I want some freedom. I can't remain boxed up here in the house. I'll need a car."

Derek considered this with a frown. "You're sure you're able to drive?"

"I'm both able and fit," she said shortly. "What about a car?"

Derek showed embarrassment. "We put your car away. All it will need is the battery installed and the tires checked and a general clean-up."

She recalled the medium-sized sedan she'd driven until the time of her illness with some affection. She'd certainly rather drive it again than something else. She said, "I'd like to drive to Dark Harbor tomorrow. I have some errands to do and some people to see."

"Very well," he said. "I'll go out to the garage and speak to Ryan. Will you want it early?"

"No. Mid-morning will do," she said.

Her husband still showed some concern on his handsome face. "You have your driving license?"

"The one I had. I think it's still valid," she said.

"That should be checked," he warned her. "I'd better go out and speak to Ryan right now."

He went out through the foyer and she remained there standing alone. For a moment she occupied herself staring into the mirror which reflected the dark foyer clearly in its broad surface. Then she glanced down to the fireplace and saw that Regina had left the living room by the lower door and that Mona was crossing the room to join her.

The redhead offered her a wry smile. "We missed you at dinner," she said.

Joyce looked at her very directly. "Of course you know why."

"The trouble about Timmy?"

"Regina unfairly accusing me of killing that poor cat," she said.

"It was the scarf," Mona said. "That's probably what decided her it was you."

"That's so unfair," she protested. "Anyone could have taken that scarf and used it as they did."

Mona seemed to remain coolly unconvinced. She shrugged and said, "Mother will get over it. I'd just ignore the situation if I were you."

"Thanks," she said with some bitterness. "That isn't always easy with your mother."

Mona said, "Are you really feeling well again?"

"As well as I can expect. It takes a long time to regain one's health," she said. And by way of changing the subject: "I hear you are doing another book."

"Yes," Mona replied. "The last one did so well they were anxious to have another one right away."

"That must be flattering."

Mona looked unimpressed. "I suppose it is. But I find writing more of a chore and less fun than it used to be."

"What is your new book about?" Joyce said, trying to make some sort of conversation with this girl she disliked and whom she knew had a hatred for her.

The redhead smiled coldly. "In a way the leading character is a lot like you. I suppose you suggested her to me. A woman who loses her husband's affection and then has a breakdown."

She felt herself tense. "That's not exactly my story. Derek and I are still very much together."

"Yes, you are," Mona said slyly, as if she didn't expect that to be of long duration.

A kind of chill came over Joyce for no reason at all. It was as if an eerie coldness had suddenly surged into the room around her. And as she prepared to reply to Mona she let her eyes wander to the huge mirror on the wall opposite her. Staring at her from the shadows of the foyer was a ghostly face. The pale countenance of the woman with blood streaming down one side of her face from her eye. Joyce's whole being froze as she stared at the phantom face and she fought with herself not to cry out.

CHAPTER FIVE

"Is something wrong?" It was Mona who put the question to her in a tone with barely concealed excitement.

Joyce was still transfixed by the bloodied face in the mirror. Then it vanished as suddenly as it had appeared. She tried to hide the terror the strange vision had brought her as she turned to the other girl.

"What did you say?" she asked.

Mona was staring at her oddly. "I asked you if there was something wrong. We were talking and suddenly a kind of rigidity seemed to come over you. You began staring straight ahead of you with a frightened look on your face."

"I'm sorry," she apologized. "An unpleasant thought came to me." It was a lame excuse but the only one that came to mind at that moment.

The redhead seemed skeptical. She said, "I thought you were having some sort of attack."

"No!" She was trying to erase the memory of the phantom face from her mind.

Mona asked her, "Will you be checking with Dr. Taylor from time to time?"

Henry Taylor was the island's doctor. He had ministered to the needs of the Mills family for a good part of his seventy years. In spite of his age he was still active and she guessed that Derek had taken her to him or at least had him see her before she was shipped to the mainland for treatment.

She said, "I had no instructions from the hospital. But I may see him on my own. He's a fine old doctor."

Mona gave her a derisive look. "I'd try and avoid those unpleasant thoughts if I could. You certainly looked strange."

She lied, saying, "I didn't notice." She dare not tell the hostile Mona the truth.

"At least you're back in time for the big event of the summer social season," the redhead said.

"Oh?"

Mona raised her attractive eyebrows. "Hasn't Derek told you about it? I would have expected him to."

"We haven't had much time together."

"The museum is holding a costume ball to raise funds. Derek and Faith are heading the project and it is well advanced. They're having it at the museum."

"Won't that cause difficulties?"

Mona shrugged. "I understand they are clearing the big main lobby of everything and holding it there. It's large enough and has a marble floor."

"Yes," she agreed, still shaken. "I suppose that it might turn out very well."

"I'd expect he'd put you on the committee at once," Mona said with a malicious smile. "He can turn to you for help rather than Faith Patterson."

She gave Mona a sharp glance. "Why hasn't he asked your help?"

Mona continued to smile. "You know how he has always been with me. He invariably turns to someone else for companionship or advice."

"I wasn't really aware of it." Nor did she think Mona had offered a sound point.

It was then that Derek had come back into the room. As he joined them Mona told him, "I've just been mentioning the costume ball to Joyce. You must tell her all about it." And with that she left them to go upstairs.

When they were alone Derek gave her an embarrassed look. He said, "I've made arrangements for you to have the car. It will be ready in the morning."

"Thanks," she said.

He gazed after Mona in some annoyance and told Joyce, "I can't imagine why, she was in such a hurry to tell you about the costume ball!"

"Why shouldn't she tell me about it?"

"No reason," her handsome husband said, looking guilty. "I just don't consider it all that important."

She thought about the ghostly face which she'd seen for that brief moment in the hallway and wondered just what was important. She asked him, "When you came through the hall just now did you see anything?"

"See anything?" he asked, blankly.

"Or anyone," she quickly added.

He frowned. "No. Why?"

"I just wondered."

"Without any reason?" he asked suspiciously.

"You might say that," she said, not daring to admit that she'd had another eerie vision.

"Did Uncle Henry bother you with a lot of talk?" her husband worried.

"Why do you ask that?"

Derek said, "He likes to cause trouble and he hates all of us. Especially Mother! He works for the estate and lives here but he has the idea he's been cheated by us."

"I know."

"And it simply isn't true," Derek went on indignantly. "He wasted all the money my grandfather left him and then he expected to get my father's money."

Joyce said, "It isn't important to me."

"I simply wanted to explain," Derek told her. "I have an

idea he'd like to cause trouble between us."

"I doubt that," she said. "Mona might have more interest in that. I can tell she's still madly jealous of you."

"Mona?" he said with disbelief.

"Yes, Mona. And I'm sure you know it whether you are willing to admit it or not. And what is this about the costume ball?"

He spread his hands. "We're having it next week. At the museum. It's a project to raise funds. Faith got the idea and I've helped her develop it."

"I see. Mona seems very jealous of you and Faith working together. That's likely why she mentioned it to me. Hoping I'd object."

He smiled incredulously. "But that would be silly on your part! This is just a project for the museum. A pleasant one, I'll admit but still part of our job." He was at pains to make this long explanation but she felt he was protesting too much. There was guilt in his manner.

"I imagine it has meant your seeing Faith a great deal," she commented.

Now his guilt seemed more pronounced. He said, "Not anymore than the others on the project. You might just as well accuse David Chase. He's doing all the special decorations and they've had a lot of sessions about that."

She said, "It happens that David is not a married man."

"I can't see that makes any difference," her husband protested.

"It could be where gossip is concerned," she pointed out.

"It's not worth arguing about," Derek said unhappily. "Not when you consider all the other things that have happened."

"Perhaps not," she said. "What sort of an affair is it to be?"

"It's tied in with the history of the island," he said. "The museum is helping out with costume designs. We're bringing in a band from Boston and the lobby will be completely decorated for the occasion. It should be the social event of the season here and bring the museum a great deal of money."

She gave him a questioning smile. "Am I to be allowed to attend?"

"Of course. You'll be an honored guest. I was saving it for a surprise," her husband said.

Joyce somehow doubted this but she accepted it at face value. "I'll see later if I feel up to attending," she said.

They talked for a little longer and then went up to their respective bedrooms. Derek kissed her goodnight with a certain air of gentleness but he left her alone as he had on the other nights. And once she was in her room by herself the vision of the woman's face covered with blood came back to haunt her. It was the second weird experience she'd had in one evening. And yet she hadn't been able to confide in Derek. She prepared for bed and then waited a long while for sleep to come.

That night her dreams were of the island. The entire island. The Brant Point Light and the foot of Old North Wharf. Stately mansions on Union Street and the weird old monastery which had once housed a leper hospital. The old cemetery where Lucie was buried in the Mills family plot on a hill overlooking the town.

In her dream she lingered in the cemetery, moving among the worn gravestones until she came to the one marking the tiny green mound under which her beloved child lay. She stood before the small tombstone inscribed with Lucie's name and birth and death dates. Below there was the quotation, "Suffer little children to come unto Me."

As she stood there a storm suddenly came up. There was rain and wind and sharp flashes of lightning. She crouched under the severity of the storm. The clouds had turned so dark that it was like night and the lashing rain beat across her face and soaked through her thin clothing. The wind howled and the ancient trees shading the graves leaned and groaned under the impact of the howling storm.

Joyce fell to her knees and clutched the gravestone of her child for sanctuary. The storm grew in intensity. She sobbed her fear aloud. Next, as a great flash of lightning lit up the cemetery, she saw Captain Peter Mills in his uniform appear among the gravestones and come marching towards her. She crouched behind Lucie's gravestone whimpering with terror as the phantom drew near!

Then she awoke. Her room was dark and silent. There was not a sound in the old mansion. She sat up and stared into the shadows with her dream still vivid to her. It was a nightmare she'd had at least two or three times before.

She'd experienced it at the mental hospital while she was a patient and it had disturbed her so that she'd sought out Dr. Beckett to ask his advice about it.

The British doctor had listened with more than usual interest until she finished. Then he said, "It has symbolic meaning, my dear Mrs. Mills. The act of clutching at your dead child's gravestone is symbolic of your reaching out for her. The storm is the lashing punishment which you feel life has offered you. And so you crouch before it and seek sanctuary at your child's grave."

She'd frowned. "If all that is true where does the ghost of Captain Peter Mills come into it? Why am I so afraid of him? I know nothing about him other than the legend that has been repeated down through the years."

"But in the legend he is pictured as a wife murderer," the doctor said.

"Yes."

Dr. Beckett had given her a meaningful look. "So you

identify this long ago murderer with your husband for some reason. Perhaps because you fear your husband's anger. You think he blames you for the death of your child."

"Yes, I do!"

"That is what is behind it all. Your conviction that the death of the child came about through your neglect. You mustn't believe that. It was an accident. Accidents happen and often we can't do anything to prevent them. The sooner you realize this and cease blaming yourself the sooner you'll recover. Life is like a golf game, my dear, follow the rules and your chances of getting in the rough are slim. But it can happen! It can always happen!"

She glanced in the direction of the door leading to Derek's room. The door was lost in the darkness at this moment. But she knew that on the other side of it her husband lay asleep. Had he ever forgiven her for what had happened that tragic afternoon? Was he merely being kind to her because of her illness? And had he turned to Faith Patterson in his despair to blot out the memory of losing the child he'd loved and to try and forget her ugly illness?

She didn't know. These were things she had to try and find out. And that was why she felt the need to remain in this haunted mansion on Pirate Island. With a sigh she lay back on her pillow and once again sought sleep.

In the morning she had breakfast alone and then went upstairs and dressed for her drive in to Dark Harbor. She had two or three errands she wanted to do and she definitely wanted to call on Captain Zachary Miller. She felt the old man's advice would be valuable and Derek had said the captain was still alive and active.

Ryan had her car out in front of the garage waiting for her. He'd polished it so that it shone and it looked very good indeed.

She thanked the garage man. "You've done a wonderful job," she said.

The elderly Ryan beamed at her. "Glad to be able to bring it out, Mrs. Mills. Didn't seem right for a fine car like that to be collecting dust in the rear of the garage. But those were the mister's orders. But no matter! She's all shipshape and ready to drive again."

"That's truly good news," she said, opening the door and sitting behind the wheel. It felt comfortable. She started the engine and headed in the direction of Dark Harbor.

She had turned the windows down and a lovely summer morning breeze wafted through the car. There was truly something about the island air. It could be miserably damp at times but when the days were fine there was nothing to quite match it.

Within a few minutes the castle was a distance behind her and she was speeding along the main road toward the town. It had been more than a year since she'd been in Dark Harbor on her own. Once she'd enjoyed almost daily shopping trips to the town. And now she felt a growing excitement as she neared the rows of weathered houses that marked the outskirts of the village.

Once it had been the most prosperous whaling port in New England. The wharves of Dark Harbor had been lined with the great vessels with their rich cargoes of whale oil. Generations of sailors had shipped out of Dark Harbor to spear the huge monsters of the ocean as far away as South America and the Pacific Coast. The money from their whaling expeditions had built the fine houses on the island, including the Mills castle. But those days had vanished and Dark Harbor depended on its fishermen and its tourist business.

Reaching the bottom of the cobblestoned main street she

drove on until she came to the intersection and the side street which led to the door of the modest cottage of Captain Zachary Miller. And she was delighted to find the old man seated in a chair next to his front door contentedly puffing on a clay pipe. He hadn't changed much except to perhaps shrink a little in size; his keen, sympathetic eyes were still bright in the weathered old seaman's face.

Just seeing the courageous old man made her feel better. She swung out of the car in a hurry and crossed the dirt sidewalk, opened the gate in the spotless white picket fence and made her way along the flagstone walk to where the old man was seated.

"Good morning, Captain Zachary," she said with a smile.

The old man struggled to his feet and removed the clay pipe from his mouth. Then he stared at her rather shortsightedly for a moment with eyes that had seen all the oceans and countless foreign lands. It took him a few seconds before his wizened face broke into a smile.

"Mrs. Mills," he exclaimed with delight. "You're back! Welcome home!"

"Thank you," she said, feeling happier than at any time since her return. "I had to look you up."

"I'd have been upset if you hadn't," the old man assured her. "Let's go inside where it's more comfortable."

"Anywhere will do," she told him.

The little old man proudly led her into the living room of the cottage he owned and maintained himself. It was shadowy inside from shutters only partly opened and the room smelled of spices and tea. The walls were papered in a pretty floral pattern and lined with framed photos of another era.

The old man waved her to a battered leather chair and sank into a high-backed chair with a worn needlepoint covering. He studied her with a pleased look on his wizened face.

"I said you'd get well," he told her.

"Thank you," she said. "For a while I didn't know."

"You have the spirit," he said. "Takes a lot to level you."

She said, "There wasn't much fight left in me when they took me to the mainland."

"You went through a lot," the old man said sympathetically.

Joyce nodded. "Now I begin to wonder if it's over."

Captain Zachary Miller showed interest. "Don't tell me things still aren't right at the castle."

"Far from it," she said, her face shadowed with her despair. "I sometimes wonder if anyone is pleased by my return. Certainly not Regina or Mona. And I'm even a little dubious as to how Derek really feels."

The old captain's shaggy eyebrows lifted. "You think that your husband mightn't have wanted you to recover?"

"I'm worried by his attitude."

"In what way?"

"He's been very withdrawn since my coming hack. And when any arguments come up he sides with his mother. He seems to still see me as the mentally ill wife he took to the mainland. He can't accept that I'm myself again."

The captain pursed his thin old lips. "That is too bad."

"There is gossip," she went on unhappily. "His Uncle Henry told me that. He is my one friend at the castle."

"I know Henry," the captain said, not making it clear by his tone whether he approved of him or not.

"Henry told me that my husband is involved in an affair with Faith Patterson."

"Faith Patterson?" the old man stared at her blankly.

"You must know her. She's blonde and very attractive in a lush way. She's married to Brook Patterson at the museum.

She's from one of the old families here."

He nodded. "I know now. I used to buy her hard candy when she was a little tot. I remember Faith well! Long yellow curls and a flirt's smile."

Joyce smiled ruefully. "The long yellow curls have gone but she still is a wicked flirt. She's given her husband a bad time."

"And he's a mainlander."

"He owes everything to her family," she said. "So he lets Faith do about as she pleases."

Captain Zachary gave her a sharp look. "Do you really think there is anything in this?"

"I don't know." She hesitated. "I still have the feeling that Derek has never forgiven me for Lucie's death. That inwardly he may be boiling with hatred of me."

"I doubt that."

"I know I shouldn't think about it but I can't help it," she said in despair. "And I feel that his hidden hatred and his agony may have made him enter into an affair with Faith."

"That isn't good," the old man in the chair opposite her said.

"I know. I don't want to believe it and I tell myself if I see this through I may win back Derek's love and respect."

"Perhaps you only think you have lost it," he told her. "Derek may not doubt you and there may not be any love affair."

"I think there is," she worried. "And to top it all weird things have been happening at the castle. I've been seeing ghosts."

"Ghosts?"

"Yes. You know the story of Captain Peter Mills and how he stabbed his wife to death in a jealous rage and then hung himself in the cellar of the castle."

"Everyone on the island must have heard that tale," the old man said.

She leaned forward and looked at him earnestly across the shadowed room. "You must know the details of it better than anyone!"

Captain Zachary Miller furrowed his ancient brow. "I've seen tintypes of him. My grandfather had one he picked up somewhere. Captain Peter Mills was a tall, thin man with a narrow face and high cheekbones."

"And a small black mustache!" she found herself saying.

The old man stared at her in surprise. "How do you come to know that?"

She didn't reply for a few seconds. Then she said, "Because I've seen his ghost."

"Remarkable," the old man said dryly. "I've heard that his ghost haunts the castle and the grounds around it. But you're the first one I've ever talked to who claims to have seen him."

"I have," she said. "I'm sure of it. Tell me more about him. He wears a cap with braid and some kind of leather visor and his coat is cut tight at the waist and has wide lapels and two rows of shiny metal buttons."

Captain Zachary Miller was clearly impressed. He said, "You have very well described the regulation outfit of a sea captain in that day. But then you must have seen such outfits at the museum."

"Maybe," she admitted. "But I'm describing what the phantom figure I've been seeing wears."

"Have you told anyone else about this?"

"Only Uncle Henry and he has promised to keep silent. He also has warned me not to tell others. That they may think me still mad if I do."

"That's sound advice," Captain Zachary agreed. "It could

be a hazard. People are always suspicious of anyone who has had a mental illness."

"David Chase told me that."

"Who is he?"

"A young artist working at the museum for the summer. He's living at the castle."

"I see," the old man said. "Well, he's a wise young man. The tag of madness is a nasty one. Few who have been tainted with it are ever regarded the same by others again."

"But that's ridiculous!" she protested. "People can recover from mental illness just as they recover from physical ailments."

"It's the nature of the illness," the old captain said. "It goes back to the early days when mad people were said to be possessed by the Devil. The old superstition lingers on."

"There's nothing I can do about it," she told him. "I know I'm sane and yet I have no way of convincing anyone that I am."

"You must be especially discreet," he advised. "That is where Henry and that young man were wise. You must be particularly careful not to give any hint of madness."

"And saying I have seen a ghost would suggest I am still insane?"

"I'm afraid so."

"But I have seen these phantom figures," she said bitterly. "A man and the other night, a woman!"

The old captain looked solemn. "I'm not questioning you nor do I think you mad. But others might."

"Tell me more about Captain Peter Mills," she insisted. "Tell me anything you can remember hearing. I must know!"

The old man gripped the carved arms of his chair with his bony, heavily-veined hands. "Captain Peter made a fortune. He was away from the island a long while. He made his first voyages as a whaling captain like all my own folk. But according to the stories that didn't appeal to him. He couldn't bear the stench of the blubber and he hadn't the patience to wait over a period of some years to become wealthy. So he settled for a different kind of trade, with a stench that has been strong in men's nostrils over the long years."

"What sort of trade?"

"Black ivory."

"Black ivory?"

The old man nodded. "Yes. The slave trade! They claim he ripped out the insides of his ship and rebuilt her for that special cargo. Then he made a dozen or more trips to the African coast. When he finished he was able to come back to the castle as a young man and retire."

"Do you really believe he was in the slave trade?"

"He had plenty of money and he was young to retire. People of that day regarded him with suspicion. None of the fine families here on the island would allow any of their daughters to associate with him. So he went to the mainland and bought himself a beautiful highborn wife. They say she was the only daughter of a Boston banker whose business failed. At any rate she was a beauty and soon the castle became the social center of the island."

"But she fell out of love with her husband?"

Captain Zachary Miller nodded soberly. "The talk was that he was crazy jealous of her from the start. The servants told stories of his beating her in the night after many of their parties and her screams echoing through the old house."

"So he was cruel as well as jealous?"

"Yes. But then a man would have to have a bad streak to be a slaver, wouldn't he?"

Joyce agreed. "Yes."

"It was natural that his girl-wife should turn to one of the young bloods on the island for true love and understanding. And it was just as much to be expected that he would eventually find out what was going on."

"And then he killed her!"

"The version of it I heard described him coming back from the mainland when he wasn't expected. He caught the two of them together in a room in the castle. The young man was unarmed and Captain Peter Mills always carried a dagger concealed on his person. Maybe he had fears of some of his slave trade cronies coming to the island to attack and rob him. In any event he used the dagger to stab the young man through the heart."

She was startled. "I didn't know there had been a double murder."

The old man's eyes were bright as he recalled it all. "Yes. He killed them both in that room. After he stabbed the young man he turned on his wife. And it seemed he wanted to destroy her beauty more than really kill her. He made a lunge at her face with his knife and somehow it went deep into her eye!"

"Her left eye!" Joyce said tautly. "And the blood streamed down her cheek!"

"You know all that?" the old man asked in awe.

"Yes. Go on!"

He hesitated. "Captain Peter Mills saw what he'd done and it seemed to horrify even his cold heart. He fled from the room and raced downstairs. Then he rushed out of the house and across to the chapel his religious grandfather had built."

She said, "He didn't go to the cellar at once?"

"No. Neither did his wife die right away. Somehow she managed to stagger downstairs. And the servants discovered her standing down there with the blood streaming down her face and clothing. Then she collapsed and died."

Joyce felt an icy chill run down her spine and in a low voice, she asked, "Was it in the front hallway that she died?"

"Yes," the old man said. "Why?"

"I knew it had to be there," she said.

"There is a secret passage between the chapel building and the castle," the old captain went on. "I don't know whether it still exists. It may well be blocked off by now. But there was one in those days. And Captain Peter Mills used that passage to return to the cellar."

"And there he hung himself?"

"From a ceiling rafter, using his belt as a hangman's rope. He had no other choice. All that he had wanted was lost to him. His beautiful wife, his high social position on the island, all that he valued. He would not face the court for his murders, so he pronounced sentence on himself. Perhaps the most commendable act in his evil life."

She sat back with a sigh. "How long after that did the ghost legend start?"

"I guess almost right away. But how much was based on fact and how much on fancy I wouldn't care to say." He stared at her with his shrewd old eyes. "And yet you say you have seen the ghosts. And you seem to know more about them than I'd expect!"

"And you don't think me still insane?"

"I do not," Captain Zachary said.

"I know about those two," she said. "Because I have seen their phantom figures. That is how I can describe them." And she went on to tell him of her several experiences.

The old man seemed shocked. "You were actually attacked by Captain Peter's ghost once?"

"Yes."

He frowned. "That makes me wonder."

"What?"

"If this might be some wicked hoax," he said.

"What do you mean?"

He looked unhappy. "I don't want to dispel one set of fears to substitute them with another, but what you've told me does bother me."

"Go on," she told him.

He sighed. "You have come back to the island with the taint of madness to battle. You are in the position of having to prove yourself, prove your sanity to the satisfaction of your husband and his family."

"So it seems."

The wizened face was troubled as he went on, "Now suppose there is someone who doesn't want you to be able to prove that. Who wants to destroy you and send you back to the hospital as hopelessly mad. Someone who really hates you!"

Faintly, she told him, "I can think of more than one who might hate me that much."

"Very well," the old man said. "Wouldn't the ideal way to do this be to play on your nerves? Make you believe you were seeing phantoms while humans played the various roles. Murder that poor cat and use your scarf to make it seem you did it. Cause you to scream for no apparent reason?"

His words made sense to her. In fact they sent new fear surging through her. In a taut voice, she said, "You're telling me this may all be an evil game someone is playing on me. Their intention to eventually drive me to madness."

"Exactly."

"I don't know. The ghosts are so real. I can't think of them as being staged."

"The attack on you makes me suspicious."

"A ghost might attack me," she said in mild protest.

"Perhaps," Captain Zachary Miller said grimly. "But I see

it as more likely some criminal human was responsible."

"Who?"

"Who has a motive?"

Again her fears assailed her. In a weak voice, she said, "I don't know. A lot of people. Regina, Mona, even Faith or Derek himself."

The old captain listened with a resigned look on his wizened face. "It could be any one of them or a combination of two or three of them."

Her eyes widened in terror. "The Mills family arrayed against me!"

"It could be. If I were sure of that I'd tell you to flee the island at once. But Derek may know nothing of this. He may well still be in love with you. That is what you must first find out."

"I don't expect that to be easy," she said.

"Nor do I," the old man said. "But I can sense grave trouble ahead. There is bound to be a crisis. Another tragedy! I hope you escape it this time."

"I'm hardly likely to," she said, "since it all seems to center around me."

Captain Zachary Miller told her, "I shall worry about you. You must keep in close touch with me."

"I shall," she promised. "I've taken too much of your time."

"Not at all," the old man said.

She smiled ruefully. "And done nothing but burden you with my troubles."

"I'm interested in you."

"Thank you," she said rising. "I won't bother you anymore today. I must get on to the museum. I want to see Derek. And I do thank you for listening to me."

The thin old captain got to his feet stiffly. "Come back at

any time. I'm always here and I have a good deal of influence in Dark Harbor. I'll be glad to help you in any way possible."

He saw her to the door of the cottage and stood on the step to wave her on her way when she drove off. She left him with the warm feeling that she had at least one friend on the island on whom she could count. She also valued the old man's sharp mind. And this brought her to the troubling thought that he might be right about the spiritual visitations being staged to drive her to madness.

It was baffling to the point of frustration. She drove along several of the tree-lined back streets until she reached the museum. It was plain in outward appearance, constructed of red brick and three stories high. It was a deceptively large building made to look singularly unimpressive by its very ordinary front entrance. There were a few cars parked outside it and when she parked her own car there and started for the entrance she glanced at her watch and was surprised to see that it was a few minutes before noon. She'd had a longer session with the captain than she'd realized.

She entered the museum and stepped into the reception hall. She was greeted with a smile by a teenage girl at the desk. It was someone she'd never seen before and who plainly didn't recognize her.

"Welcome," the girl said. "Is this your first visit to the museum?"

"No."

"Oh?" the girl seemed a little let down by this. "Well, we have some new things. As you can see there's a display by several of our summer water-colorists going on in this room."

"I see," she said, noting the groups of paintings which decorated the room's walls. There were also several tourists moving about studying the paintings. She told the girl, "Actually I'm here to see the Director, Derek Mills."

The girl looked at her dubiously. "What is it about?"

"It's personal," she said, grimly amused and determined to play the odd game to its end.

The girl looked more upset. "Well, I'm not sure he's in. He often leaves by the rear door. Do you know where his office is?"

"Yes," she said, "I'll go look for him." And she left the girl and went on into the main lobby of the museum's ground floor. As soon as she entered it she saw that it had been stripped of all displays for the summer ball to be held the following week. It looked immense with its walls and all the floor space bare. She walked across the tile to the stairway conscious of her heels clicking loudly on the hard surface with every step.

As she reached the bottom of the wide stairway she saw someone she knew coming down. It was the balding Brook Patterson, looking neat and correct in a gray flannel suit.

"Hello, Joyce," he said with a friendly smile as he came down to her.

She said, "I'm looking for Derek."

"You won't find him."

"No?"

"He and my wife have gone off somewhere," the balding man said matter-of-factly. "They're very busy getting ready for the big dance next week."

"I've just heard about it," she said, and glancing around, she added, "I can see you're all ready to decorate here."

"Yes," Brook Patterson said with a slight frown on his slender face. "I wasn't all that enthusiastic about the project. I mean, I don't see stripping the museum in the middle of the tourist season, then having to put it all back together again. But Faith sold Derek on the idea and I was more or less left out."

"I can imagine," she said. It was impossible to hide her disappointment at not finding Derek there. She had badly wanted to talk to him away from the castle.

The balding assistant at the museum asked her, "Have you any lunch plans?"

"Not exactly. I expected to meet Derek."

"I know," he agreed. "So why not have a bite with me? There's an interesting new place along the shore. You can always get a good table there at this time of day."

She hesitated. "You tempt me."

He took her by the arm. "Then come along," he said. "We'll use my car and maybe when we get back here my wife and your husband will have returned."

A few minutes later she found herself beside him in the front seat of his sports car as they drove along the shore road. He kept his eyes on the road ahead as he told her in a somewhat strained voice, "Actually I'm glad to have this opportunity to talk to you alone."

She glanced at his lean profile, rather startled. "Is that so?"

He gave her a grim glance. "You must know what is going on between Faith and your husband."

CHAPTER SIX

Joyce hardly knew how to answer him. She felt she must be tactful since there might be nothing more to it all than mere gossip. So she said, "I'm out of touch with island things. I've been away almost a year you know."

His face was grim as he gave his attention to the road once again. "I realize that. But surely you must have heard some talk since you've been back."

"I've heard a lot of things," she said. "I don't always take too much stock in what I hear."

Brook Patterson said, "I've tried that for a long while. But eventually there comes a time when you can ignore things no longer. I'm convinced Faith has been untrue to me and this is not the first time."

"I'm sorry," she said.

"What really pains me is that Derek is the man involved in the present affair," Brook went on.

She gazed at him. "Are you really sure?"

"I'd say so."

"Have you spoken to your wife about it?"

"Yes."

"And?"

He smiled bitterly. "She told me I was imagining things and threatened to leave me if I brought the matter up again."

"So you didn't find anything out."

"No more than I knew," he said. "Faith has driven me to a point where I've actually considered murdering her. You may find that hard to believe but it's the truth."

Shocked, she said, "That would be a poor solution even if things are as bad as you seem to think."

Still giving the wheel his close attention, Brook said, "The human mind can only stand so much before it breaks. You should know that better than most people."

She made no immediate reply as they had reached the large restaurant overlooking the ocean. She noted that there were not too many cars in the parking area.

"It can't be crowded," she observed as Brook opened the car door to let her out.

"No," the man in the gray flannel suit said. "Most of the people remain on the beach during the day. It's in the evening they really do a large business. But I like it when it's quiet as it will be today."

She managed a wan smile as they began walking towards the double glass doors of the restaurant entrance. "I also prefer to avoid the tourist rush."

They went inside and a pleasant, matronly woman greeted them and guided them to the main dining room. There were plenty of empty tables by the broad windows on the ocean side and she sat them at one.

Brook Patterson asked her, "Is that all right?"

"Very pleasant," she said. She was still on edge from their previous conversation and wondered if now the lunch would be a succession of banalities with both of them hiding their true feelings.

Brook consulted with her about the menu and then ordered for them. After that he gave her a serious look and at once resumed his discussion of his wife's infidelity.

He told her, "I've mentioned this to you because I feel you should know. Should be prepared."

"I understand," she said in a quiet voice.

The balding man's pleasant face showed his anguish. "I

have had to keep silent about this and as you may imagine it hasn't been easy for me. It's a relief to be able to talk frankly to you."

"I don't mind," she told him.

Brook said, "I've always regarded you as a friend I could trust. And I don't have too many of them on the island. Unless your family has been here a couple of hundred years you're always a mainlander."

She smiled wryly. "I know all about that."

"You've done very well," he said. "But then I think it is easier for a woman. You don't have to adjust to the business life of the community as well as the social one."

"True."

He frowned. "Faith's parents took me over and bought my way into a couple of island business deals. And then they used their influence to get me this job at the museum. I could have managed well on my own on the mainland. I had a good job there that they made me give up. Faith wouldn't think of living anywhere else but on the island."

"You must have known that when you asked her to marry you."

"No. She didn't make it clear until we were on our honeymoon. Then it was too late. I foolishly gave in to her and her parents and now I'm paying for it."

Joyce asked him, "Are you still in love with Faith?"

He considered for a moment. "I suppose so. A lot of the old feeling is gone. But I keep hoping that this will end and it won't happen again." He gave her a sour smile. "But we both know that it will."

She made no comment. It was clear that Brook Patterson was suffering enough. As for herself, she hadn't decided what she would do. She felt that her breakdown and the loss of Lucie might have driven Derek into an affair which he might even now regret. She could not act hastily.

They sat in silence over cocktails and then the waitress brought them lunch. They began to talk again and this time it was a purely routine conversation about things which meant nothing much to them. It was only when they reached the stage of iced coffee that Brook Patterson spoke frankly once more.

He said, "You're not going to do anything about it?"

"I think not," she said carefully.

"Maybe you're wise. This could be a onetime thing for Derek and he may learn his lesson. I can't hope that with Faith. In due time there will be another man in her life. That's almost predictable."

She felt sorry for the troubled Brook. She said, "Even if the worst that you think is true I wouldn't give up hope. Faith may one day tire of these rather pointless affairs."

"I wonder."

"It can happen," she encouraged him.

He was staring at her. "I find you changed and for the better. You're no longer so high-strung, so vulnerable!"

She gave him a forlorn smile. "Don't be too sure. I still have my moments. But I also learned some valuable lessons in that hospital."

"That's obvious."

"I'm still sensitive to certain things. Loud or monotonous sounds grind on my nerves. I had a bad time coming across on the ferry with its pounding engines. And I'm not too easy in crowds as yet. The babble of conversation makes me terribly edgy."

"That's not because you have any mental problems," he said, "it's because you've always been a sensitive person."

"A little more than that," she said wryly. "People who are merely sensitive don't give way and scream when the pressure gets too great. I still can be guilty of that."

Brook seemed concerned. "But your mind is clear?"

"Yes. I don't hallucinate anymore. Yet I find living at the castle extremely hard on me."

He arched an eyebrow. "Regina?"

"She gives me a lot of trouble, but she's not the only one. There's Mona and the general atmosphere of the old house." She gave him a questioning look. "You do know that it's a haunted house, don't you?"

Brook looked embarrassed as only a staid New Englander can. He said, "Well, I have heard the legend but I pay no attention to that sort of thing."

"Really?"

"No. Such stories leave me cold."

"And you are a historian," she said. "I should think you'd be more flexible in your convictions."

He was staring at her. "You sound as if you've reason to believe in the castle ghosts. Have you seen them?"

Remembering the advice given her by Uncle Henry and Captain Zachary Miller she said at once, "It's just that I always feel such legends must have some basis in fact." She felt that to be a suitably evasive answer.

Brook Patterson pushed aside his empty iced-coffee glass and said, "The legend about Captain Peter Mills has. It began with the double murder by him of his wife and her lover, and then his suicide in the castle cellar gave the story a suitably gruesome ending. The events caught the imagination of the people and they've kept the tragedy alive with stories of the ghosts showing themselves down through the years."

"I see what you mean," she said.

He gave her a knowing look and in a taut voice said, "I hope our present era doesn't provide another such tragedy to build a legend. It well might."

She knew what he was thinking and it frightened her. She said, "You shouldn't allow yourself to think such thoughts."

"They come unbidden," was his bitter reply. "I suppose it is time to return to the museum."

"Yes. Thanks for the lunch."

He shrugged. "You had to listen to a lot of unpleasant talk along with it."

"I don't consider what we've discussed unpleasant in that sense," she told him. "I agree with you that it is important we have brought the matter out in the open and know how we both feel about it."

"Thank you, Joyce," he said humbly. "You're being very generous. I may have brought you needless pain in an effort to ease my own feelings."

"No."

He rose to help her with her chair. "I'll admit to being a coward in this. I suppose I always have been where Faith is concerned. It's because I'm too afraid of losing her."

They left the restaurant and began the drive back to the museum. It was still a bright, sunny day and she sat back and relaxed as much as she could while Brook Patterson drove silently on. When they reached the museum they went in by the rear door and the first person they met in the lobby was the artist, David Chase, standing on a stepladder measuring out areas on the lobby's vast bare walls.

He paused to smile down at her. "Hello," he said. "I haven't seen much of you these last few days."

She smiled. "I'd begun to wonder if you'd left the castle."

"No. I've been busy. The time for the summer ball is getting nearer and there's so much to be done."

Brook Patterson showed a tight smile. "David has full charge of the decorating. Do you think you'll have everything ready on time, David?"

"I will have if we get the materials I've ordered," the young artist said. "Everything is deadly slow getting here."

"One of the disadvantages of being located on an island," Brook told him and then he and Joyce went on upstairs to the offices.

They found Derek seated at his desk in his shirt-sleeves with Faith standing next to him with some letters in her hand. Both Derek and Faith showed surprise as Joyce came into the office with Brook at her side.

Derek said, "I didn't know you were here, Joyce."

She told him, "I missed you. So Brook and I went to lunch. We had a very pleasant time."

The blonde Faith gave her a grimly amused glance. "Where did you go?"

"The Nautilus," Brook said. "It was quiet."

Derek sat back in his chair. "We went to that Greek place in town as we didn't want to waste time. It was crowded and hot."

"Better than wasting another half-hour," Faith said crisply with the air of a dedicated worker. "There are still so many details to be worked out about the ball."

Derek gave her an admiring smile. "I don't know where she gets the energy," he said. "Not only is she working with me on my end of things she's also helping David with the decorations."

"I enjoy it," Faith said. "And David doesn't really know much about the island's history so he needs a local to advise him."

Her husband gave Faith a scathing look. "When you set your mind on anything you never rest until it's taken care of," he said. "I would say that it's not only your chief virtue but your main vice."

Faith crimsoned and then turned to Derek and said, "I'll leave these letters with you. They'll all need answering."

Derek nodded. "Thanks," he said quietly.

Faith gave Joyce a defiant glance and then marched out of the office with Brook silently following her. Derek got up and closed the door of the office to give himself and Joyce privacy. He still looked ill at ease as he returned to stand facing her.

"Did you have a good morning?" he asked.

"I benefitted from getting away from the castle."

"How is the car working?"

"Very well, so far," she said.

Derek was studying her closely. "So Brook took you to lunch."

"You and Faith had left. It seemed a logical arrangement."

"I quite agree," Derek said. "In fact, I'm glad. I've found Brook in a sullen mood these days. The luncheon ought to have done him good. What did you two talk about?" This last came very subtly.

She wasn't to be trapped by him. She said, "Any number of things."

"I see."

"I'm not sure he's entirely sold on the summer ball," she said.

Derek sighed. "I know. He has some very conventional ideas. When you do something unorthodox he gets very uptight."

"You have had to tear down a lot of displays in the midst of the tourist season."

"Only for a week or so," her husband argued. "And the money we hope to make from the ball will make it well worthwhile. It's to be a costume affair, you know."

"So I gathered."

Her husband's handsome face showed a thoughtful expression. "I must speak to Mother and have her check some of the trunks in the attic. It would be excellent if we were able to come up with enough outfits stored away up there to give us all authentic clothing. A lot of the other island families are trying to do the same thing."

"What about sizes?" she asked.

"We'd have to trust to luck," Derek said. "Small alterations could be made easily enough. But I'd better make sure the clothing is looked up before it is too late."

Joyce warned him. "Don't worry too much about me. I'm by no means sure I'll feel like attending. Crowds still bother me."

"It won't be that large a group."

"Just the same I prefer to wait and see how I feel on the day of the ball before making any plans," she said.

"We should find you a dress anyhow. It can be of any period as long as it's over thirty years old."

She said, "I hope it's a success. You and Faith have been working so hard at it."

Her husband said, "Everyone has been doing his share. It takes a lot of cooperation."

"I'm sure of that," she agreed. "You're busy so I won't stay."

"You can if you like."

"No."

"Are you feeling some better about things at the house?" he asked.

"I'm afraid not," she said frankly.

"Mother doesn't mean to be hateful," he said worriedly. "But that business about the cat really upset her."

"Yes, I soon discovered that."

"She had no right to blame you," Derek went on with uncertainty. "It might have been anyone."

"I tried to make her see that but she wouldn't listen."

Derek said, "I'm sure now that she's thought about it she's had second thoughts. Try and get along with her for the sake of us all."

"I won't make any rash promises," she warned him. "Part of it depends on her."

Derek frowned. "I know." And he took Joyce in his arms for another of his brief embraces. Next he rather hurriedly took her to the door as if the gesture might have embarrassed him. He saw her to the head of the stairs and then returned to his office allowing her to go to the ground floor on her own.

When she reached the lobby David Chase had come down from the ladder and was putting on his jacket. The artist gave her a smile of greeting. "You're leaving?"

"Yes. I'm driving back to the castle."

He looked at her shyly. "May I trouble you for a lift?"

"Of course, I'd be glad to drive you," she said. "I keep forgetting you have no car."

"I have the use of the museum station wagon at times. But it is in use today."

"Then come with me by all means."

They strolled out through the front door this time and the girl at the reception desk gave them an interested look.

As David settled in the front seat at Joyce's side, he gave her a sly smile. "I'm amazed that your husband felt you were able to use a car again."

She exchanged a knowing glance with him. "Don't think I didn't have to battle for the privilege. He was full of doubts."

"But you won out."

"Yes," she started the engine.

"I'm glad for you," the young artist said in his friendly

way. "I feel as if it were a personal victory. I have gone through it all myself."

Joyce backed the car out onto the road. "Your confiding in me about your own breakdown has helped me more than you may realize."

"I had an impulse to tell you," he admitted. "As you know I don't mention it to most people."

"And I have found out why," she said bitterly. "The tag of having been mad is a hard one to lose."

"They want to brand you with it," he said. "By the way I've been told there's a monastery at the other end of the island which is very interesting."

She glanced at him. "The old leper hospital? Haven't you seen it?"

"No, but I must."

"It's only about a ten-minute drive from here," she told him. "If you'd like to see it I can take the next turn to the left rather than going straight back to the castle."

David Chase hesitated. "I don't want to waste your time."

"I have plenty to waste," she told him. "And I'd enjoy the drive. The idea of rushing back to the company of my mother-in-law and sister-in-law doesn't exactly thrill me."

The young artist laughed. "Very well, then," he said. "I'll accept your generous offer. Mind if I smoke?"

"No." When they came to the branch road she took it and they began heading for the southern tip of the island.

He said, "I'm told the monastery is perched high on a cliff and that it's owned by some rich young man now."

"You're right," she said. "He has a hippie colony there and the place is as carefully shut off from the public as it was in the days when it was a leper hospital."

"He doesn't want any intruders?"

"It seems that's the story. You hear all sorts of bizarre tales about it. One Boston newspaper ran an article saying it was a temple of black magic and drug experiments. But I'm sure they made too much of it."

"How do the rest of the island people feel about it?"

"No one thinks much about the monastery," she said. "At least they didn't up until the time I went away to hospital. And I haven't heard that anything has changed."

"Do you have police here?"

She smiled. "A single constable with the New England name of Titus Frink. He's fairly old but he does his job well and he can always call on the State Police when he needs help."

David Chase said, "It's strange but that's the first time I ever thought about police here. It would almost seem you have no need of any."

"There have been times when we have," she said. They had left the village behind them now and were driving along a shore road with occasional big summer homes along it. The hills were covered with rocks and there were only a few trees.

He looked out at the country they were passing through. "It isn't as busy on this end of the island," he said.

"No," she agreed. "When all the summer people are here it is fairly lively. But from October on it is almost deserted."

"The lepers came here before the monastery was built, didn't they?" the young artist asked.

"A ship was wrecked on the reefs along this shore," she said, her eyes on the road. "The sailors remained here and mixed with the local people. Then to the horror of the local doctor it was found that a large percentage of the men had been infected with leprosy and some of them had passed it on to young men and women of the island. The doctor explained that those with leprosy had to be isolated from the rest of the people on the island. So those infected moved out here and built primitive shacks and lived in them."

"How long ago was this?" David Chase wanted to know.

"About a century and a half ago," she said. "A frantic call was sent out for medical and nursing aid. It was answered by a religious order. A group of Catholic monks were willing to come to the island and build a monastery and give the stricken people care. Despite Pirate Island being a Puritan and Quaker mixture in its religious views the inhabitants welcomed the monks."

"And so the monastery was built?"

"Yes. The leprosy wrought great havoc among its victims. But many of them lived on to old age though horribly mutilated by the dread disease. And from time to time new patients were sent here from the mainland. The monastery flourished with financial support from the government. Then, about fifty years ago, with most of the patients dead and the government treating new cases of leprosy in its own hospitals, the monks found themselves without a mission."

"What then?"

"The order sold the property to a wealthy man who was in love with the location and didn't mind the history of the place. He converted it into a luxurious summer place though retaining the outward lines of the monastery. He used to consider it a joke to inform his house guests that they were spending their weekend in a leper colony."

David said, "Sounds like a cruel sense of humor."

"I'd say so," she agreed. "In the end tragedy overtook him. He killed himself and most of his immediate family died soon after. That started plenty of rumors about the place being cursed. It remained empty for years until the present owner bought it."

"Thanks for filling me in on its history," David said.

"We're almost there," she told him. And a moment later

the black, forbidding hulk of the monastery outlined against the sky ahead was revealed to them. She said, "We can't get close to it. It is completely fenced in except on the ocean side and you have to climb a precarious cliff to get to it from there. But I can park in the field next to it and we can walk to the edge of the cliff to get a better view of it."

She turned the car off the road and drove along a small side road that finally ended in a turning place near the cliffs. She shut off the engine and told the young artist, "End of the trip. This is where people come to study the monastery. That is how the road happens to be here."

"So quite a lot of people must take the pilgrimage," he said.

"They do," she agreed.

They got out of the car and stood gazing at the tall, grim stone building which clearly showed its origin as a monastery. Its top story was set in from the several stories below and it appeared that this might have made a kind of lookout and balcony.

David Chase said, "I see no sign of life there."

She shaded her eyes from the sun with the palm of her hand. "They may all be away," she told him. "They sometimes go to the mainland and aren't here for weeks at a time. But they do remain here all through the winter, at least some of them."

"Interesting."

"If we go to the edge of the cliffs you can see it a little better," she told him.

They walked on to the very brink of the high gray cliffs and stood staring at the other side of the monastery with the pounding of the waves from below sounding loud in their ears. David looked amazingly young as he stood there intently gazing at the monastery with the wind riffling his long, wavy hair.

He murmured, "A page of history standing there in stone."

"So true," she said. "I hadn't thought of it that way before."

The young artist turned to her. "Thank you for bringing me here. The place fascinates me. I must delve further into its history."

"I'm sure it would repay you," she said.

"I suppose I have a touch of the morbid," he admitted. "But the tragedy surrounding it makes it more appealing to me."

"I think we all show interest in the morbid," she said.

He smiled at her. "How nice that we've been able to do this together. You know I've come to feel very close to you, Joyce."

She smiled. "And I to you."

"The others don't know that we've been companions in misery," he said. "And I think that has drawn us together."

"It is a comfort to know that someone else has had a similar bad experience and come through it. Especially come through it as well as you have."

He shook his head and turned to look out at the ocean. "Not all that well. I have times when a curtain of blackness descends on me. I get moods of melancholy I can't shake off."

"So do I."

The young man sighed. "Then I force myself to shut out all the past and somehow I manage to go on living again. Until I have another spell. I imagine it will be like that for the rest of my life."

"Dr. Beckett told me that time helped and keeping busy. He had a fetish for golf."

"My painting has helped," David Chase admitted. "Without it I couldn't go on."

Joyce fixed her eyes on his tanned, pleasant face. "How are you progressing with your portrait of Faith?"

He looked somewhat surprised. "I'm almost finished with it. The trouble at the moment is that she's too busy preparing for the summer ball to take time out to sit for me."

"I can imagine."

"It is her project."

"So I've been told," she said. "Do you like her?"

"Faith?"

"Yes."

He made a gesture of resignation. "She's all right in a strictly superficial way. She has no depth."

"You feel that way?"

"Yes," the young artist said with a strained look on his face. "She has none of your sensitivity and character. But then I suppose that's a plus for her. She'll never wind up in a mental hospital as you and I did."

She nodded. "My husband seems to agree with you."

His eyebrows raised. "Why do you say that?"

"Surely you know."

"I'd rather have you tell me."

She felt her throat tighten with pain as she said, "Surely you know that my husband and Faith are having an affair. It's common knowledge."

The young artist looked at her with sad eyes. "It's nothing I would want to tell you. Especially not at this time when you're making such a battle to recover."

"You needn't worry," she said, quietly. "I've known about it almost from the time I returned. Uncle Henry told me."

"Stupid old man," David Chase said tensely.

"Not really," she said, quick to defend Henry Mills. "He wanted me to hear it from him rather than anyone else. And he was right. It hurt less. It has left me better prepared."

"Joyce!" There was great tenderness in the artist's voice. And almost at the same instant he reached out and drew her to him. His kiss was more ardent than any she'd had from Derek since her return and he held her to him so closely that it almost hurt. At last he let her go and she saw the torment in his eyes as he whispered, "I shouldn't have done that. Will you forgive me?"

She nodded, not equal to words at the moment.

"I always fall in love too late," he said. "I do love you, Joyce, and I despise Derek for the way he's treating you."

Joyce said, "Try to understand. The things that happened may have driven him to Faith. I try to believe that and also believe that the affair isn't important. That it will pass."

The young artist sighed. "It could be you're right about the thing not lasting. That still doesn't make me feel any better about your husband."

"Thank you, David," she said in a voice filled with emotion. "I will always consider that fate sent you here when I so needed a friend."

He took a step away from her and then turned and said, "Why don't you leave Derek and the island. That house of ghosts can't be good for you! Let me take you away from it."

"No," she said. "I must be honest. I still love Derek and if anything can be salvaged of our marriage that is what I want most."

"You know that isn't pleasant for me to hear," David said.

"I'm sorry," she said with sincerity.

"You're determined to stay on with Derek?"

"Yes."

"Knowing how much his mother and sister hate you?"

"I don't care."

He hesitated. "There is also another party concerned in all this."

"You mean?"

"I mean Brook Patterson," the young artist said. "I have watched him in the last few weeks and I can tell that he's close to desperation."

She didn't attempt to deny this since she'd already heard it from Brook himself. So she said, "He's been through it before. This is not the first time Faith has shown interest in another man."

"But it could be the time he finally reacts," David warned her. "What then?"

"I hope the whole thing will be over before anything like that happens," she said.

"You're taking a terrible risk."

"I have no choice," she said. There was the sound of a car coming near them and she glanced back and saw that another car had pulled up near hers. And as she watched she saw a group of adults and children get out. She turned to David, "A carload of tourists! We're lucky they didn't get here sooner!"

He shrugged. "I wouldn't have cared."

"I would have," she said. "There's enough gossip on the island now. We must start back to the castle."

David gave her a worried look. "You don't think any less of me because of what I've said and done?"

"No," she said, offering him a smile of reassurance. "I'm grateful to have you here. But now you understand how I feel. We shouldn't have to discuss it again."

"I understand," he said with a heavy sigh.

They returned to the car and drove away as quickly as they could before the group of tourists could give them too much attention. They were both silent on the drive to the castle, each of them lost in his own thoughts.

Joyce went directly to her own room after returning and washed and then rested for awhile. Her afternoon nap was interrupted by a knock on her door. She got up and went over and opened it to find Mona standing there with a gown draped over her arm.

She said, "Derek asked me to give you this. He called earlier and had Mother and me go through several of the old trunks. He wants us to use authentic dresses for the ball. This is a very nice one and I think it will fit you."

"Thank you," Joyce said, taking the gown. It was of red velvet with a flowing skirt and had decorations of gold tape down the front and around the collar and puffed sleeves.

"It's a very old one," Mona said with an unusual show of friendship. "If it will fit you it should be striking."

"It is lovely," Joyce agreed. "Though I'm not yet certain I'll be up to attending the ball."

Mona gave her a meaningful look. "I'm sure Derek will be let down if you don't."

"I'm hoping to attend," she said, still holding the dress. "I'll try it on and look after any alterations that may be needed."

"Fine," the blonde girl said. "And, by the way, you may be interested in the history of this dress."

Joyce was at once suspicious of the note of mockery in Mona's voice. She had felt all along there must be something behind her facade of friendliness. She said, "What about its history?"

"It once belonged to Ann Mills. She lived about a century ago."

"Oh?"

A smile played on Mona's lips. "You may not know her by name but she was Captain Peter Mills' wife. The one who was murdered."

Joyce glanced down at the dress with a feeling of revulsion sweeping through her. She was certain that Mona had pressed the ornate velvet dress owned by the murdered woman on her as a macabre joke.

She said, "Really?"

"I knew you wouldn't mind. It is a lovely dress. She had quite a few of them. And she was evidently just about your size."

"I see," Joyce said.

"Well, I must go," Mona said briskly. "I'm trying on one of the older dresses myself. I'll see you later." And she went off down the shadowed hall.

Joyce went back into her own room and closed the door. Then she began examining the red velvet dress. She knew it was silly of her to allow Mona to upset her this way. She should brazen it out and spoil any satisfaction the blonde girl might be deriving from her mean prank. The dress could do her no harm and it was very attractive.

She took off the robe she was wearing and slipped into the velvet dress. Then she stood before the long mirror on the door of the closet and studied herself in it. Mona had been correct in at least one thing. It did fit her.

Earlier in the day she had heard many new details of the tragedy which had taken place at the castle a century or more ago. She learned from Captain Zachary that the murder had taken place in one of the upper rooms but that Ann Mills had managed to stagger down to the foyer where she'd collapsed and died. And it was in the foyer that Joyce remembered seeing the ghostly face with the blood dripping down one side of it! Just as the old captain had described it to her.

In fact everything he'd said had fitted in with the ghostly experiences she'd had. She had known what he was going to tell her before she'd heard his words. It was very strange that the phantoms involved in that tragedy of the past should choose to reveal themselves to her. Could this have any special meaning for her? Was tragedy about to strike in the castle again?

These thoughts made her uneasy. And she worried whether to wear the dress of the murdered woman if she did attend the ball. It surely was attractive on her and wearing it would show Mona that she did not fear the dress. That she had control of her nerves and would not allow this link with the ancient tragedy to upset her.

With this in mind she decided to let Mona see what the dress looked like on her. And she went to the door leading to the corridor and opened it. As she stepped out into the shadowed hallway she suddenly was confronted by the white-haired, Uncle Henry.

Seeing her, he halted with a gasp. "Joyce!" he exclaimed. "For a minute you looked like a ghost to me."

She smiled faintly. "It's the dress I may wear to the ball. Mona claims it once belonged to Ann Mills."

The old man raised his eyebrows. "And you don't object to wearing it?"

"I think not," she said.

The old man looked annoyed. "Of course Mona purposely gave it to you. Hoping it might upset you."

"I thought of that," Joyce admitted. "And that is why I feel I must wear it. To spoil her plan."

Henry Mills nodded. "You may be right." He glanced in at her room. "There is one other thing you should know. I've kept it from you. But I feel I ought to tell you."

"Yes?" she felt a slight chill ripple through her as she waited for whatever revelation he had in store for her.

"I'd say Regina deliberately assigned you to that bedroom

for the same reason. It has always been rumored that is where the double murders took place. In fact, if you look, you'll find a dull stain on the floor that they claim was made by Ann Mills' blood!"

CHAPTER SEVEN

Joyce tried to put the business about the room out of her mind. But she could not forget what Henry Mills had said. And later that afternoon she made a thorough search of her bedroom floor. And when she rolled back the shag rug before the dresser a fairly large black stain showed on the wide floor boards. She stared at it in fascinated horror and concluded that Regina had without a doubt assigned her the murder room.

She was finishing dressing for dinner when Derek joined her at the end of the day. He came into her room and asked her, "Did Mother find you a suitable dress?"

Joyce paused in brushing her long black hair and glanced at him over her shoulder. "Yes," she said, with a knowing look. "Your mother gave me a very nice red velvet dress. Just one thing about it, I understand it belonged to Ann Mills who was murdered here years ago."

Derek's handsome face showed embarrassment. "I can't believe that," he protested.

"Mona told me," she said.

He crimsoned. "Well, does it really make all that much difference? As long as it's a nice dress."

"I suppose not," she said. "But I've also found out that this is the room where the murder took place. Have you been aware of that all along?"

"No one really is sure about that," her husband said, looking more uncomfortable every minute. "I know there's a stain on this floor and the rumor is that it is blood. But I'm inclined not to believe it."

"I see," she said quietly and went back to brushing her hair.

Derek came up behind her and placed his hands on her shoulders. She looked in the mirror and saw the strained look on his handsome face. He said, "I hope you're not going to make a lot of fuss about this."

She kept staring in the mirror at the two of them. "You dislike fuss no matter how much it is justified," she said.

"I know how easily upset you are these days."

"I'm trying very hard not to be," she said.

He frowned. "I wouldn't like this to start your seeing another round of ghosts. You mustn't let your nerves upset you. If you don't want to wear that dress I'll have Mother get you something else."

"I'll wear it," she said.

"You're sure?"

"Yes."

He gave a sigh of relief and removed his hands from her shoulders. "Don't worry about this room. I'm sure the story they tell about it has no basis whatsoever."

"Perhaps not," she said, putting the brush aside and rising.

Derek was gazing at her earnestly. "You're not angry with me, are you?"

"No."

"You're behaving strangely," he worried. "Giving me short answers with no clue to what you're really thinking."

Her eyes met his in a reproving glance. "Do you really care?"

"Of course I do. I was glad you came to the museum today. It is good for you to get out and around. It will help you fight all those morbid thoughts."

"I am better off with the car," she agreed.

He went on uneasily, "And I'd like you and Faith to be better friends. She's really a very nice young woman when you know her."

"I could tell she's very devoted to you," Joyce told her husband pointedly.

He raised a protesting hand. "Any gossip you may have heard about us is untrue. With you away in hospital and Faith coming to work at the museum as my assistant it could be expected that there would be talk. But I certainly don't expect you to pay any attention to it."

She said, "What about Brook? He doesn't seem too happy."

"Brook is neurotic," Derek said. "But I'm sure he knows his wife well enough not to listen to the talk of troublemakers."

"I wonder," she said.

Derek showed exasperation. "What's the use of trying to talk about it. It's a subject on which we seem unable to communicate. So let it rest."

"Perhaps that would be wisest," she agreed.

Later they went downstairs and joined the others on the patio for cocktails. Everyone was there including David Chase. Joyce felt he was still embarrassed for having declared himself so openly earlier in the day as he made it a point to avoid her now. He spent most of his time with Regina, discussing plans for the ball.

Mona at once latched on to Derek to ask him a lot of questions and that left Joyce with Uncle Henry. The old man seemed in a doleful frame of mind.

"Weather's been too good," he warned her. "There's supposed to be a change tomorrow and we're to be in for a week of fog and wet. What do you think about that?"

"I suppose we'll have to accept it," she said.

He glanced around to make sure the others were out of earshot and asked her, "Did you speak to Derek about that room you're in?"

"Yes."

The old man squinted at her as the dying sun's rays hit their end of the patio. "What did he say?"

She grimaced. "The usual thing. He considers the story a lot of nonsense."

"I expected he'd say something like that," Uncle Henry replied grimly. "To the best of my knowledge that is where the murders took place."

"I found the stain. Near the dresser."

"That's the one," Henry agreed.

"Perhaps that is why I've been seeing the ghosts," she suggested. "It began the night I first came back here and slept in that room. I'd never seen them here before."

The old man reminded her. "You did when you were really sick, before they took you to the hospital."

"I could have imagined seeing anything then," she said. "I was hallucinating. It's different now."

"I suppose so," Henry Mills said with some doubt in his voice. "You took my advice and didn't mention seeing those phantoms to anyone else?"

She knew she'd discussed it with Captain Zachary but she didn't feel this was any of the old man's business. So she said, "I've not mentioned it to anyone in the house except Derek. And I've stopped telling him since he seems to lack faith in me as much as the others."

"You have to be careful," Derek's uncle warned her. "Regina and Mona would like to make out you're still crazy."

She smiled forlornly at his bald words. "Do you think someone might be staging the ghost appearances to work on my nerves? To try and frighten me back into insanity?"

The idea seemed to startle him. He said, "Do you really believe someone would try that?"

"They might if they wanted me out of the way badly enough."

"I suppose so," he agreed reluctantly.

"And if Derek is carrying on with Faith as you've suggested he must want to be rid of me. All his concern for me could be merely a pose."

The old man eyed her nervously. "Everything you say could be true and then again it needn't be."

"Don't you think your nephew capable of that kind of villainy?" she asked him.

"Maybe," he said with caution. He glanced down to the other end of the patio where Regina was in conversation with David Chase and said, "I'd be more inclined to think she'd favor that kind of scheme."

"You could be right," she said.

"We'll see if any more ghosts bother you," Henry Mills said. "Then maybe we can discover their origin."

She took a sip from her glass. "I'd settle for seeing no more."

"I know," he said. "Are you definitely going to the ball?"

"I feel I should support it," Joyce said. "If the noise and crowd bother me too much I can always take a taxi back here."

"So you can," the old man agreed. "I think you're looking better than when you first returned."

"I'm afraid I don't feel much different," she told him. "But at least I've made some sort of adjustment."

"Better than I ever hoped," the old man said earnestly. "Just watch out for Regina. She was fuming about your having a car today."

This came as no surprise to her. She knew that her mother-in-law was set against her and would continue her campaign to do her any harm she could. But she was now adjusted to that as well.

Dinner proved another occasion for Regina to hold forth

on all her favorite topics. The older woman dominated the table conversation so that about all the others could manage was to agree with her.

She told Derek, "I've heard some criticism of your having this summer ball," she said. "It seems not all the members of the museum board are in favor of it."

"The majority are," Derek assured his mother. "Faith took a poll of them."

Regina listened with an impatient gleam in her eyes. Then in her arrogant way, she said, "Of course the project is really Faith's idea so we must expect her to bring in favorable opinions about it."

"I don't think she would lie," Derek said unhappily.

"Perhaps not," his mother replied. "But I know the people I've talked to have had mixed feelings about it."

David Chase, who was seated across from Joyce, raised his eyes from his plate to give her a look of recognition. She felt warmed by his glance, knowing she had at least one unbiased friend at the table. But she said nothing.

When dinner was over she went out on the lawn for a stroll. Derek made no attempt to join her but went to the study to make some phone calls. She walked on alone until she reached the chapel. It was first time she'd been there since her strange experience when the phantom had attacked her there. Now she studied the old building with calmer eyes.

The door was open and a framed printed sign was nailed to the door, which gave information for tourists visiting during the day. She mounted the two stone steps to the entrance and read the sign. It stated that the chapel, like the castle, was almost two centuries old. It had been constructed by the first of the successful whaling captains in the Mills family and the property was still owned by descendants of the original builder.

She stepped inside and saw the dark, narrow, winding stairs that led up to the belfry. She had never been up there. To the left was the entrance to the sanctuary. She ventured in remembering her talk there with Uncle Henry after he'd saved her from the ghost of Captain Peter Mills. She recalled how he had persuaded her not to mention the scary experience to any of the others.

Standing in the shadows of the vaulted chapel she felt a familiar sense of fear creep through her. It seemed she was becoming more and more deeply involved in the tragedy that had happened at the castle so many years ago. Was this a pattern over which she had no control? Were these ghosts of long ago gradually gaining power over her?

A board squeaked behind her and she turned with a start to see Brook Patterson standing there. He said apologetically, "I didn't mean to frighten you."

"I didn't hear you come in."

"I came over to pick up Derek," he said. "We're working at the museum tonight. This way he doesn't have to bother with his car."

"I see," she said.

"Occasionally he picks up Faith and me," Brook went on rather nervously. "So it works out."

"Of course," Joyce said.

He stood there a few feet from her in the shadows looking uncomfortable. "I hope I didn't upset you too much today."

"It's all right," she told him.

Brook Patterson confessed, "I thought about it later and worried most of the afternoon. You've had enough trouble without my bringing you more."

"There are some things I have to know," she said.

Faith's husband sighed. "You mustn't worry about it. That's what I wanted to tell you. I saw you coming in here when I drove up and I felt it might be a chance to speak to you in private. We don't get much chance."

"I know," she said.

"I painted a pretty bad picture about Faith and Derek," he went on. "But it most likely will work out. I was in a down mood at lunch today. I said more than I intended."

"We can both forget about it," she suggested.

"I think that's what we should do," he said in quick agreement. "Please don't ever mention what I said to Derek. It would make my working with him impossible."

"I understand," she said. "You can count on my discretion."

"Thank you," Brook Patterson said with a look of relief and gratitude on his plain face. "I'd better go now and find Derek or he may see my car and wonder what has happened to me."

"Yes," she said.

With a parting nod the assistant director of the museum made his way out of the chapel leaving her alone in the dark, silent place again. It was incredible how he'd come in behind her so quietly without her hearing him until the board squeaked. He had plainly been in an upset state and she couldn't help wondering if his weakness of character wasn't a contributing factor to his wife's infidelity. After all his denunciation of Faith and Derek to her earlier in the day he was now begging her to forget what he'd said. This bothered her.

Captain Zachary Miller had said there was a secret passage between the chapel and the castle. But he'd given her no idea where it might begin in the chapel or end in the old mansion. He had suggested that perhaps the passage was blocked and no longer in use and she felt that was probably the case. She knew the chapel was not in use by the family any longer. It was now merely a tourist attraction.

Before leaving the chapel she decided to go down to the altar where she'd talked with Henry Mills. She mounted the carpeted steps to the murky upper level of the altar and touched the candelabra.

Just being there gave her an eerie feeling. As her eyes lowered to study the area at the bottom of the altar she saw a neatly-folded bundle of clothing. Something about it made her catch her breath and she reached down to pick up a captain's braided cap and a long blue coat with brass buttons. The very same type of uniform she'd seen on the ghost! She held the cap and coat before her and stared at them in fear. At once she remembered what Zachary Miller had said about the whole business being a plot to send her mad!

Had someone used this outfit to play ghost and torment her? Was that why they had left it neatly folded here? So that they could pick it up quickly when they wanted to wear it to terrify her? It seemed all too likely!

She was debating this as she stood before the altar when she became suddenly aware that she was no longer alone. A shock of fresh fear went surging through her as she gazed down to the other end of the chapel and saw a tall figure standing in the aisle.

The figure spoke and it was Derek. In a taut voice he asked, "What are you doing up there?"

She was too tense to reply for a second or two. Then she said, "I just came in here for a moment. Why?"

Derek began advancing down the shadowed aisle towards her. Coming towards her with a menacingly, steady pace, he said, "Brook told me he saw you come in here. I didn't believe him. Why would you come to this dark and deserted place at this time in the evening?"

She still held the cap and coat before her. She said, "I was strolling and came in here on an impulse. Why shouldn't I?"

He was far down the aisle now, gazing up at her sternly. "I don't think it is good for you. It can be no treat for your nerves to come in here. I don't like your showing this morbid streak. I hope it's not the signal of another breakdown!"

She held up the cap and coat. "I found these."

"Indeed!" Derek's voice was icy.

"Yes," she said, aware that she was trembling. That at this moment she was afraid of him. "It's a cap and coat exactly of the sort the ghost wore."

"Really?" Derek said in a jeering voice as he mounted the carpeted stairs to stand directly before her. "What do you make of this unique discovery?"

"I don't know," she said miserably.

"You're trembling," he said accusingly.

"I can't help it!"

"That bears out what I've just said. This dark place is not a suitable spot for you to visit." As he finished speaking he took the cap and coat from her. "About these!"

She stared at him and was barely able to make out the expression of annoyance on his handsome face. "Yes?" she said in what was little more than a whisper.

"They are mine," her husband said.

"Yours?"

"Yes, I left them here this afternoon when I came home. I brought them with me from the museum. Henry told me there was a brass piece missing from the altar. That some of the tourists must have taken it. I came in here to see for myself, put down the clothes while I made my search and forgot about them when I left."

She listened to his lengthy explanation not knowing whether she should believe him or not. "What are you doing with them?" she asked.

He smiled coldly. "These items are to be part of my costume for the ball. And let me advise you there'll be at least a dozen other captains of the same period attending. These outfits are suddenly very popular. Everyone is searching them out. So your ghost will be right in style!"

"You shouldn't make such jokes!" she protested.

"And you, my dear, shouldn't indulge in such nonsensical thoughts," was his reply. And as he said this he took her by the arm in such a tight grip that it made her wince. "Now let me see you safely out of here."

"Please let me go," she said, trying to escape the cruel pressure of his hand on her arm.

"No," he said. "I can't leave for the museum without being sure you are out of this place. It should be locked in the evenings. No tourists come here after dusk."

She knew she had angered him and so she gave way to his roughly escorting her outside. It was dusk as they emerged from the chapel. He let go of her arm on the steps.

He said, "Brook is waiting for me. I want your promise that you'll go straight into the house and not wander around out here in the darkness."

"Very well."

Her husband went on sternly. "You are not supposed to test your nerves in this fashion. Do you want to end up back at the hospital?"

"No."

"Then you must use some judgement," was Derek's grim advice. "I'm sorry you forced me to be somewhat unkind to you in this but I'm thinking of your welfare. Do you understand?"

She nodded.

"Very well," he said. And he bent and kissed her on the cheek. Then with the cap and coat still in his possession he walked over to Brook's car and got in. She remained standing on the lawn until the car drove off. Then she walked slowly in the direction of the castle.

Her mind was in a whirl. For at least a long moment in the chapel she'd been certain that she'd found the secret of the ghost and that her husband had been impersonating Captain Mills to terrify her back into insanity. And then Derek had come forward with what was certainly a logical explanation for the clothes being next to the altar.

Now she didn't know what to believe. Either Derek was a villain and an accomplished liar or she had badly misjudged him. She did know that the confrontation with him in the chapel had given her a bad fright. And she felt this indicated that she no longer really trusted him.

And yet she didn't want to lose faith in him. If it turned out her love for him was misplaced and that he was trying to rid himself of her so he could be free to carry on with Faith, she would feel she no longer had any reason for living. She had cost Derek his beloved child and failed him by her period of mental illness, so she was willing to forgive him almost anything. But she needed the prospect of his returning to her to sustain her.

Unhappily she could no longer be certain that he would give her his full allegiance again. He had pretended concern for her tonight and used this as an excuse for his harsh attitude. But had it been only pretense? She could not help but wonder.

As she reached the entrance of the castle she saw David Chase standing on the steps waiting for her. She felt an immediate sense of relief, a sense of not being alone.

"Hello," he said, standing there in the dark. "I saw you and your husband coming out of the chapel."

"Yes. I was in there. He brought me out. He doesn't approve of my going in there at this time of night."

"And that's why he brought you out so promptly?"

"Yes," she said in a wry voice. "He considers my wandering in the darkness in there a sign of morbidity. He thinks it might encourage me to have another mental collapse."

The young artist said, "He could be right."

"I suppose so."

"What did make you go in there?"

She hesitated, "I can't really say. It wasn't dusk yet and I decided I wanted to take a look inside." She didn't want to tell him that it was because she'd been attacked by the ghost there. She'd told only Henry and Captain Zachary that and they'd been skeptical.

David said, "I can understand that the chapel would attract you. It has great interest for me. I'd like to do some pen and ink sketches of it inside and out one day."

"You should," she agreed.

"There's so much material on the island," he went on. "It's hard to make a choice. And then I've been busy doing the ship paintings for the museum."

"I know," she said, feeling better just for standing there talking to him.

"I don't suppose you're interested in my problems," he said with wry humor.

"I am," she told him. "Go on talking. It will get me out of my black mood."

"You're in a black mood?"

"I'm afraid so."

"Because of what happened over there? I thought Derek had an angry air about him when he came out. But I couldn't see too well."

She said, "He was very strange for a few minutes. I found myself frightened of him."

"Why?"

"He seemed somehow sinister. I can't explain. And then the moment passed."

"And everything seemed normal again?"

"Almost."

He gazed at her in the darkness. And he told her, "I may find myself on Derek's side in this. The way you've acted isn't a good sign. Going in that dark, isolated place and then having a fit of nerves. You'll have to take care."

"That's what he said."

"Better take it seriously," he advised her.

She glanced up at him. "What are you going to pick for a costume at the summer ball?" She was still thinking about her find in the chapel.

David said, "I've decided to go as a whaling skipper. A lot of the men are going to do the same. Makes a good outfit and those fellows were the ones who made the island famous."

"That's true," she agreed. And she noted that what David had just told her fitted in with what Derek had said. Perhaps he had been truthful after all.

He said, "I understand you have a dress. That all the ladies here are wearing authentic dresses discovered in the attic."

"Yes," she said. "Though I'm still not certain if I'll attend the ball."

"You must!" the young artist insisted. "The least you can do is dance with me!"

"We'll see," she said.

"I want your promise," the young man said. "I shall at least want that much of you to remember when I have gone away from here."

It hadn't struck her that he might be leaving. She said, "When will you be going?"

"At the end of the summer if not before," David Chase said. "Just as soon as my work here is done."

"I see," she said, thinking how different it would be when

he had taken his leave. She had come to depend on him a lot. As long as he was at the castle she felt there was someone to turn to.

"I won't soon forget this summer nor you," the young artist continued. "I think the summer ball should be the highlight of the season. That is why I'd like us to enjoy it together."

She smiled mirthlessly. "There's been little enjoyment for me since coming back here."

"I know," he said. "I listened to your mother-in-law and some of the others at the dinner table. They have no consideration for you. This will never be a true home for you and Derek."

"He'll never leave the island."

"Then make him find you another place to live," was David's suggestion. "In your nervous state this is the worst possible place for you."

"I'm on the point of believing that," she said.

The door behind them opened and it was Regina Mills. The older woman gave them a bleak look. "I was sure that I heard voices out here but I couldn't imagine who it might be," she said.

David gave her a polite nod. "Your daughter-in-law and I are having a chat about the ball."

"Indeed?" Regina sounded skeptical, as if she might have really heard what they'd been saying.

"Most of the talk on the island will be about it since the big event is only a matter of days off," David continued.

Regina's face remained an arrogant mask. She said, "I'm not one who dwells much on such trifles. But I'm sure it will prove interesting for the young people."

David said, "But you are attending?"

"I have little choice since I'm on the committee," Regina

said in her overbearing way. "Ordinarily my son would have had his wife head the women's committee but with Joyce in such precarious health he turned the responsibility over to me."

With that she went back in the house and they followed. In the dimly-lighted foyer Joyce paused to smile wryly at David Chase and say, "As you mentioned, I'm not rated too highly in this house."

His eyes were serious as they met hers. "I think you must do something about that yourself. You must not so easily accept the tag of mad woman. Regina is never going to let up on you if you do."

"I know you're right. But it's difficult."

"It is always difficult," the artist said. "I found that out from my own experience. The first thing you must do is throw off all your guilt feelings."

"I'll try."

"It's a must," he said. "After that you need to fight for your rights. With Derek as well as the others. If you are willing to accept his unfaithfulness he'll go on behaving that way. You are the one to end it."

"You make it seem so easy," she said in mild rebuke.

"I know it can't be that," David Chase said earnestly. "But I have been through this and I want to help you."

She gave him a look of warm admiration. "I know," she said. "And it does mean a lot to me having you here."

With this confession made she left him to go upstairs. She found herself in a bewildered and melancholy mood. David was so sympathetic and understanding in contrast to Derek's coldness. When she'd returned to the island she'd expected Derek to give her support but he hadn't. He seemed much more interested in pleasing his mother than her.

The elegant red velvet dress was draped over the easy chair

in her room. And she went over and examined it. The gold trim set the dress off and it showed very little sign of wear. Perhaps the unhappy Ann Mills had not worn it at all or at the most only a few times. She knew so little about the young woman who had supposedly been murdered in the very room in which she now was standing.

She had seen the faint outline of a bloodstained head that night in the lower foyer where Ann was supposed to have finally collapsed and died. She wished she knew more about the story. How it had all come about. Why Ann had been unfaithful to her husband? And what sort of person had Captain Peter Mills been. From the little she'd learned it struck her that he must have had an evil streak in his character. He had waited for the opportunity to slay his wife and her lover and taken full advantage of it.

Putting the dress back on the chair she let her eyes wander to the rug under which that dull brown spot lay covered. She began to become tense and wished that she had not been given this room. She did not like being in it alone now that she knew its tragic history.

Deciding that rest might help her frayed nerves she began to prepare for bed. All the while her thoughts were of other things. Her meeting with Derek in the chapel had strange undertones which bothered her and which she felt she did not fully understand. Her fears had returned to torment her and she knew she would never be free of them as long as she remained at the castle.

With the lights out she lay waiting for sleep. From a distance she heard the monotonous chant of the Gull Point foghorn. It had been clear when she'd come back to the house but sometimes when a day had been very warm a blanket of fog moved in around midnight. She wondered if it were that late and why Derek wasn't home. He couldn't be working this long at the museum!

She closed her eyes and at last sleep came to her. A tortured kind of sleep in which she had one nightmare after another. Most of them were centered in the old chapel with Derek behaving cruelly towards her. She saw his face, cold and menacing, and in her nightmare he not only seized her arm but threw her to the ground.

She cried out her terror as he stood over her in the shadows. Then her nightmare changed to the cliffs and she was standing there with Lucie again. Her child was hovering on the edge of the cliff waving to her and laughing as she had on that tragic day when she'd fallen to her death. Joyce ran towards her and as she did the child raised a hand, cried out and toppled over the edge. Joyce cried out in agony and twisted unhappily in her bed.

Now it was Regina who thrust an anger-distorted face in hers and told her she wasn't fit to be a mother. Screamed at her that she was a madwoman. Not fit to be part of a fine family. Joyce sobbed in protest and covered her face. She wakened to the darkness of her bedroom and to the sound of her door slowly opening.

Staring at the door as it came open she felt herself freeze with terror. From the shadows of the doorway a figure gradually formed. It was all too familiar to her. First she made out the head with the captain's cap and then the coat with the brass buttons and this time the ghost of Captain Mills had something in his right hand. The long dagger!

The dagger which he had used to kill his wife and her lover! She saw the phantom glide closer and noted that its face was a pale blue blur. She couldn't move or cry out. The phantom seemed to be floating in the darkness and now the dagger was above her, seemingly about to be plunged into her.

She closed her eyes and it seemed to break the spell for it enabled her to scream. She screamed at the top of her lungs, over and over again. She had no idea of how long it was before she heard voices and the movement of others in the hallway. Then there was a knock on her door.

Opening her eyes she saw the phantom had vanished but she cried out, "Help!"

The door burst open and Henry Mills came into her room in pajamas and dressing gown, followed by David Chase dressed in the same way.

Henry Mills came to her bedside. "What were you screaming about?"

She was sitting up now, sobbing uncontrollably. "The phantom! He came again!"

David, at the foot of her bed, asked, "The phantom?"

"The ghost of Captain Mills," she said between sobs. "He came in here after me. He had a dagger."

Mona had entered the room and switched on the lights. There was a look of derision on her attractive face.

Addressing Joyce, she said, "What is it now?"

Joyce fought to control her sobbing. "It doesn't matter!"

Mona glanced at the others and then at her again. "I'd say it does since it seems you feel you have the right to scream madly and rouse all the house!"

Joyce said, "I saw something."

Uncle Henry gave her a warning look. "You probably had a bad dream. We all get them now and then." He told Mona and David, "You two may as well go back to bed. Next thing we'll have Regina in here and the fat will really be in the fire."

Mona gazed at him defiantly. "I feel I have a right to know why she screamed!"

"She had a nightmare!" Uncle Henry said stubbornly.

David Chase gave Joyce an understanding look. "You're

sure there is nothing I can do?"

"No," she said. "Please go! Both of you!"

Uncle Henry's lined face was stern. "You heard her. Now get along. I can take care of this." And he herded the other two out and then closed the door after them. When he'd done this he turned and gave her a grim look.

She said, "Thank you for saving me from myself! I was about to go on babbling about the ghost!"

He moved back to the foot of her bed. "I could see it coming and that was why I stopped you."

"Thank goodness you came! But I did see something!"

"You think you did."

"I know I did!"

The old man glanced at the door which connected her room and Derek's with annoyance written on his weathered face. He said, "What's wrong with your husband? Why didn't he come in answer to your screams?"

"I don't know. He wasn't here when I went to bed."

Uncle Henry grunted. "He ought to be here now." And he went over to the door and opened it. He stood there with surprise on his lined face. "You're right. He's not in his room."

"I'm not surprised," she said.

The old man came back to her. "Why do you say that?"

"He's been acting strangely. And you know about him and Faith. He's likely off somewhere with her."

"Could be," Uncle Henry murmured. "The best thing you can do is go back to sleep and forget all about this."

"I'm not sure I can," she said with a tiny shudder. "I was having awful nightmares."

"And you woke up to one."

"More than that," she insisted. "When I woke up the door was opening and then I saw him!"

"Captain Mills!" the white-haired man in robe and pajamas scoffed. "He's a product of your imagination. A result of your illness."

"No!"

"You must accept that," Uncle Henry warned her. "If you keep on telling everyone you're seeing things they'll put you back in the hospital."

"It was either a ghost or someone acting like one," she said.

He frowned. "Who would do that?"

Her eyes met his. "Perhaps Derek. He isn't here and he does have a proper uniform to play the ghost. Maybe he wants to drive me mad!"

The old man gave a weary sigh. "No matter what you say you have no proof that anyone was in here. I saw no one in the hall and the door you say had been opened was shut."

"Someone did come in!"

"Prove it to me," he said.

She hesitated, realizing she had come to a blank wall. And then she let her eyes wander to the chair and she saw the red velvet dress was no longer on it but had been thrown to the floor. And she could see that it had been slashed almost to ribbons!

CHAPTER EIGHT

Joyce pointed to the dress and in a horrified voice cried, "Look!"

Henry Mills turned in a rather bewildered fashion and stared at the dress. "What happened to that?" he asked.

"The phantom!" she gasped. "The phantom had a dagger in his hand. I thought he was going to attack me but it seems he tore the dress to pieces instead! Ann's dress!"

Henry gave her a grim look. "Now you're saying that the avenging ghost of Captain Mills came back here and ripped the dress his wife once wore to pieces!"

"Doesn't it all add up?" she asked, still sitting in bed.

The old man said nothing for a moment as he went over and lifted up the ruined dress. He stared at it. "Whoever went at it surely did a thorough job," was his comment.

"It had to be the ghost!"

His eyes met hers. "Or someone playing the ghost!"

Her face shadowed. "Yes." She was thinking of Derek and how easily he might have played this macabre trick on her.

Uncle Henry held out the dress. "I'll tell you another variation of this," he said. "I'll give you Regina's version. You know what she will do, don't you?"

"What?"

His lined face showed disgust. "She'll accuse you of destroying the dress and say you did it because you're crazy."

She listened with dismay. And she realized it was all too likely. That Regina could and probably would jump to that conclusion. She said, "But I'd already agreed to wear the dress. Why should I destroy it?"

"Regina won't need any logical reason," he warned her.

Joyce knew this was true. And once again she felt trapped. The dress would have to be explained and this would certainly result in a scene. Regina would be delighted to take advantage of the situation.

She said, "What can I say to her?"

The old man grimly put the dress on the easy chair. He shrugged. "Right at this minute I don't know."

As he said this the door from her husband's room opened and a troubled-looking Derek came in to join them. He looked at his uncle in amazement and then at her.

"What is happening here?" he asked.

Joyce countered with, "Where have you been?"

His handsome face bore a sullen expression. He said, "I was detained at the museum. You haven't answered my question."

His Uncle Henry looked uncomfortable. The old man said, "You two don't need me here." And to Derek, "Joyce can tell you all about it." And with a good night he went out and closed the hall door after him.

An upset Derek came over and questioned her, "Tell me what has been going on?"

She grimaced. "I made a scene again and you weren't here to help me."

"What sort of scene?"

"I woke and saw the ghost in my room."

"Not again!" he said irritably.

"I'm afraid so. This time he had a dagger in his hand. I finally managed to scream out for help. It frightened the phantom off and brought half the household here. Uncle Henry shooed the others off and remained to comfort me."

Derek gave a small groan. "Did you rouse Mother?"

"No. She was the only one who didn't show up. But Mona

was here and I'm sure she'll give your mother a lively account of it all."

"It's too bad," he said.

She couldn't help but derive some enjoyment from his obvious discomfort. And she felt if he had played the ghost role he was an accomplished actor. She found herself doubting that he could have and now give such a show of amazement.

She said, "That's not the worst. The antique dress your mother found for me to wear to the ball is ruined."

"Ruined?"

She nodded at the easy chair. "You can see for yourself. The phantom must have slashed it with his dagger. After all it was his wife's dress. The wife he murdered in this room!"

He shot her a reproving glance. "You can't be sure of that!" And he went over to the dress and lifted it up. He seemed shocked by the damage. "You're right. It's beyond repair."

"When your mother finds out there's bound to be trouble," she told him.

He put the dress back on the chair and came over and sat down on the edge of the bed. Staring at her with troubled eyes, he asked, "Just what does all this mean?"

"I wish I knew," she said. "And I wish you had been here. You should have."

Derek looked guilty. "I left the museum before twelve but when I went to my car it wouldn't start. Something was wrong with the battery. I had to phone the garage in Dark Harbor and get them to bring me another. That's what kept me so late."

She listened to his explanation and studied his face and knew he could be telling her the truth or just a well-made lie. More and more she found herself feeling that this man she loved was a stranger to her. Could it be that she had never really known him? That she was in love with someone who didn't really exist!

She said, "If you'd been here I could have called on you and I'd not have had to disturb the others."

"Tell me about it," he urged her.

"I had trouble getting to sleep. Then I had a series of bad dreams. As I came awake from one of the nightmares I saw the door opening and the phantom entering."

His eyes were troubled. "You know what I think?"

"I can almost guess," she said bitterly. "You think that the phantom was part of my nightmare."

"Yes."

"I'm sorry to spoil your theory," she said. "But there's the dress! Who ripped it to ribbons?"

Her handsome husband didn't reply for a few seconds. Then very soberly, he said, "Joyce, don't you think you might have torn the dress yourself. You didn't like the idea of wearing it and in a kind of rage you may have done all this to it."

She sat back with a gasp. "You're actually accusing me before your mother has a chance. I didn't think it possible!"

He looked upset. "What do you mean by that?"

"Your Uncle Henry predicted that Regina would say I tore the dress in a crazy rage. And now you're saying it first!"

"It's not that I don't believe in you," he protested.

"Oh, no!" she said scornfully.

"Joyce!"

"I understand," she said wearily.

He stared at her with new concern. "We'll somehow alibi for your screaming. We can say you had a bad dream."

"Of course."

"And my suggestion is to not say anything to Mother about the dress. Just find something else to wear. There must be lots of things upstairs. You can give any logical reason for not wanting to use the dress. Get rid of it without them ever knowing it was torn to bits."

She shook her head. "I don't think it will do."

"Why not?"

"I'm sure that Mona saw it when she was in here. It was on the floor and she was standing right next to it."

"Let's hope she didn't notice it."

"Hope anything you like," was her reply. "But don't be surprised if your dear adopted sister should spread the word. You know she has it in for me anyway."

Her husband eyed her worriedly. "There are times when I think Dr. Beckett made a mistake in releasing you so soon."

Joyce automatically lashed back. "I suppose it has been inconvenient for you and Faith. You two have been getting on so very well."

He sprang up from the bed and stood there angrily. "I don't have to listen to that kind of insinuation!" he declared.

"I thought I was only repeating fact."

"Good night, Joyce," he said stiffly. "I hope you're in a better mood in the morning." And he stalked into his own room and slammed the door after him.

As soon as she found herself alone she regretted having angered him. It had been a meaningless victory to hurt him. Now she felt more desolate and alone than ever before. No one believed her story about the phantom and she was equally sure that most of the others in the castle suspected that she was slowly drifting back into insanity. Her husband had not been too subtle in his hints just now.

She'd even seen doubt and fear in the eyes of David Chase, who should know better, and Uncle Henry, who up to this time had been her chief defender. Worst of all it made her wonder about her mental state and begin to worry that they might be right. That she was living in a fantasy world and twisting all these things to fit her hallucinations. It was in this troubled frame of mind that she put out the lights and sought sleep.

The rest of the night passed without event. And when she got up the next morning she found that fog had come sweeping in from the ocean. It lay over the island so thick it was almost like a light drizzle of rain.

One of the first things she did was knock on Derek's door. But he wasn't there. He'd already left for the museum. She went downstairs and had breakfast. She was congratulating herself on escaping a confrontation with her mother-in-law. But she counted on this too soon. As she was crossing the foyer Regina appeared from the living room and glared at her.

"Are you feeling better this morning?" her mother-in-law asked with sarcasm.

"I wasn't ill last night," she said as calmly as she could.

Regina smiled nastily. "I heard about your screaming and assumed you were."

"I had a scare," she said, clenching her fists at her side and striving to keep control.

Her mother-in-law nodded condescendingly. "Yes. You're given to them. I suppose they are part of your medical history."

"This was nothing imagined! It was a real scare!"

"Of course you would think so," Regina said. "But all this talk of ghosts is nonsense. I have lived in this house nearly all my life and I have never seen anything to suggest the house is haunted."

Joyce came back with, "It could be that you are not sensitive to the psychic."

"Why mince words!" Regina said crossly. "You are given to mental breakdowns. You've had more than one and it is likely you're on the verge of another. That is the explanation of your wild screaming in the night!"

Her throat became so full she felt she might choke on her hurt. But she battled off the desire to break into sobbing or even to allow herself the joy of rage. Either would be regarded as signs of mental weakness in her.

So she forced out a small, "There's nothing for me to say since you have me so well diagnosed." And she turned to hurry up the stairway and escape the arrogant older woman.

"One moment!" Regina called after her in an authoritative voice.

She hesitated and slowly turned. "Yes?"

"About the dress."

"Yes?" she spoke more faintly this time.

"The expensive antique dress that I loaned you to wear for the ball and that you so brazenly have destroyed. Are you going to pretend that wasn't madness on your part?"

"Mona told you!"

"Yes, she did," Regina said angrily. "I cannot forgive such vandalism, even though you are evidently still mad. And I promise you that you'll get nothing else from our stock of clothes in this house."

Joyce said, "I don't suppose you'd believe me if I told you I didn't destroy the dress."

"I would not!"

"Then there is no point in my saying anything," Joyce said wearily.

"You are so right," her mother-in-law declared. "If I were in your place I'd cease to be an embarrassment to my husband and voluntarily place myself in the hospital again!"

"You'd like that, wouldn't you?"

"I'd consider it sensible on your part!"

Joyce smiled bitterly. "I'm sure you would. But don't

expect me to do it!" And she turned and resumed mounting the stairway.

As she climbed the stairs her mother-in-law cried angrily after her, "It was a sorry day for my son when he married you!"

She went on to her own room with her head reeling. The scene had taken a great deal out of her even though she had actually been expecting it. She had one overwhelming desire and that was to escape the old mansion. She found her raincoat and a kerchief and then picked up the ripped velvet dress and started back downstairs. She left it for Regina on a chair in the living room. Then she went out into the wet, foggy morning and got her car. It wasn't a pleasant day for driving but anything was better than remaining at the castle.

On the drive to Dark Harbor she turned on her headlights to be sure of being seen by other cars in the thick fog. She debated what she should do about a costume for the ball. She had no intention of accepting one from the Mills collection even if Derek persuaded Regina to change her mind. And she recalled that the day she'd been at the museum Brook Patterson had mentioned that the dry cleaning shop had brought in a group of period rental costumes from Boston for those who had none otherwise. And so she headed for the hilly main street and the dry cleaners.

The Dark Harbor Cleaners were located next to the Inn owned by Matthew Kimble. She drove onto the main street and followed its wet cobblestones up the hill until she found a parking place in front of the tavern. As she got out of the car and put a coin in the meter Matthew Kimble came marching up the street.

He was hatless and coatless. He had on a sports shirt and dark trousers. When he saw her a look of curiosity came to his lantern-jawed face.

He nodded to her. "Good morning, Mrs. Mills."

"Good morning," she said. "What a foggy day!"

"We need them every so often," he said, his eyes fixing on her in a strangely evasive way that was peculiar to him. Shifty-eyed would be the best term to describe him, she thought. He added, "I thought you were still in the mainland hospital."

"No," she said. "I've been home for a short time."

"Feeling better?"

"Yes. Much better."

"That's good," the big man said. "Nice to know you're back." And he nodded and moved on.

She started for the cleaners. She'd heard a lot of ugly stories about Matthew Kimble but he'd always been civil and a gentleman as far as she was concerned.

The dry cleaning shop was not large and she entered its single glass door and found herself facing a counter with a young girl behind it whom she'd never seen before.

She told the girl, "I'd like to look at the rental costumes for the ball."

The thin young woman indicated a small side room. "In there," she said. "There's a few left."

"May I look for myself?"

"Sure, if you find something you like you can try it on. There's a dressing room at the back."

"Thank you," she said. And she went on into the room where the costumes were hung on racks on two walls. On the street side the rack had all men's costumes and the inner wall had another long iron rack with women's dresses. She began to work her way through these, examining each dress briefly as to style and size.

As she went about this she became vaguely aware that someone else was in the dressing room behind the green curtain which served to give some privacy to whoever was using it. She kept on looking at the dresses until she came to one in pink chiffon which impressed her. She took it from the rack with the thought of trying it on when the dressing room was free.

She was waiting with the dress over her arm when the green curtain was pushed aside and she was startled to see Faith Patterson emerge from the dressing room also carrying a costume.

Faith saw her and showed slight embarrassment. "I had no idea it was you out here," she said.

"I see we're both on the same errand," Joyce said. "Did you find something?"

"Yes. I like this." Faith held up a dress with a high bodice which was all lace and ruffles. It had a fussy look like Faith herself.

"That should look good on you," she said, working hard to make some sort of genial conversation.

"And you have one," Faith said awkwardly.

"If it fits."

"Mine is fine," Faith said. And then apologetically, she added, "I'm sorry I kept Derek so long at the museum last night. But we never did seem to get a start on our work until after Brook went home. And we're so far behind I made him stay and catch up on all his correspondence."

"Was that it?" she asked coolly.

"I can imagine you were worried about him," Faith drawled.

"I had expected him to be home earlier," she agreed. "I had the impression he had trouble with his car and that was what kept him."

Faith's pretty face turned scarlet. "Oh? I didn't know about that. Perhaps it happened after I left. I drove home first and he stayed to lock up."

She could tell that Faith was rapidly improvising. But she said, "That could be."

Faith still looked shaken. She said, "Well, I must go out and arrange for the rental of this dress and go back to work. I asked for a half-hour off to come here and I don't want to stay longer."

"I understand," Joyce said, just as anxious to be rid of her as Faith was to get away. She went on in to the dressing room and tried on the dress she'd selected.

By the time Joyce had put the dress on and changed back to her own things Faith had left. Joyce went out and at once arranged for the rental of the costume she'd picked out. She paid the clerk and was given the dress in a cardboard box.

The thin young woman behind the counter reminded her, "The dress has to be returned the day after the ball or we'll have to charge you extra rental."

"I understand," she said. "I'll return it promptly."

Joyce went back out onto the foggy main street. She stopped at a couple of other small stores to make purchases and then returned to her car. It was still too soon for her to want to go back to the castle and she didn't want to drop by the museum with Faith there, so she decided to fill in some time by paying a short visit to Zachary Miller.

She drove on up the cobblestoned main street with her headlights on for safety and turned into the lane where the Captain had his cottage. There was no sign of him outside so she knocked on his front door.

After a little she heard his slow step and then he opened the door to her. His wizened face lit up at once as he saw who it was. "Mrs. Mills, what a pleasant surprise," the old man said.

"Can I come in for a moment?" she asked.

"For as long as you like," the old man said warmly. "This is a bad day. Makes a man want companionship."

She followed him into the shadowed house and to the library which was at the rear. When they reached it they sat down as they had before.

The old man said, "I enjoy your visits."

Joyce smiled wanly. "I'm afraid I bring you nothing but my troubles."

"I find it a challenge to try and help you solve them," the old man said with a twinkle in his bright old eyes. "What have you new today?"

"Let me tell you," she said. And she did, beginning with the weird account of her visitation by the phantom the night before and the dress being torn.

The Captain listened attentively and when she had finished, he said, "From all you say I'd gather that things are not any better at the castle."

"They aren't."

"And you and Derek are still at odds."

She nodded. "We're not reaching each other."

"That's a pity," the old man said with a sigh. "You need him badly in this crisis."

"I'm beginning to wonder if he isn't contriving the crisis," she said. "There was something very strange about last night. Derek could have come in dressed as the ghost and destroyed that dress as well as terrifying me. Then he could have easily turned up later pretending to know nothing about it."

"You say he seemed very sincere in his surprise."

"Yes. But it still could be feigned."

"I wonder," the old man mused. "I thought something of the sort when you were here before. And because of his affair with Faith he has a motive for wanting you to have another mental collapse. Do you feel he is guilty?"

"I don't know," she admitted. "I suppose I don't want to believe it."

"Yet the evidence is very strong against him," the old man said.

"I realize that more each day."

"And you stay on."

"Possibly because I must learn the truth."

"Perhaps you are seeing ghosts," Captain Zachary Miller said seriously. "It could be that in your sensitive mental state these phantoms are getting through to you."

"I keep thinking that."

The old man gave her a shrewd look. "In addition to Henry you have this young man who is interested in you."

She blushed. "Yes. David Chase, the artist."

"I gather he is in love with you?"

"He says he is."

"It's not something a man says lightly so I imagine we should take him at his word. He thinks you should leave Derek?"

"Yes."

"Do you feel you could fall in love with him?"

"I might," she said. "I like him. Maybe I care for him more than I realize even now."

The Captain showed interest. "It may be that you'll escape from the castle and all its terrors for you one day and go off with this young man."

"He'll be leaving soon," she said. "Probably in another month."

"Then you should think this all out and make up your mind before he leaves," the Captain said.

"I'm almost too mixed up to do that."

"Try," he said.

"I will," she agreed. "But I doubt if I'll have any luck. Now

I suppose I must drive back to the castle."

Captain Miller advised her, "I wouldn't allow Faith to frighten me away from the museum. Why don't you go there and make Derek take you to lunch somewhere?"

"Knowing what is going on I hate to face them."

"Forget that you know," the old man said. "That's the best way. You are going to the ball, aren't you?"

"Yes, I think I should if only to annoy Regina and Mona," she said.

He chuckled. "I agree. But I think you should be there anyhow."

"Are you attending?"

He shook his head. "I'm a mite too old for that. But there was a day when I wouldn't have missed it. Too bad about the weather. I have an idea we're in for a spell of rain and fog."

"You really think so?"

"Yes. Been fine too long. Now my joints are giving me the bad weather signal and I tell you they never fail."

She smiled as she rose to leave. "You have the island in your bones. You're so much a part of it."

He looked pleased at this. "It's a barren spot, Pirate Island," he observed. "And there are towns not nearly so gray and hilly as Dark Harbor. But in spite of the barrenness it has produced strong people. Men of this island have gone from the coast of Japan to Baffin's Bay in search of whale. Rounding the Horn in a two hundred ton vessel didn't faze them at all. And there are plenty of stories to tell about pirates and cannibals, mutineers, scurvy and shipwreck. Not half of it has been told. One day you must read some of the logs and letters I have stowed away in my sea chest in the cellar."

"I'd like to," she said with sincerity.

"It would take your mind off your troubles for a spell and give you a different picture of this place," he assured her.

"The castle is only a part of it and so are the Mills family. This island has produced more than its share of characters."

"I'm sure it has."

Captain Zachary Miller's wizened face had taken on a glow as he reminisced. "Men like Crevecoeur, the elegant French noble who was all for liberty, fraternity and equality. And Reuben Chase and the giant Long Tom Coffin who cared for nothing but the sea. Ratliff, the British bluejacket, spinning his tales about his cruise to St. Helena with the Great Emperor Napoleon. And Billy Clark, the town crier, tooting his horn and ringing his bell!"

"They sound so colorful," she said. "But what about the women? There must have been some characters among them as well."

"To be sure."

"Can you name any?"

"Plenty," the old man chuckled. "There was Mary Starbuck who was a queen among women with a fine mind, Keziah Coffin who was mean and ruthless and a great whale of a woman named Deborah Chase who would toss luckless suitors up on a rooftop or into a keg of oil! And there was Maria Mitchell who became a great astronomer and Lucretia Mott who made a name as a crusader. And my own dear Mamie who was at my side until only a few years ago when she died. I could go on with the list but you should be starting for the museum." He got to his feet.

"Do you think I should go?"

"I do or I wouldn't have said so," Captain Miller told her. "If you want to measure up to the island women you've got to have spunk."

She smiled in spite of her misgivings. "I'll see what I can do," she said.

The old captain escorted her to the door and once again

she went out to drive in the fog with her headlights on. She reached the museum shortly after twelve and this time made her entrance through the rear door which was used mostly by the staff. She was at once impressed by the excellent job of decorating which had been carried out.

Splashy, colorful sketches of the island had been done on paper and tacked to the wall at intervals. And there was bunting and displays of whaling and marine equipment set up at various spots in the lobby.

She was standing there admiring the decorations when Brook Patterson came down the stairs to join her. He showed a smile on his lean face and said, "Do you approve?"

"Very much so. You're doing a marvelous job."

"Special lighting will help. I think it will create a true island atmosphere. And that is what we want."

"I'm sure everyone will be impressed," she said. And then she asked him, "Is Derek still here?"

Brook nodded. "He's upstairs in his office. Faith and David Chase have gone off somewhere to look up some additional marine props for lobby decorations."

"I see," she said. "I wonder if Derek is going out for lunch or if he planned to have something sent in."

The balding man said, "I really couldn't say. You'll have to ask him."

"I shall," she said. And before going to the stairs she asked him, "How are things with you?"

Brook Patterson looked bleak. "No change. About the same."

She could only take this to mean that the affair between his wife and her husband was still in full bloom. Very quietly, she said, "I see." And she left him to mount the stairs.

Derek was at work in his private office when she entered. He looked up at her from his desk with an expression of surprise. "I wasn't expecting you here today," he said.

She stood before his desk. "Do you mind my coming?"

He at once changed in his manner. "No. Not at all," he said. "Please take a chair. I'm just going over some accounts. If one doesn't keep at them they become mountainous."

She took the nearest chair and sat very upright in it. She told him, "I went to the cleaners on Main Street and found myself another costume."

He stared across the desk with a slight frown. "Wasn't Mother able to find you a dress at the house?"

"She refused to. She made a scene this morning. And of course she accused me of destroying that dress."

Derek seemed upset. "What did you say to her?"

"Very little considering how unjust she was to me," Joyce told him. "But I made up my mind I'd find a costume somewhere else."

"You should have come to me first."

"I didn't want to bother you," she said. "I thought you'd be relieved to know I found something. I met Faith there and she had picked up a dress."

Her husband at once became more friendly. "I am glad you did locate one. But I know there must be a wide selection available at the castle. I'm sure mother would have gotten over her upset shortly and been glad to help find you a dress."

"I've been through that before," she said. "I'll feel much happier this way."

"As long as you are satisfied," he told her. "I was very shocked at your condition last night."

She gave him a knowing look. "Our conversation didn't end on a very happy note."

"I did leave abruptly, forgive me," her husband said, looking sorry.

Joyce said, "Perhaps I didn't handle things as well as I

might have either, but I felt you should be more understanding."

He looked at her with worried eyes. "Any hint of madness seems to frighten me these days. And you were talking and acting strangely last night."

She knew they would do best to avoid a replay of all they'd said to each other the previous night. So she asked him, "Are you going out to lunch?"

"I've been too busy to think about it," he said. "I can."

"Don't let me upset your work," she begged him.

He shoved his papers he'd been studying aside. "No. I need a break. Where would you like to go?"

"Anyplace."

"Most of the island spots are open," he said. "Let's drop by the Inn. It's not the most pleasant spot in town but it is on the main street and I want to check with the cleaners on how the costumes are going." He got up from his desk.

She said, "I met Matthew Kimble on the street today and he actually stopped and inquired about my health."

Derek heard this with a slight frown. "Don't get too friendly with him. He's not too well-liked on the island but he does try to keep in with the older families."

"What is the story about him?"

Derek put on a trench coat and escorted her out and down the stairway. He said, "His parents were respectable enough. But Matthew always has been a black sheep. The story is he served a prison sentence on the mainland and this broke the hearts of his parents. His father died before Matthew showed up on the island once again. By that time his mother was old and feeble and he took over the management of the Inn."

"So that's it," she said. And as they came to the lobby, she said, "I think the decorations are fine."

Her husband hesitated for a moment to admire them. "So

do I. Faith has done an excellent job."

Joyce did not miss this tribute to the wife of Brook Patterson. She said, "I understand she and David are out looking for more things."

"Faith wants everything perfect," Derek smiled. "And the time is getting short."

"Have you any sketches of Deborah Chase?"

Derek eyed her with astonishment. "Deborah Chase? How do you come to know that name?"

Joyce shrugged. "I have a little knowledge of the island's history. Wasn't she a powerful Katinka type, a three hundred pound woman who tossed her suitors around like toy soldiers?"

"She was indeed," he said with a laugh. "I must ask Faith if she has any reference to Deborah in the decorations. It would be an oversight if she hasn't."

"And Long Tom Coffin," Joyce added, aware that she was impressing him.

"You know all the famous characters!" he gasped.

"And some of the stories," she said. "Is it true that when one of the whaling captains returned after a three-year cruise, his wife met him at the door with a bucket, and said, 'Go fill this at the well and then come on in to your dinner.' "

Derek chuckled. "I can't vouch for the story. Nor can I for the one where the whaling captain left his house and started down to his ship and then realized he'd forgotten to say goodbye to his wife. But he told himself, 'It's only going to be a one-year cruise!' and so he didn't bother going back!"

They both laughed at this and she realized that perhaps for the first time a sense of warm communication had been established between them. She mentally thanked old Captain Miller for his good advice and she began to believe that it might be practical to build a new bond between them by stressing what seemed unimportant. If they could carry on light conversations maybe they could later approach the more serious problems without being frightened and self-conscious.

Leaving the lobby of the museum they went out into the fog again. Derek used his car to drive them to the village. When they had found a parking place on a side street he took her to the inn. It was dark inside and very plain but it wasn't crowded with tourists. And it also had a kind of charm with its ancient panelled walls and the prints of ancient whaling ships at intervals. A single middle-aged waitress presided over the booths which lined both walls of the tavern and Matthew Kimble was nowhere in sight.

Derek ordered for them and then told her, "I'm glad you came to meet me. We seem to do better away from the castle than we do in it."

"I do feel some kind of shadow over me when I'm there," she admitted. "Perhaps that is to be expected. But Dr. Beckett thought I would manage all right there. I'm not sure that it has turned out to be the case."

Derek wrinkled his brow. "Perhaps we haven't given it enough time."

"Perhaps not," she said. "What did you do with your coat and cap which I found in the chapel last night?"

"I put them away," he said with a touch of his old sullenness returning.

She said, "It's strange but when that apparition came into my room he seemed to have on an identical cap and coat."

"Which merely leads me to believe the whole thing was part of your nightmare," her husband said almost curtly. "You mustn't be so ready to give in to your imaginings."

"The ghost seemed real enough. And the dress was ripped to ribbons."

Derek looked unhappy and she saw they were losing much of the ground which they'd earlier gained. He said, "I don't want to make it seem to you that I always agree with Mother but I have a strange feeling that you might have done that damage yourself."

She stared at him in despair. "I couldn't have. To do that I'd have to be as mad as I was before I left the island for treatment."

"You might have occasional mild relapses still," Derek argued. "In fact they might be expected. And during these spells you perhaps think you see things and do things that aren't quite rational."

Joyce felt her desolation and fear returning again. "You see me in that light. As still a damaged person?"

Derek showed concern. "I don't see why that should upset you so. You know you were sick for a while. Why expect to be so completely cured now?"

"Because it is important to me that you can see me as a normal person. Realize that I've been cured. That's the big hurdle for people like me. You still want to tag us mad. Someone warned me about that not long ago."

"Who?" Derek asked.

"It doesn't matter," she said, determined not to break her word to David Chase about keeping his mental illness a secret. She was glad to note the waitress coming with their food and ending the discussion.

CHAPTER NINE

Captain Zachary Miller's prediction about the weather proved only too true. The days that followed until the day of the summer ball were all either foggy or wet. It was far from ideal summer weather. As the pace of preparations for the ball went forward and the time grew shorter it seemed that the outstanding social event was filling everyone's mind.

As a result Joyce found life at the castle more acceptable. She had none of the weird visions which she'd experienced earlier and for the most part both her mother-in-law and Mona left her alone. Derek was mildly attentive to her in the short intervals when they were together, but the big summer dance was taking up more and more of his time.

His Uncle Henry seemed to be the only one not caught up in the preparations. He told Joyce with slight disgust, "I'm willing to attend the affair but I'm not doing any work to make it possible. Let Derek and his colleagues do it. It's their idea."

She asked him, "Don't you think it will make money for the museum?"

"Maybe a little," the old man said. "But have you thought what it will cost? They're going to have to spend plenty."

"I suppose so," she agreed. But she was still inclined to be on her husband's side in the matter. She saw the summer ball as a fine money-raising scheme which was apt to be carried on annually.

The day of the ball began with rain in the morning. This tapered off to a drizzle in the afternoon and then the fog rolled in. She spent most of her day getting her dress ready and went to Dark Harbor in the afternoon to get her hair done. There were a lot of extra people on the island in spite of the weather and she guessed that many of them would be attending the ball.

A buffet dinner was to be served at midnight in a side room off the museum lobby. She and Derek were to be on hand with Brook and Faith Patterson to receive the guests. Joyce couldn't help wondering how much gossip had been making the rounds about her husband and Faith and whether the fact that the two couples made up the reception line would attract further comment.

Derek arrived home late with just time to take a shower and get quickly dressed. He appeared very much on edge. She had taken several of the tranquillizer tablets which Dr. Beckett had given her and hoped that she would manage the evening. She was already in her dress by the time he arrived from the museum and she did what she could to help him dress.

As he fumbled with his string black tie he gave a disgusted cry. "My fingers all seem numbed," he declared. "I'd say you are much less nervous than I am."

"I did take some medicine," she reminded him. "Let me help you with the tie." And she did.

His handsome face was pale and he eyed her nervously. "You look very well. I feel strange getting into this outfit. I wish I'd made it a black tie affair rather than a costume ball. But that was Faith's idea."

"I think it will work well," she said as she brought him the blue coat with the two rows of brass buttons. He put it on and then the captain's gold-braided hat.

He scowled in the mirror. "I look ridiculous."

"No," she said, "you are quite handsome." What she didn't tell him was that he so resembled the spectre that had several times terrified her that the sight of him made her uneasy.

She had expected him to be in a happy, bright mood in anticipation of the party but instead he was in this curious, tense state. It made her wonder if he and Faith might not have had a falling out. She was to drive with Derek in his car while Mona and Regina followed in the family limousine with Uncle Henry and David Chase.

Joyce had a brief chance to see the two other women in their costumes and saw that they were more elaborate than hers. They kept aloof from her and paid her no compliments on the simple gown she'd rented. Regina had chosen to almost completely ignore her since the incident of the ripped dress and Mona had followed suit.

But both Uncle Henry and David Chase took the time to compliment her on her appearance. Uncle Henry was wearing an outfit of a town crier and carried a prop bell with him. And David Chase had on a whaling captain's outfit almost like her husband's except that the coat and cap were light green rather than blue.

David smiled at her. "This is going to be an important night for you."

"I'm starting out well but I'm terrified I'll be nervous later," she admitted.

"Never," he said. "Try to forget yourself and enjoy the occasion. The costumes ought to make it seem as if we were celebrating a hundred years ago."

"I know," she said. She gave a glance up the stairway watching for Derek to come down. And she told the young artist, "Derek is in a strange mood. I don't know what to make of it."

"What sort of mood?"

"Nervous and irritable," she said.

179

"Maybe he's afraid for you," David suggested.

"It could be," she admitted. "I'd never thought of that." As she spoke Derek appeared on the stairs and hurried down to join her.

The fog was thick again and the drive to the museum not a pleasant one. Derek seemed strangely quiet and only made a comment or two on the weather and wondered whether it would make a difference in the attendance. They reached the museum early and went inside.

Brook and Faith Patterson arrived at the very last minute. And it seemed to Joyce that she and Derek were not on the good terms they had been. There were no smiles exchanged between them. Tension was in the air. Faith frowned as Brook took what seemed an endless time to pin on her corsage. Derek stood with his back to Faith while this was going on and Joyce again felt this was not by accident.

Then the first of the patrons of the ball began to arrive. The lighting in the museum lobby was soft and enhanced the decor and costumes. On a stand at the far end of the room the Boston orchestra began playing a lively dance number. Once the people began to come they arrived in a veritable flood.

Joyce's hand was stiff from shaking the hands of the guests. And for a long while after the music began they were forced to remain at the entrance to greet any last minute guests. At last Derek suggested they had waited long enough and asked Joyce to have the first dance with him.

He'd removed the cap as soon as he'd come inside and now he looked extremely handsome in the blue coat with its brass buttons and fawn trousers. He and Joyce danced for a long while and she thoroughly enjoyed it. At last the music ended and he took her to one of the bars for a drink.

As they were standing there, she said, "I'm sure everyone is having a wonderful time. Aren't you?"

The familiar cold expression had returned to his handsome face. "Of course," he said in his aloof way. "It's a perfect evening." Then he turned to her and added, "I must speak to Brook about something. Please excuse me for a moment."

He left her standing alone and then the music started and still he did not return. She began to worry as she searched the big lobby for some sign of him and could not find him.

She was standing there in this troubled state when David Chase came up to her and offering a low bow said, "Will you dance with me, ma'am?"

Joyce smiled. "You're very much in character tonight."

"It is the proper time for it, Mistress Mills," the young artist said with mock gravity. And he swung her out onto the dance floor.

It was about then that her head began to ache, though not badly. David was a good dancer and she enjoyed herself. The floor was crowded and she kept looking for Derek but there wasn't a sign of him. This bothered her and her headache grew more pronounced.

When the dance ended David escorted her back to the bar. She hoped that Derek would be waiting there for her but he wasn't. Instead a frowning Brook Patterson was standing there. He had on a rather shapeless Puritan style jacket and wore a white jabot at his neck.

Brook asked her, "Have you seen Faith?"

"Not since the first dance," she said.

"Nor have I," Brook said irritably. "And Derek is missing as well."

"I know," she agreed. "Where can they be?"

"That's difficult to say," her husband's assistant said dryly. "They probably feel they've done their duty and now they can act as they like."

"People expect them to be here mixing with the guests," she pointed out.

"I hope you tell them that when you see them," Brook said, staring at the dancing couples with a face pale with anger.

"They can't be far away," she protested.

"Let's dance in any case," Brook said. "At least the people here will see that we're doing our part."

She danced with him but her head was aching so now that she didn't really enjoy it. She also had the feeling that everyone was watching them and gossiping about them and the absences of their spouses. She was relieved when the dance ended and he returned her to the area of the bar.

He left her and she stood alone, exchanging a few words with passing couples whom she knew. Everyone seemed to be having a great evening except for the committee. She stood there waiting and gradually feeling more ill until at last she moved away from the noise of the music and the talking. She went all the way to the rear door where she was surprised to find the single island policeman, Constable Titus Frink, had taken a stand.

The middle-aged policeman tipped his cap to her. "Out here for a breath of air, Mrs. Mills?" he inquired sympathetically in his nasal fashion.

"Yes. I have a dreadful headache," she said. "I think it's the noise back in there. I'm only able to stand it for so long."

The constable looked worried. "You're really sick, then?"

She nodded. "I'm afraid so."

The aging Titus Frink was concerned. "I'd better go inside and locate your husband and tell him."

"No!" she protested. "I don't know where he is and I wouldn't want to bother him in any case."

"You can't stay here if you're ill?" the constable said worriedly.

She covered her eyes with a hand. "It's my head! I can't seem to think! It's paining so!"

Constable Titus Frink said, "Dr. Taylor is here somewhere. Maybe I can have him look at you."

"That isn't necessary," she said in a strained voice. "I just need to get away from here where I'll be more quiet. I took some pills but they don't seem to have done much good."

The constable said, "I'll be glad to drive you home, ma'am. I'm not needed here and it will only keep me away a short time in any case."

She gave him a grateful look. "Would you?"

"Of course," he said. "You just wait here and I'll go get my car and come back for you."

She remained in the doorway as he walked off into the fog. The damp had restored her a bit and she was able to think more clearly. She tried to keep her mind off Derek and her concern for his welfare. All evening she'd sensed something was wrong without actually being sure what it was.

Headlights showed in the fog and a moment later the constable drove up. He opened the car door and warned her, "Mind your dress. Hold it up so it won't drag as you get in."

She did, and thanked him as she sat in the front seat beside him. "It's very good of you," she said.

"Part of my job," was his laconic reply. He rapidly drove away from the museum.

She lay back against the seat with her eyes closed and within a surprisingly short time the car came to a halt and she looked out and saw they were at the front door of the castle.

"You lost no time," she told him.

"I know the road well."

"I suppose so."

"How are you feeling?" the constable wanted to know.

"A little better."

"You think you'll be all right."

"Yes."

"Should I tell your husband that I've brought you home?"

"Please do. Tell him I had a bad headache. He'll understand."

The constable said, "Yes, ma'am." And he helped her out of the car.

She stood in the driveway and watched the red taillights of his sedan as he drove off towards the museum once again. She enjoyed the cool air without minding the damp and remained standing there in the darkness broken only by the lights on either side of the front entrance.

She still worried about what had happened to her husband and Faith. Her headache was growing worse again to the point that it made her dizzy. She was really ill and yet she didn't want to go inside. She was afraid she'd collapse before she managed to get up the stairway.

While she was debating what she'd do she heard distant, muffled voices that seemed to belong to a man and woman. Her reason blurred by her headache she began to move in the direction from which the voices seemed to have come. Leaving the semi-lighted area of the entrance for the thick fog of the lawn, Joyce stood staring into the darkness and trying to make out what the voices were saying.

Then she saw that she was not far from the chapel and it was from the entrance of the chapel that she'd heard the voices. As she watched a figure came running out and started across the lawn in front of her. It was the figure of a woman in a costume of another era, that was all she could make out. And then a man came out of the chapel to pursue the woman.

She raised her hands to her mouth and gasped. For it was the ghost she was seeing, Captain Peter Mills in cap and familiar jacket racing after the fleeing woman. In a moment he'd caught up with her and the woman cried out in terror. Then she saw the phantom's hand raise as if he were about to plunge a weapon into the unfortunate woman!

Joyce cried out a terrified warning and then, taxed beyond her strength, she collapsed on the wet grass in a dead faint. When she came to it was totally dark and she was thoroughly soaked from the wet fog and grass. She raised herself on an elbow trying to recall what had taken place.

And as memory returned to her she was stricken with a trembling caused partly by the wet cold and partly from her terror. She had watched the phantom of Captain Peter Mills in a re-enactment of the long-ago murder. Somehow she managed to struggle to her feet and with teeth chattering and a dry sobbing she stumbled back in the direction of the castle entrance.

When she reached the door she groped for the bell and rang it several times. A few minutes later when the startled housekeeper opened the door Joyce fell forward into her arms. Then she fainted for a second time.

The next time she opened her eyes she was in her own bed. A grave-faced Dr. Taylor was standing by her bedside still in costume from the ball, as was Derek waiting only a short distance behind him.

Dr. Taylor wore horn-rimmed glasses and had a rather kindly face. In his deep voice, he asked, "How do you feel now, young woman?"

"I'm all right," she said weakly, staring up at him.

"You didn't seem so when I first arrived," he told her. "You've had some sort of seizure."

Her eyes widened with memory of her experience on the

lawn and she said, "I was terrified."

"Terrified?"

"Yes!"

"Of what?" the old doctor questioned her. "From what I've heard you were taken ill at the party."

Derek came forward still in the black string tie, and blue captain's jacket. He looked at her earnestly and said, "That is what Constable Frink told me. He drove you home, didn't he?"

"Yes."

Derek went on, "He said you complained of a bad headache but that you seemed better when he left you."

She gave the two men standing by her bedside in the dimly-lit room a frightened look. "It was afterward."

"Afterward?" Dr. Taylor encouraged her.

"Yes," she said, still communicating with difficulty.

"Go on!" Derek ordered her almost impatiently.

"By the chapel," she said.

"What about the chapel?" Derek demanded. "What were you doing out there in the fog and wet?"

She said, "I heard voices."

"Voices?" Dr. Taylor repeated.

"Yes. The voices of a man and woman quarreling."

Derek's handsome face was ashen. "Who?"

"I don't know."

Dr. Taylor said, "You heard voices but you couldn't make them out clearly enough to tell who they belonged to or what was being said. Is that right?"

"Yes."

"And they drew you to the chapel?" the old doctor went on in his patient way which helped her more than Derek's angry questioning.

"I went closer to see what was happening," she said.

Derek said, "And what did you see?"

She looked up at her husband, almost afraid to go on. Knowing that he would surely show anger with her. She said, "I saw a woman. She came running out of the chapel."

"Go on!" Derek urged her, the nerves in his cheek twitching.

"And then a man came out. It was a moment before I recognized he was the phantom!"

Dr. Taylor raised his eyebrows behind his horn-rimmed glasses. "The phantom?" he said in surprise.

Derek showed embarrassed annoyance. "My wife has had some strange spells since she returned from the mental hospital. At times she sees a figure she identifies with Captain Peter Mills. He killed his wife here over a hundred years ago!" His whole tone was meant to suggest that she was not responsible and her story should not be listened to.

She spoke up resentfully. "I have seen the ghost many times and the murder was committed in this room!"

Dr. Taylor showed further surprise. He turned to Derek and asked, "Is this true?"

Derek raised his hand in an impatient gesture. "Rumor has it the murder did happen in here. I don't believe it myself. As to my wife seeing the ghost I put it down to her mental state."

"No!" she cried, raising up on her elbow.

"Don't excite yourself!" Dr. Taylor placated her. "Nothing is to be gained by that. We'll stay with the bare facts. You believe that you saw two figures on the lawn. And that one stabbed the other. The young woman? Am I correct?"

"Yes."

"Now if these were real people there should be a body out on the lawn? You agree to that, Mrs. Mills?"

"I suppose so," she said wearily.

"So there we are," the veteran doctor said. Turning to Derek he told him, "I suggest that a search be made of the lawn at once. There could be something in her story, you know."

Derek showed annoyance. "Two figures out of the past, a man stabs a woman on the lawn! It's ridiculous! It has to be fantasy on my wife's part."

The old doctor studied him from behind his thick glasses. "I don't think we should leave any doubt. There were a number of people around in costume tonight at the ball. Suppose two of them came over and had a quarrel. It's possible."

Derek seemed to be suffering from a strong emotional reaction to the idea. He gave an exasperated sigh. "Do you really want the lawn searched?"

"It can do no harm," Dr. Taylor said. And he asked her, "In what section of the lawn did you witness this attack?"

"Between the chapel and the cliffs," she said.

"There you have it," Dr. Taylor told her husband.

Derek glared at them both. "Very well," he said. "I'll go out myself and have a look. But I know it's nonsense."

"At least it will put your wife's mind at ease," the veteran doctor suggested.

"I doubt that," Derek said snidely as he left the bedroom.

Dr. Taylor turned to her with a baffled look and said, "This is a very strange business, Mrs. Mills. I remember your breakdown. It was I who suggested that you be sent to Dr. Beckett's sanitarium."

"I know," she said. "Dr. Beckett turned out to be excellent."

"I feel he's a good man," Dr. Taylor agreed. "But I'm very surprised to learn that he dismissed you when you are still suffering from spells in which you see phantom figures."

"I wasn't having them when I left the hospital," she said. "I only began to see ghostly figures after I returned to this house. And in spite of what my husband told you I'm not subject to spells. I have seen things I don't understand. And once I was attacked by this phantom figure."

The old doctor frowned. "What does the phantom look like?"

"I have never seen his face clearly," she said. "But he dresses in a whaling captain's uniform and cap just as my husband and some others did at the ball tonight."

"Interesting," he said. "What about the figure of the woman?"

"I have only seen her twice. Once in the foyer downstairs I saw a fuzzy outline of her bloodied face. Tonight I saw her attacked."

Dr. Taylor listened to her attentively. He said, "I remember vaguely the story of Captain Peter Mills. He committed a double murder and then hung himself, didn't he?"

"Yes."

The solemn eyes behind the horn-rimmed glasses fixed on her. "And you think his ghost may be re-enacting the crime here at various times?"

"Something like that," she agreed. "I don't know why I should be able to see the phantoms and none of the others notice. It may be because of my precarious nervous state."

Dr. Taylor gave her a shrewd look. "Of course you know it could be someone pretending to be a ghost to terrify you back into a state of madness again."

"I know," she said. "That has been suggested to me before. I find that more repulsive than the ghost theory."

"I agree," the old doctor said. "But I don't think you can afford to rule the possibility out."

"What if Derek finds no body out there?" she asked the doctor.

"Then we'll know that you saw ghostly happenings or that you imagined the whole business. And I won't exclude the other possibility that the scene might have been staged to frighten you."

She gave him a despairing glance. "The only thing which would clear me of any hint of insanity would be if a body is found out there."

"Then it will be a case of murder or vicious attack if the woman is still alive, with you as the sole witness," Dr. Taylor said. "You might also find that a difficult position."

She heard Derek coming back up the stairway and a moment later he came through the open door. He stood at the foot of her bed with a sullen expression on his face. "There was no body! Not a sign of a body!"

Dr. Taylor showed no surprise. In his calm voice he said, "Well, at least we've settled that."

Derek said, "I think my wife needs medical treatment. The simple truth is that tonight proved too great a strain for her. The sound of the music and the pressure of being in such a large crowd of people. I worried about her and it seems that my fears were justified."

Dr. Taylor turned to her. "You did have a bad headache and that was why you decided to return."

"Yes."

"So what your husband says may indeed have some truth in it," the old doctor went on. "The party may have been too much for you. I shall give you a sedative. And in the morning I'll come by and see you again. Then we can decide whether or not you should consult Dr. Beckett once more."

She said bitterly, "You mean whether I should be sent back to the mental hospital or not."

The old doctor eyed her solemnly from behind his horn-rimmed glasses. "Well, of course you'd have to go there to be under observation since he does not give outside treatment."

Derek said, "I'd say your advice is wise, Dr. Taylor. Give my wife the sedative and we'll try to forget this nightmare and all get a good night's rest. Or at least rest for what is left of the night."

Dr. Taylor nodded and turned to his bag and searched until he found a bottle with some yellow pills. "Two of these should suffice," he said. "I'll leave the bottle and your husband can give them to you with a glass of water."

She said, "Thank you, Doctor. I didn't mean to sound ungrateful or distrustful just now."

"Of course I understand that," the veteran doctor said in a kindly voice. "Your husband is right. What you both need most at this moment is rest."

He closed his bag and he and Derek left the room and went down the stairs. She could hear their voices fade as they discussed something in low tones. She lay back on her pillow and stared up into the murky light of her room. Derek had left only the bedside lamp on and the circular reflection of its glow cast a faint area of light on the ceiling.

Derek would give her the pills and she would sleep. And in the morning Dr. Taylor would come and make a decision about her. It was all too likely that he would suggest she go back to the hospital again. And her continuing horror was that once she went behind the hospital doors this time she would never emerge. She would gradually lose her desire to return to the outside world and become a permanent patient like Mrs. Allain.

What had she seen out by the chapel? Had it been a mad hallucination on her part? Or had she seen ghostly figures as she firmly believed? It had turned out to be a disastrous night for her and she could tell that Derek was angry with her.

He came up the stairs again and joined her in the room. He said nothing at first, merely pouring a glass of water from a pitcher on the bedside table and taking two of the yellow pills from the bottle. He offered them to her along with the glass of water. Then he told her. "You'd better take these."

She was sitting up in bed. "First tell me where the others are. Your mother and sister and the other two, Uncle Henry and David Chase."

He looked solemn. "I made them go to bed. It is very late. I didn't leave the party until after one-thirty. It was all over before I received word about you. The housekeeper sent the message. And I at once got in touch with Dr. Taylor and brought him here."

"I see," she said. "I'm sorry I was so much trouble. I spoiled the party for you."

"Not at all," he said, though not too convincingly.

She stared at him worriedly. "You seemed tense and strange all evening long."

"I was concerned about you. I feared you mightn't last the evening."

"But you left me. I couldn't find you anywhere!"

"I'm sorry," he said. "I was around. You just must have missed me!"

She saw how terribly tense he still was and she said, "Brook Patterson couldn't find you either. And he couldn't find Faith. You'd both vanished."

"That's not true," her husband argued. "We had to keep circulating. It was our duty. But we were there."

"We couldn't find you," she said. "And I thought Faith wasn't herself either. When we first met in the reception line she was terribly upset. You could tell."

Derek looked incredibly weary. "Let's not waste time

talking about Faith's state of mind this evening," he said. "Take these tablets and let's get some sleep."

"Very well," she said quietly. She took the two pills and drank some of the water. Then she returned the glass to him. "Are you going to send me back to the hospital?" she asked.

He stood up impatiently. "I don't plan to send you back anywhere! If you need treatment you'll have to have it."

"I know," she said. "Did Brook find Faith and take her home after the ball?"

"I'm sure he did," Derek said. "I can't say that I noticed. I was too upset about the news concerning you."

"Poor Derek!" she said gently. "I'm sorry."

"It's all right. Try to get to sleep."

"The party was a wonderful success, wasn't it? You'll likely be doing it again, won't you?" she said. "Faith deserves a lot of praise for the idea."

"It was a success and she's been congratulated," Derek said. "We can talk about it later. I'm going to my room now. And I hope those tablets will soon work."

She was already starting to feel drowsy. In a sleepy drawl, she told him, "They are beginning to work now. Good night, Derek."

"Good night," he said and he bent down and kissed her on the lips. It was a dutiful kiss rather than an ardent one but she was grateful that he'd shown even this much tenderness towards her.

He went into his own room and closed the door. She lay back on her pillow with the bedside lamp still on. Her eyes began to glaze and her thoughts grew less coherent. Something was nagging at the back of her mind. Bothering her and urging that she shouldn't forget. She tried to think what it was.

And then it came to her even though she was becoming

more drowsy every second. Derek and Faith had seemingly been missing from the party when she left it. And when she'd returned to the castle she'd seen the two quarreling and saw the man in the captain's outfit stab the young woman. Wasn't it entirely possible that Derek and Faith had returned to the chapel to be together and had quarreled and that the phantom figure she'd seen stabbing the girl had been Derek stabbing Faith! But if that were true what had happened to the body? Or had Faith merely suffered only a minor injury and somehow had made her way back to the ball? It was too confusing. Her eyelids dropped shut and almost at once she fell into a deep, dreamless sleep.

It was another gray morning when she woke up. Rain was lashing against her window. For a few minutes she had no desire to waken. Then memory of all the terror of the night before came rushing back to her and she began to come fully alert.

The door from the hallway opened and Derek came in fully dressed, with a breakfast tray. He said, "I'm taking the morning off so I decided to play lady's maid and bring you breakfast in bed. Are you feeling better?"

"I think so," she said, sitting up. "How about you?"

"I slept like a log," her husband said, removing a napkin from the tray as he sat it on the bed. "You'll find orange juice, cereal, toast and coffee there. That's about what you always have, isn't it?"

She smiled ruefully. "It's actually a lot more than I generally have." And she started breakfast by sipping the orange juice.

"It will do you good to have something in your stomach," her husband said.

"How about you?"

"I had breakfast downstairs with Mother and Mona."

She arched an eyebrow. "Oh? I imagine that was fun! I suppose they feel I disgraced myself and all of you last night."

"I can't think why," he said. "No one realized you'd left."

"I'm glad of that," she said.

"There were a lot of people there and so much going on," Derek told her. "I don't think anyone paid too much attention to anyone else. And I think that's good."

"So do I," she agreed. "So your mother and Mona didn't discuss my madness."

His face shadowed. "Don't talk that way! They know you felt ill after coming back here and I had Dr. Taylor come and see you. That's all."

Her eyes searched his handsome face. "You didn't tell them about my seeing ghosts again?"

"No. I felt that should be a secret between you, me and the doctor."

"That was considerate of you."

Derek said, "I try to do my best for you even though you don't like to give me any credit."

She managed a forlorn smile. "I give you credit now," she said.

Derek eyed her closely. "I can tell that you feel much better for your rest."

"I do."

"I hope that now you've changed your mind about last night," he said earnestly. "That you're no longer so confused."

"I wasn't confused from the start," she protested.

Derek said, "Meaning what?"

"I did see two ghostly figures coming out of the chapel, a man following a woman with a kind of dagger in his hands."

Her husband at once looked let down. He said, "I'm sorry

you see things the same way. It might have been better if you'd tried to think of that interlude as a bad dream."

She stirred her coffee. "But I can't do that."

Her husband got up and stared out the window at the rain gloomily. "A rotten day!"

"So I see."

He turned from the window and began to pace slowly at the foot of her bed. He said, "The doctor will be coming to see you this morning."

"So he said."

"He'll be taking note of what you say and deciding what your treatment ought to be."

"And?"

Her husband halted and looked at her with anguish on his face. "Joyce, I'm frightened. I don't want to have to send you away again. Do you have to stick to that preposterous story of seeing ghosts?"

She fixed a steady gaze on him and asked, "Suppose I didn't see ghosts but living people?"

"What would they be doing out there?"

"Who can tell? Arguing about something. There must have been a quarrel or he wouldn't have tried to stab her."

Derek took a step closer to the foot of her bed. "It couldn't have been real people anymore than it could have been ghosts. There was no body out there when I looked."

"There still could have been real people there," she said, her eyes not leaving his pale face.

His jaw twitched. "I don't see how."

"The girl might not have been badly hurt. She might have gotten away on her own."

"That's as wild as your ghost theory!"

"I'm telling you what I believe," she said.

"The doctor isn't going to like your story," he warned her.

"I'll have to take that chance."

Derek went on studying her unhappily. "There are times when I can't stand your stubbornness. You turn me against you!"

"I'm sorry."

"I doubt it," he said somewhat coldly. "It seems you won't allow me to try and help you so I'll have to leave it to the doctor and you."

"Fair enough," she said.

There was a knock on the door and Derek went and opened it. David Chase was standing in the hall. Politely, he asked, "May I come in before I leave for the museum?"

"I suppose so," Derek said without enthusiasm and stood aside for him to enter.

David came to her bedside. "Well, what's this I hear about your taking sick last night?"

She smiled wanly. "I made a strong try but I failed."

"You looked great every time I saw you. Not even a bit nervous. What happened?"

"I lost Derek more or less permanently for the evening and on my own my nerves began to tense," she said. "My head began to ache badly and I came back here."

"Constable Frink drove you, I understand."

"Yes."

"But he didn't stay here?"

"There was no reason for him to. He wasn't that concerned. I only had a headache."

"But afterward you collapsed?"

"Yes."

"From your headache?" David asked.

"No." She shook her head and gave him a knowing glance. "I saw something."

Derek spoke up angrily. "She had another of her visions."

David looked embarrassed. "I'm sorry I brought it up," he said.

"It's all right," she told him. "I saw someone dressed like Derek was last night stab a young woman. It was then I collapsed!"

CHAPTER TEN

There was a second of shocked silence in the room following her declaration. Derek stared at her with a tortured expression on his face while David Chase looked startled and embarrassed at the same time. She had deliberately said it to cause Derek some pain for his cruelty to her and it seemed that she had hit her mark.

David broke the silence by saying quietly, "You seem to be all right now. I just wanted to make sure."

"I'm all right," she said.

"Good," the young artist said. "At least you enjoyed most of the evening before you became ill."

Joyce nodded. "Yes."

David gave her a reassuring smile. "I'm certain there's not too much to worry about. I'll get along to the museum. All the decorations have to come down."

Derek spoke at last, saying, "Most of us are taking the morning off. The museum is closed to the public for the day. You needn't go down until noon."

"I'd rather get an early start," David said. "I mentioned it to Faith and she said she might come help me. We want to save the sketches for some future use."

"I doubt if she'll be there until later," Derek replied.

David said, "I'll take a chance on it in any case." And to her, "I'll see you later, Joyce."

"Yes," she said. "I plan to get up soon. I'll see you when you get back."

"Don't push yourself too hard," the young man warned her as he left.

Derek waited until the artist was on his way down the stairs before he sternly told her, "I forbid you to get out of bed until Dr. Taylor sees you again!"

"But I'm not that ill!" she protested.

"I don't know that," he said.

"Aren't you trying to be difficult because you're angry with me?"

"Because of your trying to make me look ridiculous in David's eyes?" he said.

She looked down. "You began it by making me angry."

"And you don't care what you say," was her husband's reply. "Mother is right. You've never been the same since the first time you were in hospital." And with those crushing words delivered he went on into his room.

Joyce sat there alone staring at the rain as it ran down the window pane. She supposed that she deserved this treatment from Derek since she'd deliberately baited him. But he had begun it with his trying to force her to refute every claim she'd made about the previous night. And she couldn't do that. Not even if it meant Dr. Taylor diagnosing her as in need of more mental treatment.

Ten minutes passed and then she heard the voices of her mother-in-law and the doctor at the foot of the stairs. Her heart began to pound in fear that Regina might come up to further torment her.

She heard Regina say, "I know my son is up there."

"Very well," Dr. Taylor said. "I'll find him. I want to have a look at your daughter-in-law."

"Yes, I know all about that, Doctor," Regina said in a spiteful voice.

Next she heard the doctor sighing as he mounted the stairs. Derek also must have heard him for he came back into her bedroom in time to meet the doctor as he entered the room from the hallway. The old doctor shut the door after him for privacy and came to her bedside.

"Well, you look much more rested this morning," he said.

"I am," she agreed.

Derek had taken a stand at the foot of the bed. He said, "I think she's just as stubborn as ever though."

Dr. Taylor shot him a reproachful glance from behind his heavy, horn-rimmed glasses. "This young woman has been fighting a series of mental problems. I think you should show her a good deal more consideration."

Derek flushed. "Sorry."

"It's all right," Dr. Taylor said placatingly. "A husbandly error. We all make them. We get so close to our loved ones that we come to expect a great deal of them. How is your headache this morning?" This last was addressed to her.

She said, "It's gone."

"Good. Nerves can cause us a lot of pain and trouble. That affair last night was too much for you. You should have stayed for an hour or so and then left. Being in the reception line alone had to be an ordeal. It would be for me."

"I was nervous from the start," she said.

"Blame that on me," Derek said. "I was so anxious for her to take her rightful place with me that I forced her. I can see now that it was a mistake."

"Without question," the doctor said.

She told him, "I feel very well. I'd like to get up and dress but Derek wouldn't allow it until you had seen me."

Dr. Taylor nodded. "I see no reason why you shouldn't get up now. You've had a complete rest."

Derek asked, "What about her further treatment? She still insists she saw the ghosts."

The old doctor looked rather gloomy. "That is a question."

"Try and talk some sense into her, Doctor," her husband pleaded.

Dr. Taylor eyed her gravely from behind his glasses. "You do believe you saw that macabre scene you've described?"

"Yes, I can't lie about it, Doctor," she said unhappily, knowing that this was a moment of crisis. A moment when her future might be decided. "It wouldn't help to take my story back even though I know it to be true."

"No, that wouldn't do at all," the old doctor agreed.

"So?" she said.

He shrugged. "We either have to come up with some explanation for these visions you have or conclude that you are so mentally disturbed that you require further hospitalization."

Derek said, "She just has to change her attitude about this house and its people. She insists on listening to every ghostly legend and believing in it. If she'd strive for a healthier viewpoint she wouldn't go around frightened, ready to see a ghost in every shadow."

Dr. Taylor heard him out. Then he said, "You are speaking as if she had a healthy mind. But the probability is that she hasn't. And that changes the entire picture."

"You're saying she must return to Dr. Beckett."

"I'm thinking about it," the old doctor said. "It's not a decision to be made lightly. I want a few days to make certain tests and also to see if your wife has any more of these visions."

"I'm certain she will," Derek said unhappily. "She's been seeing things ever since she returned here! Screaming about nothing!"

From her bed Joyce said, "That's not fair!"

"I'm telling the truth," Derek said angrily.

The old doctor held up a hand for peace between them

and said, "Nothing is to be gained by this quarreling. I will make the decisions and I will not be influenced by the opinion of anyone but myself. Is that satisfactory to you both?"

"It is to me," she said sincerely since she trusted the old doctor.

"What about you?" he asked Derek.

He turned away and moved back to stare out the window. Then he said, "All right," in a low, tense voice.

"Very well," the doctor said. "We have that established."

Before he could continue there was a knock on the hall door and then it was opened and a troubled-looking Brook Patterson in raincoat came a step into the room.

"Pardon me for intruding," he said, in response to their startled looks.

Derek faced him sternly. "What is it?"

The balding man was clearly in a near-frantic state. His clenched hands working nervously at his side he asked, "Where is Faith? Did she spend the night here?"

"No," Derek said. "Why do you ask?"

"She's missing!" Brook said bitterly. "She didn't come home all night. She was missing when the party was over and I assumed she would be coming home in your car. You've seen so much of her!"

"I didn't see her after the party ended," Derek said, his cheek twitching nervously again.

Brook's narrow face was shadowed with doubts. He said, "You are sure she hasn't been here?"

"Quite sure," Derek said.

"I don't understand," Brook said, now clearly more concerned than ever.

Dr. Taylor spoke up, "Has your wife any other friends whom she may have decided to visit for the night?"

"No," Brook Patterson said in a choked voice.

"When did you last see her?" Joyce asked.

He shot her a worried glance. "Not after the time we danced together. She was missing for most of the evening." He turned to Derek. "And so were you. That is why I assumed you must be together."

Derek shook his head. "I didn't leave the museum all night."

"I looked for you several times and couldn't find you," his assistant said accusingly.

Derek's handsome face was troubled but he answered calmly enough, "I'm sorry about that. I still say I was there."

Brook gave a deep sigh. "I'd counted on her being here. Now I don't know what to do."

"In my opinion you should report her missing to the police," Dr. Taylor said.

Brook frowned. "I don't want any scandal," he worried. "I don't want to cause a lot of talk that won't be hushed up. This island is a small place and gossip is a main commodity."

"I can't argue with you on that point," the doctor said. "But your wife is missing. She could be in serious trouble. I don't think you have any choice but to tell the authorities."

"I agree," Derek said. "You ought to go downstairs and put a phone call through to Constable Frink at once."

Brook turned from one to the other of them, still hesitating. Then in a taut voice, he asked, "You really think I should contact Constable Frink?"

"At the very least," Joyce said from her bed, where she was sitting up propped by pillows.

Brook considered this for another long moment. Then he said, "Very well." He turned to Derek. "You don't mind if I use your phone?"

"Not at all," he said. "Use the one in the study. I'll go

down with you." And he told the doctor. "Will you excuse me, I'll only be a few minutes."

"Of course," Dr. Taylor said, waving them on their way.

The two men left the room and Joyce found herself alone with the doctor again. Events had taken such a strange turn that she didn't know what to think. And she could see the news had also made a distinct impression on the old doctor.

She said, "I hope nothing has happened to Faith."

Dr. Taylor gave her a knowing look from behind his glasses. "She has always been a very lively girl and none too careful in her choice of companions."

It was a discreet way of saying that Faith had been promiscuous and with many men of undesirable character. The thing which now was worrying Joyce most was that Derek might be involved. There had been gossip about her husband and Faith. And she had accepted that the two had carried on an affair during her stay in the hospital.

She said, "Where could she have gone?"

"That is difficult to say," Dr. Taylor told her. "I think she should be sought by the police." He gave her a shrewd glance. "And especially in view of your experience last night. You were sure you saw a young woman being stabbed by someone."

"You don't think?" she said and stopped, since she was thinking the same thing. She was trying to visualize the two she'd seen in the fog and darkness of the lawn and think whether they resembled Derek and Faith that much!

Dr. Taylor's lined face wore a frown. "I think in view of this development we should postpone any judgment on your condition. Let us see what happens."

She gave him a frightened look. "But there was no body found here!"

"Bodies can be moved," the veteran doctor reminded her.

"And while we may be all wrong in assuming foul play has been done I still say let us postpone any action until we learn what has happened to Faith."

"You will tell Derek that?"

"Yes," Dr. Taylor said with a sigh. He picked up his medical bag. "You have the tablets I gave you for sleep. You seem in good enough health in every other way. Unless I hear from you I'll assume you're making a recovery."

"Thank you, Doctor," she said gratefully.

"Get up and dress," he told her. "Don't push yourself too much. Just coast along easily."

"I will," she promised.

His sharp old eyes met hers again. "And if you need me for anything or have any of those spells again, please don't hesitate to get in touch with me."

"I won't," she said. "You've been very helpful."

"We'll see," the old doctor said cautiously. He moved to the door. "One last word of warning. Don't get too involved. Don't try to play detective. Let the police do that."

"Very well," she said.

He left and she quickly got up, showered and dressed. She was ready to go downstairs when Derek came back to join her again.

She said, "Where is Brook?"

"Gone back to his own place," Derek said, his handsome face showing his worry.

"He called the police."

"Yes. They're going to begin checking on Faith," he said with despair in his voice. "I'm afraid we're going to be in for some nasty scandal. And she had to vanish on the night of the summer ball."

Joyce said, "It's very strange."

Her husband moved over to the window again to study the

rain. He stood with his back to her. In a taut voice, he admitted, "I know you've suspected something between Faith and me ever since you returned here."

"True," she said, carefully controlling her voice.

"You are wrong," he said, his back still to her.

"Are you sure?"

"Yes," Derek said emphatically. "As a matter of fact I've had an idea Faith has been seeing someone else and making it seem as if it were me. She convinced her husband of it and apparently you."

"Who has she been seeing?"

"I don't know," he said. "But I'm sure there has been someone."

She listened with a growing fear that Derek might be saying this merely to get himself out of trouble. That because he knew he was going to be suspected if anything happened to Faith, he was making up an imaginary lover to suspect. Joyce found it hard to believe there was another man. And she worried that her ghostly vision might have been a murder being committed with herself as a witness.

She said, "Have you any proof of this other man?"

He turned to her with his face a study in despair. "No. I can't think of anything I can offer. But I know there had to be someone. It wasn't me." He took a step towards her. "You do believe me, don't you?"

"I want to," she said.

He came to her and took her in his arms. Gazing down at her with tormented eyes, he said, "I know I've been cruel and inconsiderate in many ways. But I've been so worried about you. And losing Lucie wasn't easy for either of us."

"I know that," she whispered, her face a mask of sorrowful fear.

"I said things when Dr. Taylor was here that I didn't mean

or shouldn't have said," he went on. "I do love you more than you can realize. I was frantic that I might be going to lose you again."

She was telling herself that this wasn't necessary. That he didn't have to perform this sharp an about-face. Her love for him had never wavered. She would try to understand and help him even if he had become so involved with the promiscuous Faith that it had ended in violence.

She said, "I'm sure it will be all right. If there's another man she's probably off somewhere with him."

"I hope so," her husband said grimly, still holding her in his arms.

"It would have to be someone on the island, wouldn't it?"

Derek said, "She was never honest with me about it. She just made jokes about everyone thinking I was her lover when all the time it was someone else."

"Didn't that worry you?"

"Yes," Derek admitted. "We had a rather bitter quarrel about it yesterday."

She stared up at his tormented, handsome face. "And that is why you were so strange and upset last night?"

"Partly."

"And I could tell Faith was bothered about something," she went on. "It was obvious in the reception line."

"But what happened to her?" he worried.

"We'll likely know soon enough," she said. "The chances are she may have gone to this man's house for the night. In spite of all the fuss Brook Patterson is making it wouldn't be the first time Faith had done something like that."

"True," Derek agreed.

"If you're innocent, there's no reason for you to worry," she pointed out.

His eyes met hers. "Do you believe in me?"

"I always have," she said. Perhaps it wasn't a complete answer but it was close to the truth.

"Thank you, Joyce," he said earnestly. "Bless you!" And he gave her a long, meaningful kiss.

She returned the kiss worried about all that had happened. It was likely that the next few hours would tell her whether her husband was being truthful or whether he was a polished liar. She had felt earlier in the morning that he was anxious to ship her back to the hospital. Now he was claiming it was fear of having to do that which had made him act so strangely. She could only wonder until the facts came out.

Releasing her, he said, "I think I will go to the museum after all."

"Oh?"

"Yes. If any news breaks I want to be there. And David Chase is there working. He should be told what is going on."

"He should know," she agreed.

Derek frowned. "I'll drive over and stay awhile. Let me know if you hear anything."

"I will," she said. "I may drive to the museum later myself. I don't know whether I can face the day here."

"Whatever you like," Derek said.

He went on his way and she remained in her room for a little while. The rain ended but the fog came in heavier than ever. She went downstairs shortly before lunch and discovered Uncle Henry standing out on the porch grimly surveying the fog-ridden landscape. She quickly told him about Faith being missing.

The white-haired man's eyebrows raised. "Do Regina and Mona know about this?"

"Not unless Derek told them. Brook just told us about it a short while ago."

Uncle Henry gave a low whistle. "You might know something would come out of that party. I'll bet this is going to make a first class scandal."

"It could be bad," she agreed. "I'm worried for Derek."

The old man looked at her with questioning eyes. "You think he may know something about it?"

"He claims she only pretended there was something between them. That all along there was another man."

Henry's face showed derision. "I'm not likely to believe that," he snapped. "Those two were close."

"You said so."

He frowned. "I told you about them because I thought you ought to know. I've watched Faith since she was a teenager. I know her as well as anyone. There was a short time she had one of those young girl crushes on me."

She was startled. "I didn't know that."

He smiled bitterly. "It happens with a lot of old bachelors like me. We suddenly have some kind of weird attraction for the very young female. I enjoyed it for awhile but when I knew that she was ready to be unfaithful to Brook I told her I wasn't interested in playing that kind of game with her."

Joyce had listened to this with increasing shock. "And what then?"

Henry shrugged. "We had a beauty of a battle and the friendship was over. We talk and laugh when we meet and pretend it never happened. But we both know. I suppose in a way Derek had the same older man attraction for her, even though he's young enough to be my son."

"You're saying that Faith had a wide range of interest in men."

"Mostly older men," he reminded her.

"So who is it now?"

"I still say Derek," his uncle said. "I'm sorry. But that's what I really think."

"I don't know what to believe," she admitted.

"Better prepare yourself," he said. "I hear you became ill at the party and returned here early last night."

"Yes," she said. "And I had another of my ghostly experiences."

He stared at her. "Tell me about it."

She did, finishing with, "Now I'm beginning to wonder if Derek and Faith came back here and I happened to see him attack her."

Henry Mills looked strangely tense. "You certainly saw something."

"Yes."

"And no one seems to want to believe in your ghosts."

"No. So maybe they're right," she said. "Maybe I have been seeing real people in costume. People trying to terrify me. Last night's scene could have been staged for the same reason."

The old man nodded. "Perhaps. But Faith is missing."

"Yes," she said. "I'll feel better if Constable Frink finds her. I don't care whose house she may be in or how much scandal there is."

Henry eyed her wisely. "I know how you feel," he said.

She didn't remain at the castle for lunch. She had no wish to face Regina and Mona with the mystery of Faith's disappearance still unsolved. Nor did she want to be the object of a lot of cutting remarks about her illness of the previous night. So she got into her car and drove to the museum.

Since it was closed to the public she went in by the rear door. She found David Chase and Derek taking down the paper murals from the walls and stacking them.

Derek came to her at once. "Any word?"

"No," she said. "Have you heard anything?"

"Nothing," her husband said worriedly. "Brook is at home

but surely he'd let me know if the police contact him."

"I'd expect so," she said. "Can I help?"

"Dismantling the trimmings?"

"Yes," she said.

"If you like," her husband agreed. "I suppose we ought to go have something to eat. I'm not hungry at the moment."

"It can wait," Joyce said.

"Go help David," he told her. "I'm going to give Brook a call and see if anything has happened."

She took off her raincoat and went down the lobby to where David was standing on a stepladder taking the tacks out of a paper painting that had been put up rather high on the wall.

The young man came down the ladder to greet her. "Hello," he said. "You've made a quick recovery."

She gave him a wry smile. "The pressure of events." He nodded. "This is a bad business about Faith."

"Yes."

"I've never quite understood her," David said. "And being the wife of one of my superiors I always kept a little distance between her and myself. I knew she had the reputation for being a flirt."

"It would be hard not to know," Joyce said grimly. "The island is small and gossip spreads."

David looked embarrassed. "Where do you suppose she is?"

"Your guess would be as good as mine," she told him.

"You'd think she'd tell your husband where she was going," David went on. "They were very good friends."

"You noticed?"

"It would be hard not to," he said.

"You were working closely with them both," she agreed.

"Yes."

She sighed. "I was away a full year. One gets out of touch."

"Of course," David Chase said with sympathy. "But then Faith knows so many people. I saw her yesterday in your husband's Uncle's car."

"Uncle Henry?" she gasped.

"Yes. Derek gave me his car to drive back to the house for some materials. On my way I passed his uncle's car parked in one of those scenic lookout places along the cliffs and I'm sure it was Faith who was in the car with him."

This was new and unsettling information. She said, "I know Henry and Faith were friends but he didn't say anything about being with her yesterday."

David gave her a knowing look. "Maybe he wouldn't like to mention it not knowing what has happened to her."

"Possibly," she said. But she knew that Henry should have told her and it worried her that he hadn't.

"I'd better get back to work," David said. "This is some job."

"I'll help," she volunteered but her mind was far away, filled with doubts and questions.

They worked on for a few minutes before Derek came back to them. He said, "I've talked to Brook. There's no word yet. It's as if Faith simply vanished from the island."

"I don't understand," Joyce worried. "There was no ferry she could take last night."

"And no one saw her on the morning trip to the mainland," Derek said. "You two better go have some lunch and I'll stay here."

"You'll need something," Joyce said worriedly.

"Bring me back a cheese sandwich and coffee," her husband said.

She used her car and drove to the same shore restaurant Brook Patterson had taken her to the day they lunched together. The fog was still heavy and so she drove along the road skirting the ocean slowly and with her headlights on. David Chase sat quietly in the front seat at her side.

When they reached the restaurant they found it almost deserted. The poor weather had kept the tourist trade to a minimum. She and David took a table near one of the large windows overlooking the ocean but could see nothing but the fog. They ordered and she placed the takeout order for Derek. She was still thinking about what David had told her about Henry Mills and Faith being in a parked car together the day before her disappearance. And she continued to be puzzled that he had not mentioned this to her.

David studied her across the table. "You're lost in your thoughts," he said.

"I'm sorry," she apologized. "Several things are bothering me."

He said, "I was really worried about you when I heard about your illness last night. That's why I came by this morning. I had an idea they might be about to send you back to the hospital."

She gave him a look of grim resignation. "I think that was in their minds. But this news about Faith changed the picture."

"So maybe it has done some good," David said. "It's ridiculous the way a session of mental illness tags you for life. I had the same experience where people knew me. That's why I moved to this part of the country."

"I can understand why," she agreed. "I'm beginning to think I'd do better among strangers."

"It's the only hope," the young artist said with an earnest look on his pleasant face. "That's the reason I didn't even tell your husband that I'd gone through treatment in a mental hospital. The chances are I might not have been hired by him."

"I would hope he wouldn't have held it against you but I can't be sure," she admitted. "I've never mentioned your secret to anyone. It is safe with me."

He smiled. "I knew that or I wouldn't have confided in you. Faith Patterson tried to pry information from me about myself when I was finishing her portrait. But I was too wary for her."

Joyce said, "Then you did finish the portrait?"

"I haven't turned it over to her yet," the young man said. "There are still some final touches I want to make. I don't like to be rushed in finishing a study."

"I can understand that," she said. "Faith must have offered you an excellent subject for painting. She has an interesting face."

He frowned. "The trouble is that she is all exterior. The inner person is shallow. I sensed that at almost her first sitting for the portrait. But by then I was committed to carry it through. I wasn't able to suggest any depth in her."

"I'd be interested in seeing it," she said.

"One day," he replied vaguely.

The waitress came with their order and they gave attention to their food and did little talking. Not until they were at the coffee stage did they resume their conversation.

David told her, "I'd like to do your portrait before I leave the island."

"I'm not that interesting or attractive," she protested.

"I see you as extremely beautiful," he said. "And I want to paint you."

"We can think about it later," she said. "When all this trouble is at an end."

"I'll ask you about it again," the young man promised.

They drove back to the museum and found Derek pacing restlessly in his office. He thanked her for the food she brought him and told her, "Not a word yet! I'm getting a little panicky!"

"Surely she'll send Brook some word wherever she is," Joyce said.

Derek sighed as he opened up the sandwich. "As far as we know she didn't leave the island. That's what makes it even more of a puzzle."

She was going to mention that his Uncle Henry had been in the girl's company the previous day but decided to wait until she had a chance to ask the old man about it. She remained at the museum for most of the rest of the afternoon and then drove back to the castle.

Almost as soon as she entered the castle she met Henry Mills coming down the hall from the rear of the house. She told him, "I want to ask you about something." And she took him into the study where they could close the door and have privacy from Regina and anyone else in the house.

The white-haired man stared at her with puzzled eyes. "What is all the secrecy about?"

She faced him directly and asked, "Why didn't you tell me you were with Faith before she vanished last night?"

The old man's mouth gaped. "How do you know about that?"

"Someone saw you and Faith parked in your car yesterday afternoon. Your car was in one of the scenic turnoffs along the shore road."

Suspicion showed on the ravaged face of Henry Mills. He said, "Did you see me?"

"It doesn't matter," she bluffed him. "I know you were with her. Do you deny it?"

He hesitated. "No."

"Why didn't you tell me?"

"I was afraid," he said, his face twisted with worry. "I

think she was murdered and I didn't want you to think I had anything to do with it."

"I'd have been less suspicious if you'd come right out with the truth," she said.

"It's a tricky business!" he argued. "I didn't know what kind of interpretation you'd put on the meeting."

Joyce said sternly, "I'll admit I don't know what to think."

"It was innocent enough," he insisted. "I picked her up in front of the beauty parlor. She got in the car and told me to drive somewhere. She said that she was nervous and wanted to talk to me."

"And?"

"And so I took her out along the shore road."

"What did she want to talk to you about?"

The white-haired man showed a scowl. "She said she was in trouble with some man. That she'd just had a quarrel with Derek and everything was going wrong. She didn't name the man with whom she was having the trouble but I took it to be Derek. Especially when she mentioned that they'd quarreled earlier in the day."

Joyce heard this with a welling up of fear within her. Everything she heard seemed to more and more point to Derek as a possible murderer. She began to silently pray that Faith would be found and found alive.

"I see," she said.

Henry gave her a pleading look. "You won't tell anyone."

"I don't know!"

"It won't do Derek any good and it could do me a lot of harm," he protested.

She saw that he was badly upset and yet she didn't want to make any firm promise. Better to wait and discover if Faith turned up.

So she settled for, "I won't say anything for now."

Henry was not happy about her attitude but she would promise no more. She went up to her room to rest a little and try and think it all out. Derek joined her around six and it seemed to her that her husband had actually aged during the long, worrisome day.

She asked him, "Did you hear from Brook?"

"Nothing," he said unhappily. "The last time I talked to him he was almost at the breaking point. He's convinced something has happened to her."

"Surely not," she protested. But the vision of those two figures in the fog and the man attacking the woman remained etched on her mind. And the costume the man had been wearing had been identical to her husband's.

Derek was staring at her strangely. He said, "Who knows? Maybe that ghostly vision you had last night was prophetic."

"I hope it wasn't," she told him.

"Join me at dinner," he said. "I can't go down and face them alone."

She went down with him. Cocktails were being served in the living room. Mona looked actually joyous about Faith's vanishing and Joyce realized with grim humor that she was elated because she felt that a rival for Derek's affections had been removed from the field.

Regina made scathing remarks about the missing woman and about those who had not done their share to make the museum's summer ball a success. Joyce had an idea this was directed at her though she couldn't understand why. Uncle Henry stood by saying little and drinking heavily and she could see that his hands were shaking more than usual.

David Chase was his usual mild, pleasant self and did what he could to keep things from becoming too difficult. He came and stood with her for most of the cocktail period.

"No news yet," he said.

"Isn't it terrible," she replied, her eyes wide with concern.

"I think it will work out," the young artist said. "If only Derek will take it in his stride. He's getting too uptight."

But Derek showed no sign of becoming less tense. Through dinner and afterward he was obviously suffering. Because they were all weary from the previous night at the ball everyone went up to their bedrooms early. She and Derek were no exception.

The last thing he did before coming up to join her was phone Brook. He told her, "Constable Frink is at Brook's now. They haven't found Faith yet. But her parents came back from Boston on tonight's ferry and both Brook and the Constable are going to question them. Brook feels they may be able to give him some hint of where their daughter is hiding."

"Something must break soon," she worried.

"It has to," he agreed. He stayed a few minutes in her room and then kissed her good night in a rather absent manner and left with a troubled air.

Despite all her worries and fears she was so exhausted that she fell asleep with comparative ease. She had no idea how long she slept but she awoke to stare up into the darkness of her room with a feeling of terror. Without knowing why she was suddenly grimly frightened. And then she heard the sounds of someone moving restlessly in Derek's room and the door from his room to the hallway open and close.

CHAPTER ELEVEN

Joyce lay there for a moment considering what she would do. Then she fought back her fear and forced herself to leave her bed and don a dressing gown. She next moved towards the closed door between her room and Derek's. The door was not locked and so she hesitantly touched the knob and turned it. Slowly opening the door she looked into her husband's room and saw that his bed was empty.

There was no longer any doubt in her mind. It was he whom she'd heard leave the room a few minutes earlier. But why? And where had he gone? She went back into her own room and then out into the hall. There was a single dim night light on to give a weak glow of amber in the corridor and on the stairs. Still suffering from fear she began to slowly descend the stairs.

When she reached the foyer she glanced down the other hall leading to the rear of the house. And she was just in time to see a fully-dressed Derek vanish by the door leading to the cellar steps. She waited until he was out of sight and then she made her way down the hall after him.

Reaching the door to the cellar she found it open and a light on to show the way down the steps. Certain that Derek had vanished down there she began to cautiously descend the steep wooden steps. When she reached the earthen floor of the cellar she was presented with the question of where she should go next. She had no idea where her husband had gone.

The cellar lighting was ancient and consisted of open wiring and occasional light bulbs in white ceiling sockets at long intervals. The bulbs were weak and covered with dust and grime, some had even burned out so that the vast underground region of the old mansion had an eerie, shadowed atmosphere. Her nerves tense, she began making her way between the giant support posts which divided the area and formed corridorlike effect. The air was chill and the place was deathly silent. She advanced slowly, hoping to find some sign of Derek.

She reached a section where the overhead bulbs were all out and now she was walking in almost complete darkness. She came to a point where her progress was blocked by a stack of wooden packing cases piled high and wide to form a barrier. Now she turned to the left and as she did so she was suddenly confronted with a horror which made her scream aloud!

Hanging from the rafters just a few feet ahead of her was a male body, its head to one side in the noose, feet dangling high above the earthen floor and wearing the blue coat with the double row of brass buttons! The body moved slightly as if in the last throes of strangulation. It was too much! She screamed once more and then blacked out.

"Joyce!"

She heard her name as if from a great distance and looked up to find herself gazing into the weathered face of Henry Mills. The white-haired old man was kneeling next to her and studying her with anxious eyes.

He said, "Don't give way to your fears."

She stared up at his lined face. "The ghost!"

He frowned. "What ghost? And what brought you wandering down here?"

Joyce at once raised herself up to a sitting position and turned to point out the hanging body of Peter Mills to him. But it wasn't there!

"He's gone!" she cried weakly.

"Who?"

"The ghost of Captain Peter Mills! I saw him hanging there! Just as he must have hung there years ago! Now he's gone!"

Uncle Henry looked skeptical. "I came down here to you as soon as I heard you scream and I saw nothing!"

She struggled to her feet and turned to stare into the shadows where she'd seen the body. "It was right there! Hanging from the rafter!"

The old man touched her arm and said, "Don't get yourself upset again. You'll be blacking out and I don't want that!"

Joyce turned to him in dismay. "You don't believe me, do you? You think that I'm mad!"

"Not necessarily. But I do think you're letting your nerves run away with you. You saw some shadow there and knowing that Captain Peter Mills had hung himself in the cellar you at once decided you were seeing his phantom!"

"I did see something!"

"We're not going to get anywhere arguing about it," Derek's uncle pointed out. "There's no ghost there now."

"There was!" She gave him a startled look. "How do you happen to be here? How did you know I was down here?"

The old man in black dressing gown and pajamas showed slight annoyance. "I was in the kitchen. Occasionally I wake in the night and find myself hungry. I came down to the kitchen for a glass of milk. I was on my way back along the corridor when I heard your scream from the cellar. And so I hurried down here!"

She listened to him with some doubt. It was a satisfactory enough explanation. But almost too pat. Already suspicious of the old man she found herself wondering if he were telling her the truth.

She said, "And you saw nothing when you reached me?"

"Nothing but you stretched out on the cellar floor," he said.

"I screamed because I saw the ghost. And that is why I fainted!"

He eyed her sharply. "What brought you down here in the first place?"

"Derek."

"Derek?"

"Yes. I heard him leave his room and I followed him down here," she said.

The old man frowned. "If that's so where is he now?"

"I don't know," she said. "I lost him after he entered the cellar."

The white-haired Henry shivered. "It's cold down here! You'll catch your death! Better go back upstairs."

"But where is Derek?" she persisted.

Henry looked bleak. "I don't think you'll find that out down here," he said.

She gazed into the shadows around them. "He must be here somewhere."

"I say go back upstairs," Henry Mills told her sternly. "I can't leave you here alone and I can't dare risk this chill air much longer. This cellar is always as cold as a tomb!"

She gave another look around and then reluctantly accompanied him to the stairs and back up into the main house again. When they reached the hall the old man closed the cellar door after them and led her to the stairway.

"I'll see you to your room," he said.

She gave him a frightened look. "I won't be able to sleep," she said.

"You must try," the old man said firmly.

They mounted the stairs and he went to the door of her room with her. "Feel any better?" he asked.

"Not much."

"What can I do?" he asked.

"Nothing, really," she admitted. "I only wish I knew why Derek left his room and went to the cellar. And where he vanished after he went down there."

The old man was staring at her rather strangely. "You are certain he is not in his room?"

She said, "You can look for yourself."

Before she could finish speaking the door of Derek's room opened and he came out in his pajamas looking sleepy and angry. He stared at them incredulously and demanded, "What are you two doing out here arguing at this time of night?"

For a few seconds Joyce thought she would faint again. Then her shock gave way to anger. And she asked her husband, "When did you come back?"

"Come back?"

"Don't pretend! I followed you to the cellar!"

Derek gazed at her in astonishment and then at his uncle. He said, "I don't know what you're talking about. I've been in my bed sleeping ever since I said good night to you."

"No!" she protested.

Henry Mills told Derek, "She claims that she heard you leave your room and then looked in and your bed was empty. After that she went downstairs and saw you vanish in the cellar. And she followed you."

"It's true!" she cried.

Derek eyed her stonily. "I'm sorry, Joyce. But what can I say? You must have had another of your nightmares. This sounds like a bad dream."

"But you did leave your room!" she insisted.

"Apparently I did in your mind," he said coolly. "But in fact I've been in my room sleeping all the time."

Henry Mills gave her a concerned glance. "Derek may be

right. You could have had a nightmare. Best thing you can do is go back to bed and try and forget the whole business."

She looked at them both in dismay. "But I can't! I can't!"

"Nothing will be gained by your waking everyone," Derek warned her. "Do you want my mother here asking a lot of awkward questions?"

Joyce stood there stunned. She saw that she had come up against another blank wall. She was certain that Derek was lying to her but he was doing it so skillfully and he'd covered his tracks so cleverly that she would have a small chance of disputing him.

Henry Mills told her, "You'll feel differently about this in the morning."

"You won't believe me, either of you?" she asked in a pained tone.

"My uncle is right," Derek said in a more kindly voice. "You oughtn't to be wandering around at this hour. You should be getting your rest. So should we all."

"I see," she said slowly. "I have to accept a lie. Very well. But I know it wasn't a nightmare. And I won't change my mind in the morning." And she went into her room and shut the door.

She heard her husband and his uncle talking in low tones for a moment. Then they parted and Derek went back into his room. But he did not come to her.

She knew she hadn't suffered from a nightmare. But she was at a point where she was beginning to question her sanity. Could it be that she was really sliding back into a demented state? A twilight of the mind in which everything was hopelessly blurred and confused! She was positive Derek had left his room and gone to the cellar just as she was certain that she had seen the hanging body of Captain Mills. But Derek claimed he hadn't been out of bed and he was there to prove

225

it, and Henry Mills swore that he'd seen no ghost in the cellar!

So it could be that she was moving back and forth between reality and a mad, imaginative state of mind. She would not know. Not be able to tell when she was losing reality and moving into a fantasy world. It was terrifying and made her think of her first days in the hospital when she'd continually hallucinated. What was she to do?

For the moment she had little choice but to try and sleep. And so she did. It was a fitful sleep with troubling dreams of her hospital days racing through her fevered mind. When she awoke in the morning she felt as if she hadn't slept at all. The only improvement she noted was that the fog had finally faded away and the sun was shining once again.

She got up and washed and dressed and started downstairs. She'd gotten no more than halfway down when she was met by Derek on his way up. The moment she saw his shocked face she knew that there had been news of Faith.

"What is it?" she asked.

He halted on the stairs, his hand on the railing. In a dull voice, he said, "They found her."

"Alive?"

"No."

"I'm so sorry!" Joyce said with sincerity.

"She was murdered."

"How?"

"Stabbed to death. Several times in the chest. And then her body was stuffed down an old abandoned well at her parents' place."

"Her parents' place!"

Derek nodded. "It's a big estate off the road to the monastery."

"Then it must have happened there!"

"Presumably. There were cigarette ashes in the living room and indications she'd been there with someone. She had the keys to the house and checked it when her parents were away."

Joyce asked, "Have they any idea who it was?"

"No. Constable Frink is bringing in the State Police. This is too big a case for him."

"Of course."

"I'll have to go over and see if I can do anything for Brook," her husband said.

"Yes. Is there anything I can do?"

"I doubt it. If there is I'll let you know."

"Do!" she said.

"I'd better get going," he said with a sigh. And he turned and went down the stairs again.

In the announcement of the murder everything else was overshadowed. Joyce didn't even have time to consider the eerie happenings of the night before and what they might mean. No one was interested in anything but the tragic fate that had overtaken Faith Patterson.

"She deserved it. She only received what she deserved," was Regina's comment, delivered with a sniff.

Mona had barely been able to hide her relief at being rid of her rival for Derek. "Faith was no good," she said. "I don't know why Brook put up with her for so long. Or what Derek ever saw in her."

It was Henry Mills who showed the only sorrow for the murdered girl aside from Joyce. He joined Joyce out in the garden and looking old and shaken said, "What a dreadful thing!"

"I agree," she said. "Who could be guilty of such a dreadful deed?"

"I wish I knew," the old man said with a sigh. "This is

going to be very hard on Brook. In spite of everything he loved her."

"I'm sure that's true," she agreed.

"We can only hope the one responsible is caught, and soon," the old man said. "Are you feeling more yourself this morning?"

"I'm weary," she said. "I didn't sleep well."

"I can imagine," Derek's uncle said sympathetically

Her eyes met his with frankness. "And I still say that Derek left his room and I saw that ghost."

The white-haired Henry looked embarrassed. "I can't believe it. I'm sorry."

"You don't have to," she said. "I know." She glanced in the direction of the house and saw David Chase coming towards them quickly.

When he came up to them he was almost breathless. He said, "I've just heard the news about Faith!"

"Yes. Isn't it awful!"

"It is," the young man agreed. "Who would want to kill her?"

Henry Mills said dryly, "Quite a few people."

The artist gave the white-haired man a look of reproval and said, "I mean, who actually might kill her?"

Henry Mills glanced down uneasily. "I keep thinking of Brook," he said.

David arched an eyebrow. "The wronged husband?"

"That's about it," the old man said.

Joyce protested, "No. I don't think so."

"Why?" David asked.

"I don't know. I just don't see him as a killer. He is not that sort of person."

"I wonder," Henry Mills said.

David sighed. "I was doing her portrait. I've actually

almost completed it. I was studying it just before I left my room and wondering what she looks like now. I'm sure that lovely face must have been shadowed with horror!"

Joyce said, "I understand she was stabbed several times."

Henry Mills added, "And the body stuffed in that old well. I'd say whoever did it was familiar with her parents' place. It must have been an islander."

She said, "That would narrow the suspects down considerably."

"The State Police are either here or coming on the morning ferry," the young artist said. "They should soon clear up the mystery."

Henry Mills grumbled. "I wouldn't be too sure. We've had two or three unsolved murders before. The State Police didn't perform any miracles then and I doubt if they will now. At least this time they'll get here. Last time was in winter and there was a storm and neither their patrol boat nor the ferry would risk a crossing from the mainland. So we waited for twenty-four hours before they showed up."

David Chase registered surprise. "I had no idea the island was so isolated that way."

"You should be here through a few real bad storms," Henry Mills told him. "And we were without electricity as well!"

"That's not apt to happen at this time of year," the young man said.

"Never can tell," Henry Mills warned him. "New England weather can be mighty cantankerous."

Joyce said, "I can't stand remaining here all day. I'm going into the village. I have a friend I want to see."

David asked her, "Can I ride along with you?"

"I'll take you directly to the museum if you like," she said.

"No need," he said. "Just drop me off on Main Street and I'll get a lift to the museum later. I have some shopping to do. A few small things."

"All right," she said. "I'll go get the car now."

They left the castle around ten-thirty. The sun was bright and the weather had turned warm once more. There were all kinds of pleasure craft along the shore and lots of tourist cars on the road.

David stared out at the holiday scene and said, "Everything goes on as if nothing had happened."

"I know," she agreed, busy at the wheel.

"How do you feel about the murder?" he asked as they drove on.

"Frightened," she said.

"That's natural."

"Frightened in more than one way," she amplified it for him and gave him a brief glance. "Something happened last night that has upset me terribly."

"What?"

"I had another experience."

"What sort of experience?"

She kept her eyes on the road ahead. "One which seemed very real to me but which everyone else doubted."

David said worriedly, "Another ghostly appearance?"

"Yes. Only this time there were other confusions concerning the living."

"Go on," the artist said.

Her face was shadowed with her worry. "I'm beginning to wonder if I'm really as well as I think I am. The news of the murder this morning took the attention from me. But when the first shock is over I'll be under scrutiny again."

"As to whether you're sane?"

"Yes," she said. "And this time I may not be my own best witness for I'm no longer sure. Perhaps my mind is playing tricks on me!"

"That could be dangerous thinking," the young artist in the front seat beside her said sharply.

"I can't help it! There has to be an answer," she lamented. "I can't be right and everyone else wrong."

"Why not?"

"You don't know the facts or you'd understand," she said. "And now I'm wondering something else. I had that vision about the murder. Could it be that I suffered some sort of mad spell and murdered Faith myself? I had the motive!"

"Joyce!" David Chase said in a shocked tone.

"I have to ask myself that question. I was insane. I may still be," she said.

"So you're giving in to them," the young man said bitterly.

She gave him a quick glance and saw that he was badly upset by what she'd said. She told him, "I must if my mind is sick."

"You're no sicker than I am," he cried. "I was in a hospital longer than you!"

"Some can be cured and others can't," she argued as she drove into the more built-up area just outside Dark Harbor.

"Let me tell you that I was considered incurable once," David Chase told her. "But I'm out and living a normal life today."

"You don't have blackouts or see things. I do."

"I have devastating spells of depression," he said. "You have no idea the kind of black well I can sink into. I have to fight to enjoy a normal existence."

"And I could be a murderer," she said.

"Then what did you do with the knife?"

"I don't know," she said.

"And how did you move the body and get it to that old well?" he demanded. "Have you ever tried to handle a dead body? Even one as thin as Faith's? I can tell you they are heavy and awkward. You couldn't manage it."

She brought the car to a stop at corner of the main street. Ignoring the passers-by and traffic she looked at him solemnly and said, "Then I must have seen the crime committed. The stabbing I saw must have been real. And the man in that captain's coat must have been the killer."

"It could be," David agreed. "Your husband wore a coat like the one you described. And he was missing from the dance."

"You're saying Derek killed her?"

He shrugged. "I'm saying he could have."

"You don't sound very sure," she said.

"Perhaps that is because I actually suspect someone else," the young artist said.

"Who?"

"The man I saw her in that car with the afternoon before her murder."

"Uncle Henry?"

"Yes."

She stared at him in bewilderment. "I can't see him doing it. You talked with him just now. What did you think?"

"I think he's acting suspicious," David Chase said. "But I can't expect you to listen to me."

"I'm too bewildered to know what I believe," she confessed.

David smiled grimly. "I like that expression on your face just now. If I ever paint you that is the way I mean to do it. And I shall call it, 'Fear on a beloved's face!' Do you approve of the title?"

She shook her head. "Please! Not now! Is this all right for you?"

"Fine," he said. "I'll see you later." And he got out of the car and mingled with the passers-by on the sidewalk.

She drove on to the cottage of Captain Miller. She found

the old man out studying his vegetable garden. He turned to her with a look of concern on his wizened face.

He said, "I kept thinking this had to be a bad morning for you."

"You've heard about Faith?"

"I guess the whole island has. It was on the radio."

"So there is a murderer among us," she said bitterly.

"Happens every so often," the old captain agreed.

"I'm terrified and sickened," she told him.

"Oh?" He was staring at her soberly.

She nodded, tears brimming in her eyes. "I think I've lost the battle. I believe I'm still insane."

Captain Zachary Miller whistled. "Now I never did expect to hear anything like that from you."

"I can't help it," she said. And she began to sob violently.

The little old man placed an arm around her gently and said, "Come into the house. You need something in the way of nerve tonic."

She let him lead her into the cottage and he saw her safely to a comfortable chair. Then he left her dabbing her eyes and returned a short time later with a glass of some yellowish liquid.

"Whiskey," he said. "A glass for me and one for you. It's just about the best nerve medicine I know of. Drink up!"

"It's so early in the day!" she protested. "And I never do drink whiskey."

"Then this is the time to start," Captain Zachary Miller informed her. "I'm not asking you to drink it—I'm telling you to do it."

In the face of his forcefulness she had little choice but to drink the strong liquor. Oddly enough after she'd had a little of it she began to feel somewhat better.

The old man was standing observing her. "Got over that

spell of blues?" he demanded.

"I feel somewhat better," she said.

"Keep drinking," he ordered her. "I'm feeling better myself." And he took a large swallow that almost emptied his glass.

She finished the whiskey and felt the warmth of it going through her. Her head was a trifle dizzy but she no longer felt as insecure as she had when she first arrived at the cottage.

"I'm all fuzzy-minded now," she told the old captain.

He chuckled. "That may be a very good thing for you. Now I want you to tell me what brought you here to me in such a state."

She was much more in control now and not afraid to speak frankly. So she said, "It began last night when I woke up and heard Derek leave his room." And she went into the whole story ending with her going back to the room in Henry's company and Derek showing himself and acting as if he'd never left his bed.

"That's a strange story," Captain Zachary Miller said.

"Do you wonder that I think I may be mad?" she asked.

The Captain frowned. "Let's skip that. I'm thinking about Derek. It's my belief that he's normally an honorable man. But for some reason he felt he had lie to you last night."

"You think he lied?"

"He must have," the old man said. "I think you were right. But he somehow got back to his room before you and his uncle arrived there and pretended innocence."

"Perhaps," she said.

"And that brings me to Henry Mills," Captain Zachary said. "He's always been a kind of odd, drunken character. I think there might be more to him wandering around and finding you in the cellar than meets the eye."

She nodded. "David Chase is suspicious of him!"

"David Chase?"

"Yes. The young artist who has been working at the museum this summer and who is living at the castle."

"I guess I haven't met him."

"No," she said. "He's very nice."

Captain Miller was studying her closely. "Is he a friend of yours?"

"One of my best friends."

The old man said, "Then maybe you ought to listen to him. You say he's suspicious that Henry Mills might have killed Faith?"

"Yes. He saw them in the old man's car together the afternoon before her murder."

"Uh, huh!" he said with interest.

"And Uncle Henry didn't mention it until I asked him. Then he pretended it wasn't important."

"Sounds like your friend, the artist, might be on the right track in suspecting Henry," the old captain said.

"There are times when he seems to think Derek might be guilty. He was involved with Faith. I've even worried that Derek might be the murderer and also trying to frighten me back into insanity. But now I've wound up thinking I may be insane. And guilty of any violence."

"I don't agree with you at all in that," Captain Miller said. "I think you're cured and that you should forget any ideas you may have otherwise."

She brightened. "Now you sound like David Chase."

The old man looked pleased. "From what you say that artist must be quite a smart fellow."

"He is," she said. "And there's another reason why we're so close. I promised him not to tell any of the family. But I feel I can mention it to you in confidence."

The captain's wizened face showed interest. "Please tell me," he said.

"You mustn't mention it to anyone else," she said. "But David once spent two years in a mental hospital."

"For what?"

"He had a serious breakdown. It was brought about by his smashing up a car in which the girl he was to marry was a passenger. He blamed himself for her death since they'd been quarreling at the time of the accident and this resulted in his breakdown. Just as my guilt over Lucie's death brought on mine."

Captain Zachary Miller nodded. "He is undoubtedly a sensitive young man."

"He is!" she agreed. "And he has found out the bitter lesson that I've learned. Once you're known to have had a mental illness many people look at you askance. That is why he has kept his own period of illness a secret here from everyone but me."

"I'm surprised that he told you," the old captain said.

She smiled wanly. "Sympathy. He was present when Mona made some very crude remarks about my having been insane."

"Sounds like Mona," the old man agreed.

"So I do have someone at the castle who understands my plight and has some concern for me."

Captain Zachary raised a bushy white eyebrow. "What about Derek? Don't you think he cares?"

"My husband is torn so many different ways," she said. "I feel he cares but I also think he fears my mind is still unsound."

The old captain hunched in the chair he'd settled in. He said, "I think you've made one mistake."

"What?"

"You've not given these ghostly visitations enough thought."

She gave the captain a puzzled stare. "But by all the rules of therapy that is the one thing I shouldn't do. Brood on the visions I've had."

Captain Zachary Miller sighed. "I don't know anything about modern psychiatry, but I do know the old saw about visions often suggesting portents. That's what I have in mind now. It could be these spells you've had may offer some meaning."

"I've never considered that," she admitted, fascinated by this new viewpoint on the hauntings.

"My advice is to think about them. Especially that scene you witnessed on the grounds the other night. Try to recall any details about the figures, both the man and woman. And out of it you may get some clue."

"I've been trying to block remembrance from my mind."

"Don't any longer. Try to picture that night again," the old captain advised. "It may offer you more than you can guess."

"I suppose it's worth a try," she said, not quite convinced.

The old man rose from his chair. "Now I want you to stay here for lunch with me. Since I've been on my own I've become a fair-to-middling cook. And I want you to sample my lobster bisque."

Joyce did not need much persuading to remain with the old man for lunch. Being there with him was like a reprieve from all the terrors she'd endured at the castle. For a little while she listened to his talk about the old days on the island and enjoyed the excellent lunch he'd prepared for her. But by mid-afternoon she felt she must go.

"There may be some word about who killed Faith," she

said. "I'm going to the museum. I think at least David and Derek will be there."

Captain Miller warned her. "Remember what I told you. Think about those hauntings. And take care. The one who killed Faith might decide to strike again and you could be marked as the next victim."

She gave a tiny shudder. "Why?"

"We'd have to know the killer to guess that," was the old Captain's comment. "I know Constable Frink well. If I see him I must have a chat with him about it all."

She left the cottage and began the drive to the museum. In the time she'd spent there the fog had swept in from the ocean again to once more overwhelm the sunshine and make the island a grim, gray place. Admittedly this sort of day was better suited to her own bleak mood than the sunshine had been.

She was thinking about Zachary Miller's advice and wondering if trying to remember would really help. She thought of the night of the party when she'd stood alone in the darkness and watched the two costumed figures appear from the chapel. Then the attack on the woman had been carried out before her eyes. What did she really remember about the man or the woman?

The costume the man had been wearing had fitted her earlier conception of Captain Peter Mills. But Derek had been wearing that sort of outfit for the ball and so had David. Had the figure she'd seen in any way resembled Derek? Had there been anything characteristic of Derek in the way the phantom had moved about? She tried to recall it all more clearly but wasn't able to.

When she reached the museum she saw there was a sign on the front door announcing that it was closed temporarily. This didn't surprise her since most of the executive staff were affected by the death of Faith.

The rear door of the museum was open and she went in by it. When she reached the big lobby she found it to be deserted with the colorful ball decorations still only partly dismantled. There was a strangely tragic air about the scene. She stood there for a moment touched by the macabre atmosphere of a carnival interrupted.

She was also surprised by the silence which filled the old building. Normally there were always a few sounds to be heard. Now it was grimly still. There was no sign of David nor of her husband. She mounted the stairway to the executive offices and visited them one after the other. They were all as empty and silent as the lobby. And she felt a chill of fear at being there alone in the deserted building.

How odd it was! And how much in contrast to the bustling place it had been before the ball. Where had everyone gone? She stood in Derek's private office for a moment and then decided to go back down to the lobby. It occurred to her that some news break on Faith's murder might have taken them all away from the museum to Brook Patterson's home.

Slowly descending the stairway she searched the lobby and the front reception room for a sign of someone without any results. She then started to leave by the door which she'd used to come in. As she walked along the corridor to the rear door she saw that the door that led to the cellar archives was open. She hesitated next to it. Perhaps someone was down there. She debated whether to see or not.

She finally decided to go down to the bottom of the stairs and call out. If anyone was down there she'd be certain to get a reply. Having made this decision she went down the stairs to the modern cellar with its many shelves of books and containers of special papers and records.

Joyce stood there between the aisles of bookshelves with her heart pounding hard. Her pretty face wore a look of fear as she peered down the long, shadowed corridor of the book-shelves nearest to her.

And she called out, "Is anyone there?"

There was no reply and yet she had the eerie feeling that she was not alone. She moved on to the next aisle between the bookshelves and again peered down the dark, corridor in search of a familiar face.

"It's Joyce," she called. "Is anyone working down here?"

Her voice echoed in the silent cellar and increased her fear. She decided that there could be no one there and started back towards the stairs.

As she went by the final aisle before mounting the stairs she again looked down the length of the murky corridor. And this time she saw something. But not what she expected or wanted to see. Moving up the aisle towards her from the dark shadows was the ghost of Captain Mills in cap and brass-buttoned jacket.

"No!" she screamed at the apparition and turned and raced up the stairs to the ground level of the museum. She was filled with terror and sobbing again as she breathlessly reached the corridor above.

And there she had another surprise! She almost ran into the arms of her husband. Derek had been coming into the building as she made her frantic exit from the cellar.

He halted to stare at her in astonishment. "What now?"

Joyce stumbled against him and moaned. "The ghost! I've seen it again. Down there!"

"Stop it!" her husband said angrily.

"But I did!"

Derek took her by the arms and held her a short way from him as he stared at her with stern sadness. "This has got to stop!" he said. "This madness of yours can't be allowed to go on!"

CHAPTER TWELVE

Joyce shrank from her husband's angry impatience. And then she heard something which made her cry out, "Listen!"

"What?" Derek demanded.

"On the stairs," she said. And she turned towards the open door as the sound of footsteps grew louder.

And then the phantom appeared and stood gazing at them in a contrite fashion. "I'm terribly sorry," he said. "I suppose I frightened you." It was David Chase in the cap and brass-buttoned jacket.

Derek let go of her and turned his anger on the young artist. "What are you doing in that outfit?" he said in annoyance.

David took off the cap with an apologetic air. He said, "I saw it here and put it on through impulse. I wanted to see myself in the outfit again before I gave it back. Then I decided I wanted to look at some magazines of the period with illustrations of similar uniforms. So I went down to the archives without bothering to take off these things."

"You frightened my wife badly!" Derek told him.

"It wasn't his fault entirely," she protested. "I should have taken a second look and I would have recognized him."

"I tried to tell you who it was," David said unhappily. "But by that time you were running away in tears!"

Derek looked upset. He told the young man, "You did a stupid thing in putting that on in the first place. Take it off!"

"Of course!" David said and hastily took off the long coat.

Joyce gave a deep sigh of relief. "Well, at least that's one ghostly presence explained."

Derek eyed her sternly again and said, "The chances are that all the other hauntings could be put down to your fears and some logical explanation like a shadow or reflection."

"I wish I could think so," she told him. "Is there any news?"

"Nothing," her husband told her. "I've just come from Brook Patterson's now. He's in a bad state."

"I can imagine," she said.

David stood with the cap and coat in his hands and asked in an embarrassed manner, "Do you need me here any longer?"

"No," Derek said. "I have to go up to the office and make a few phone calls then I'll drive all of us home."

He left them to go upstairs and she and an apologetic David strolled slowly into the lobby. David said, "That was downright silly of me, dressing up like that. But I never guessed anyone would come by."

She gave him a look of grim amusement. "I certainly walked into it. When I saw you I had no doubt that the ghost of Captain Peter was stalking me here."

"I don't think your husband will soon forgive me," David worried.

"Of course he will. You meant no harm."

"But I did needlessly give you a bad fright."

"It's over, let's forget it."

David gave her a grateful look. "That's kind of you, Joyce. But then you always have been kind to me."

"And you to me," she said. "I've been at Captain Miller's most of the afternoon since we parted. He's a wonderful old man."

"I don't think I know him," the artist said.

"I don't believe so," she said. "I often go to him for advice."

"Oh?"

"He came up with an interesting suggestion. He thinks that rather than try and blot out the memory of my ghostly experiences I ought to concentrate on them. To try and recall every detail of them."

David frowned. "But that could be harmful!"

"I said the same thing and he disagreed. He thinks by remembering details I may be able to come upon some clue. Some hint of the murderer's identity. He assumes that what I saw on the lawn that night was the murder."

David said, "It was much more likely to have been a hallucination on your part. I don't like to advise you but I'd be careful of that old man's dabbling in psychiatry. He might do you harm."

"I wonder," she mused. "In many ways I have a great deal of confidence."

"But this is advice of a medical nature," the artist worried. "I think it should only come from a doctor."

"Perhaps," she said, though she was still intrigued by the captain's suggestion. On the other hand she could understand David's concern. It did go against all the psychiatric theories she knew.

Derek came downstairs at this point and they all left for the castle. She drove her own car while David rode back with Derek. She was glad of this since it gave her more time to be alone. She drove along in the thick fog with her mind whirling with thoughts. She'd gotten over the minor scare of seeing David in the captain's outfit and now was reviewing the whole period of her return to the island once again.

It was strange but the thing that was most worrisome to her was the experience of the previous night in which Derek had vanished from his room and then returned to it in her absence. His denial of ever having left it troubled her more than anything else. She knew it to be a lie. And if he had lied to her once it was entirely possible that he might have lied to her many times.

Derek still remained in her mind as the most logical suspect in Faith's killing. She knew there had been some kind of quarrel between them. Perhaps Faith had threatened to destroy his reputation on the island and the Mills' pride in family was strong.

Once again she tried to practice the advice given her by old Captain Miller. She had a nagging feeling about the male figure in her vision of that night. There was something she felt she should remember about him but couldn't.

The castle was wreathed in the heavy fog when she arrived there. She parked her car and went into the house still occupied by her thoughts. Derek had already gone up to his own room and she followed him up the stairway.

He came in to join her after she'd showered and dressed for dinner and was combing her hair. He came and stood by her, keeping silent for a moment as he watched her.

Then he said, "Are you over your scare?"

"Yes," she said. "I'm fine."

His handsome face was thoughtful. "I think you ought to learn a lesson from that. Often what you think are ghosts are not."

"So it seems," she said, rising.

Derek told her, "I find you somewhat different in your manner towards me tonight. You're suddenly aloof. It is because of last night? Do you still think I lied to you?"

Her eyes met his. "You want the truth?"

"Yes."

"Very well," she said. "I'm positive you lied to me. But I can't decide why."

Derek crimsoned. "Well, I asked you to be frank."

"And I have been."

"Do you think I had any part in Faith's murder?"

"I don't want to believe it," she said. "But the way you've acted has made me wonder. And also the way you've acted since I returned here."

"I told you I wasn't having an affair with Faith," he protested. "She just made it appear that I was."

"What does Brook Patterson think?"

Derek looked guilty. He said, "I'm afraid she made him believe it, too. She was an evil woman in many ways."

"So Brook is also suspicious of you?" she said.

He spread his hands in a gesture of despair. "Everyone is under suspicion who knew Faith. And a lot more who didn't. I only hope they find her killer soon before more reputations are hurt."

She said, "I don't want it to be you, Derek. But I feel there is a barrier between us. That you're hiding something from me and I don't know what it is."

He said, "I've been put off by your illness. I try to make myself believe you're well again. But whenever anything happens to make me question, I find myself not sure about you."

"That means you're letting me down," she told him.

"You know how Mother and Mona are. All the time you were gone they drilled it into me that you'd been mentally ill before I ever met you and it wasn't likely you'd ever fully recover."

She said, "Isn't that something you must decide for yourself?"

"Dr. Taylor has no doubts about you."

"And you still do?" she said. "That seems significant. Do you want to be rid of me?"

"Why do you ask that?"

"It might explain a lot," she said. She was thinking of the ghostly intrusions and that he might be responsible for them if he wanted her declared insane.

He looked unhappy. "We never seem able to really talk. We may as well go downstairs and join the others."

"Very well," she said, giving him a significant look. "But you didn't answer my question, did you?"

Cocktails were served in the living room. Everyone was there. The fog and approaching evening had conspired to make it almost dark. There were lighted candles on the sideboards and tables around the room to give it soft, gracious lighting.

Regina stood in the center of the room and announced loudly, "I'm now at the age where I prefer candlelight. I think it so much more flattering and civilized."

David Chase stood by her and smiled his agreement. "This is a charming room and a charming atmosphere you've created."

Uncle Henry brought Joyce the martini she'd requested. He stood with her a moment, to ask, "Any developments?"

"No," she said.

"There had better be soon," Uncle Henry said grimly. "I hear there's a lot of ugly talk in the town about Faith and Derek having been lovers."

She glanced over where Derek was standing with his mother and Dave and said, "You think it may lead the police to Derek?"

"I'd be surprised if it didn't," was the old man's grim reply.

He went back to the sideboard to get another drink and she found herself wondering whether he was concerned for Derek or for himself. If the police dug deep enough they would also find a link between Henry and the attractive Faith.

"You're looking very serious!" It was Mona who had come up by her to make the comment.

Joyce regarded her sister-in-law with some surprise. It was not often that Mona cultivated her company. She said, "I was thinking of something."

There was a mocking light in Mona's eyes. "It's an odd co-incidence," she said. "But I've been thinking deeply about something, too."

"Really?"

"Yes," Mona went on almost casually. "I've been recalling all your supposed experiences with ghosts since you've been here. And of how you were so sure you'd seen Captain Peter Mills re-enact the murder of his wife the night of the party."

"Well?"

"Well," Mona continued, "since we know you've been insane I wondered if you hadn't imagined it all. And then made part of it come true by murdering Faith yourself."

It came out so calmly that Joyce was stunned. She said, "What ever gave you that crazy idea?"

"It's possible you could have done it," Mona insisted.

"I can think of a dozen reasons why I wouldn't," she answered.

"But are you really able to be sure?" Mona taunted her. "You still have those spells."

Mona then strolled away from her so that she could make no reply. And Joyce felt real fear once again. It was as if they were all banding together to prove her insane and the murderer of Faith. And if they all did stick together in their story it could be a damning one.

She had reported being frightened by the ghosts and that would be used against her. Dr. Taylor favored her but if all the Mills family exerted their influence with him he might decide against her. She glanced down the room where David was still talking to her mother-in-law and decided that he was the only one friend she could depend on.

"What are you frowning so for?" It was Derek who had come up to her.

"Was I? I didn't realize," she said.

"You've been behaving most strangely," he said, his eyes fixed on her. "I've been watching you."

A spurt of defiance made her say, "If you'd protect me from your sister perhaps I wouldn't be so nervous!"

Derek asked, "What about Mona?"

"Ask her what she said to me," she dared him.

"I will," he promised. "As soon as dinner is over."

They all went into the dining room. Again it was a trying experience for Joyce. Uncle Henry was seated beside her and he tried to make conversation but she gave him little assistance so that after a while he abandoned the effort and ate his dinner in silence.

By the time they left the dining room it was dark. She was lingering in the foyer when a car drove up in front of the castle. She at once tensed, feeling certain that it would bring some news of the murder.

The doorbell rang and because she was there she opened the door. A tall, thin man stood in the doorway wearing a long raincoat and a battered felt hat. He doffed the hat at once to reveal gray hair and she recognized Constable Titus Frink.

He spoke with a strong New England accent, saying, "Sorry to disturb you, Mrs. Mills, but I need to ask a few questions."

"Of course," she said. "Come in."

"Thank you," the tall, lanky man said and entered.

"Do you wish to speak to my husband?" she asked.

He looked rather embarrassed. "No," he said. "Not especially. I've already talked to him. Right now I'd like to check a few things with you."

She felt a little faint from fear. Was the noose already

dropping around her neck? Was this the start of a wily plot to declare her the murderess and insane?

She managed, "Very well."

He had taken off his raincoat and draped it over his arm. "Is there some place we could talk in private?" he wanted to know.

"Yes," she said. "The study. I'll show you the way."

She took him down the hall to the study. For a moment she hoped that Derek might be there and somehow help her. But he wasn't at his desk and the study was empty. She went in and the island law officer followed her.

He shut the door and then said, "I don't do this very well. Here on the island we don't have many murder investigations. So just overlook it if I make a lot of mistakes."

"It's all right," she said facing him. "I want to help if I can but I know very little."

"I understand," he said, studying her in a very intent manner.

"What can I tell you?"

He took out a notebook and pencil and opened the book. "I have let the State Police do most of this. They're a lot better at it," he apologized.

"Is there any new word of the murderer?"

The lanky man stared at her over his book. "We've got a couple of clues. But they could turn out to be useless. It's a long, trying business, Mrs. Mills."

"I'm certain it is."

His shrewd gray eyes never left her, it seemed. "You were away sick quite a spell?"

"Yes," in a small voice.

"But you're all right now?"

"Yes," she said, wilting under his continued study. "Yes, I'd say I was all right."

"According to your husband you're still very nervous."

"At times, yes."

"But not all the time?"

"No."

He hesitated. "You have been complaining of seeing ghosts, haven't you?"

She swallowed hard. "Who told you that?"

"It's known," was his non-committal answer. "What do you have to say about it?"

"What has my seeing ghosts to do with the murder of Faith Patterson?" She felt she had to somehow fight back.

The lanky police officer drawled, "That's a real good question, Mrs. Mills."

"Well?"

He continued to stare at her. "The night of the murder you were at the party?"

"Yes."

"You complained of having a headache," he went on. "And I drove you home."

"You were very kind."

"I could tell you were ill and upset," he said. "As I recall you complained of a bad headache?"

"I did," she said remembering it all.

He sighed. "According to all I can find out, your husband and Faith Patterson were missing from the party at about the same time. You were actually looking for Mr. Mills, weren't you?"

"Yes," she said. "But I can't say that he wasn't still at the party. There were so many people."

"I know," the lanky, gray-haired man said. "I left you here. It was foggy much like it is now."

"It was."

"What happened then?"

She gave him a frightened look. "I didn't go right in. I stayed on the lawn. The cold air made me feel better."

"And?"

"I wandered towards the old chapel. And then I heard voices. The voices of a man and a woman. They seemed to be quarreling."

"Could you hear what they were saying?" Constable Titus Frink asked.

"No."

"Could you tell to whom the voices belonged?"

She shook her head. "I'm afraid not. I wasn't really myself. My head was aching so. I was very confused."

The constable eyed her stolidly. "You weren't yourself?"

"No. You saw that I was ill."

"Go on," he urged her.

"Then I saw the ghostly figures come out of the chapel. The woman ran across the lawn towards the cliffs. The man dressed in a captain's costume like the one I saw the ghost of Captain Peter Mills wearing pursued her and stabbed her! I cried out and fainted!"

"The man was dressed in a whaling captain's uniform?"

"Yes."

"And the woman?"

"Some sort of dress of another era. It was foggy and dark, I only saw them a moment. I can't be sure!" Her voice broke and she sank down into a nearby chair.

"I don't like doing this," Constable Titus Frink told her. "But it happens to be my job."

"I know."

"Not that I'm all that competent at it," he said with a sigh. "There's no doubt in your mind about all this?"

"No."

"You saw the attack take place on the lawn here?"

"Yes. But I couldn't have seen the murder. Faith's body was found in the well on her father's estate at the other end of the island."

"The State Police aren't sure she was murdered there," was the reply of the police officer. "So there's no reason why the crime couldn't have been committed here and the body taken to her father's place."

"I see," she said.

"Maybe you saw the killing?"

"I thought it was a ghostly repeat of a crime that was committed here more than a century ago," she explained. "The ghosts have shown themselves to me at various times."

The lanky man looked grim. "That's not the kind of statement that would stand up very good in a court."

"I suppose not," she agreed in a despairing voice.

"Do you remember anything about the man? Anything special?"

She paused and considered. "He looked exactly like the ghost I'd seen before."

"That's all?"

"I'm afraid so. I fainted and when I came to I was in my own room with Dr. Taylor and my husband there."

The lanky man closed the notebook and put it and the pencil in his pocket. "Well, thank you," he said.

She got up from the chair. "Have I helped any?"

He gave her a strange look. "That's hard to say at this point, Mrs. Mills. It's sort of like a jigsaw puzzle. You pick up a piece here and a piece there but you don't make much sense until you get all the pieces and put them together."

"I hope you soon have the puzzle complete," she said.

"I have a feeling we will," he said. "I may have some other questions later. I'll let you know."

She saw him to the door and just as he was about to leave

Derek came down the stairs. He looked startled at seeing the constable there and quickly crossed over to him.

"I didn't realize you were here," Derek said.

Constable Frink put on his raincoat. "I just had a few questions to ask your missus. I'm on my way back to Dark Harbor now. I'm expecting an officer on the night ferry."

Derek looked worried. "Then there's nothing I can do?"

"No," the constable said. And he bade them good night and left.

As soon as Derek closed the front door after him he turned to her and asked, "What did he want to know?"

She made a small despairing gesture. "He questioned me about the night of the murder."

"What about it?" Derek's voice was taut.

"Mostly about the ghostly vision I had."

"And?"

"Nothing," she said. "He didn't seem to draw any conclusions from what I said."

Derek frowned. "I know him well enough to be certain he didn't come here without something in mind."

"I've told you all I can," she said.

"I'm going to Dark Harbor," Derek said abruptly. "I have a few things to do."

"When will you be back?"

"Soon," he said. He gave her a troubled glance. "You mustn't worry about the constable coming here. I'll find out what he had in mind." And he took her in his arms and gave her a perfunctory kiss. Then he went on out to his car.

Alone in the shadowed foyer she felt all the old fears press in on her. She had noted a strange tension in Derek's manner and she felt it had to do with the constable's visit. That her husband had been badly upset by it and especially by the fact the constable hadn't even attempted to see him. She had caught a frightened gleam in Derek's eyes as he left.

This indicated to her that Constable Frink must suspect Derek of the murder of Faith Patterson. It was not surprising that all the gossip had pointed to her husband as the murderer. And it could be that they were right. She racked her mind and tried to fit Derek in with the costumed man she'd seen attacking the woman on the lawn the night of the ball. She found it difficult to make him part of the picture.

But she could put that down to her natural reluctance to accepting the fact her husband was guilty. Slowly she made her way upstairs to her room. The house was strangely silent again and she paced up and down in her room trying to think more clearly about that night.

On an impulse she decided to venture into her husband's room. She had rarely gone in there since he'd decreed they should have separate rooms. Now she was moved by her suspicions. She entered the room and looked carefully around her. Then she opened the various drawers in the dresser and studied their contents. Nothing to suggest any guilt on Derek's part.

Next she moved to the closet. Some clothes hung there but they seemed innocent enough. She was about to close the closet door when her eyes caught the shelf. And she decided to reach up and see if there was anything there. To the eye the shelf seemed empty but you couldn't be sure.

Standing on tiptoe she reached up and felt something. Two pieces of what seemed like stiff parchment. She drew them down and they were about twenty-four-inches square. Both of them were artist's black and white sketches. One was of a woman of another century judging by dress and hairdo and the other was of Faith! And both of them had been mutilated in the same dreadful way!

A slash of vivid red paint had been drawn down from the left eye in each of the paintings. It gave the appearance of the eye bleeding and she immediately thought of the legend and how Ann Mills had been stabbed in the eye! The same mad mind which had vandalized these sketches by David Chase must have schemed to murder Faith!

She stared at the sketches in stunned horror. There was only one explanation as far as she was concerned. Derek had stolen these sketches from David Chase's room and mutilated them. Then he had hidden them away. It seemed certain her husband had gone on to stab Faith to death in the manner of the legend!

How long had Derek had the paintings hidden away? She wondered. Had David Chase missed them and said nothing about it? Kept silent in an effort to protect her husband? Determined to find this out she left her husband's room with the sketches and went directly to David's room at the other end of the hall. She knocked on the door and waited.

After a moment he opened the door and stared at her in mild surprise. "What is it, Joyce?"

"I have something to show you," she said. And she went in and offered the paintings to him. "Have you said nothing about missing these to protect Derek?"

The young artist studied the mutilated sketches grimly. "So this is what he did to them!"

"When did he take them from you?"

David turned to her. "He stole them out of my room weeks ago. One is a preliminary sketch of my study of Faith and the other is an imaginative study of a long ago lady. I suspected that he must have taken them but I wasn't sure."

Her eyes were wide with fear. "David, he must be the killer."

The artist nodded slowly. "Was it ever that much of a puzzle to you?"

"Yes. I didn't want to believe it. I love him! In spite of all that's happened, all I've found out nothing can change that."

David said, "You'll have to learn to face it."

"The constable was here just a little while ago. I'm sure he knows something he wouldn't tell me."

"Oh?"

She gave the young artist a frightened glance. "He's probably about to arrest Derek. And I think these ruined sketches should be submitted in evidence."

"Without question," David said. "And there is something else which proves him guilty beyond question."

"What?"

"I'd prefer to show you," he said. "Come with me!"

He took her by the arm and led her along the corridor and down the stairway. Then they went out into the foggy night as he continued to guide her in the direction of the old chapel.

She looked up at him. "Are you taking me to the chapel?"

"Yes. After you see what is there you won't have any doubts as to whether Derek is a murderer."

"What is it?" she asked.

"You'll see."

"How long have you suspected Derek?"

"Soon after I first came here," the young artist said. "He and Faith were carrying on shamelessly."

"When I was in hospital?"

"Yes."

They had crossed the wet lawn and were now at the steps of the old chapel. He led her into the dark doorway and told her, "We must go to the belfry tower."

"Why?"

"That is where the important evidence is," he said. "I'll go ahead. The stairs are winding and steep. Be careful."

"I will," she promised, wondering what they'd discover up there. Perhaps some items belonging to Faith.

They went up the winding stairs until they reached the top

and came out in the open. The great bell hung in the center of the open-sided tower. From where they were they could look down on the castle.

She said, "It frightens me! It's much higher than I thought."

"I know," the young man at her side agreed.

"Where is the evidence?" she wanted to know.

"One minute," he said. "I had to safely hide it to be sure he didn't come back and find it."

She gazed at the young artist barely able to tell his expression because of the fog and darkness. She said, "So what I saw that night was not fantasy? It was Derek murdering Faith!"

"Yes."

"And then he took her body back through Dark Harbor in the car. Took her to that well on her father's estate?"

David nodded. "That's right. You were the sole witness to the killing."

"Now he'll want to kill me or prove me insane," she said tensely.

"Either way he'd be safe," David said.

"All those other ghostly appearances were tricks of his as he tried to terrify me into another breakdown. He must have even used that sketch to make it seem I was seeing the face of that girl murdered here so long ago. The sketch of yours which he ruined with that splash of red paint!"

"You have it all figured out," David told her. "Now wait until I get what I came to show you."

"Hurry," she said.

"I will," he promised as he vanished down the stairway.

She stood leaning against the light railing of the tower. The windows of the castle showed as squares of amber light in the thick fog. She could hear the distant, ghostly wash of the waves on the shore. The foghorn gave its melancholy call every so often. She continued to wait and shivered from the cold.

Now she began thinking of that night again. And she remembered what David had once said to her. That she couldn't have killed Faith and disposed of her body. It would have been too heavy a task for her. But not for Derek! Then she had a second startling thought, how could David know that Faith's dead body had been so heavy?

The answer came to her just as she saw a motion on the stairway and knew it was David Chase returning. She drew away from the stairway as a startling figure emerged from the shadows.

It was the ghostly Captain Peter Mills in his full uniform and cap. He began to slowly cross to her. And she saw the grinning face of David in the semi-darkness! The face of an insane man!

"No!" she screamed.

"You didn't guess!" he exulted. "You never doubted me! And neither will any of the others! When I finish with you here tonight it will all be over!"

"You're the one! You killed her!" Joyce said as she kept moving away from him in the narrow confines of the belfry.

"She led me on and then laughed at me!" David cried insanely. "So I killed her just as I'm going to kill you!"

"You played the ghost? Why?"

His voice became low as he drew dangerously close to her. He talked swiftly, almost incoherently. "It was destined! Fate sent me here! I knew it had to be! I'm the reincarnation of Captain Peter just as you are Ann living here on earth again. And I must kill you to make it all come out right!"

"Please!" she begged him.

His answer was a wild laugh as he seized her by the throat

and a tense struggle began between them. She knew from the start it would be a one-sided affair. That she would have no chance. He was throttling her and at the same time he raised her body to let it topple over the side of the tower. She fought back fiercely enough to delay her fate. But it would only be a delay. In another few seconds the madman would send her over the side to certain death!

He had her poised on the railing, ready to send her over, when she thought she heard a shout from the stairway. Then he surprisingly let her go. She slumped down on the floor of the belfry. There were angry male shouts and then she was vaguely aware of a mighty struggle taking place in the small area of the tower.

There was a loud splintering of wood and a kind of wild, melancholy howl and then silence. In the next instant she felt someone come to her and help her to her feet. "Are you badly hurt?" It was Derek's voice, anxious and breathless.

"No," she moaned, looking up at him. "David?"

"He's down there on the ground. He went through the railing. The constable is with him. I doubt if he's alive!"

She had dozens of other questions to ask him along with her offering her forgiveness for ever having doubted him. But she could not manage to stave off fainting any longer.

When she came to she was on a chaise in the living room. Derek was sitting by her and behind him were Uncle Henry, the constable, and a shocked-looking Regina and Mona.

Derek smiled at her. "Dr. Taylor is on the way."

"I'll be all right," she said. "What about him?"

"Dead," Derek said grimly. "And better so. He was insane, you know."

"I found it out too late," she said. "How did you know?"

Constable Frink took a step forward. "I told him, Mrs.

Mills. You see Captain Zachary came to me and repeated a conversation you'd had with him. Once we knew David Chase had a psychiatric record it led to other discoveries. Including that he'd been the one carrying on with Faith Patterson. Her husband found an incriminating note from him in his wife's drawer this afternoon. Before that he'd blamed your husband. Faith had made it seem that way."

"I know," she agreed. She glanced at Derek, "How did you come to have the sketches and why did you mutilate them with that red paint?"

Derek smiled grimly. "I took the sketches from David's room to give them to the constable. You found them before I could do it. I didn't mutilate the sketches, David did that himself. Part of his madness. If you look upstairs you'll find the complete portrait of Faith is damaged in the same way."

"When I found the sketches he must have known that you were on to him," she said.

"Yes," Derek agreed. "So he made up his mind to get you out of the way quickly."

"He would have pretended that it was a suicide," she reasoned. "That I had leapt from the tower during one of my spells."

"Very likely," Derek agreed. "But it would have done no good. The constable was ready to arrest him for Faith's murder in any case."

"Saves us the trouble of a trial," the constable said with New England wisdom. "I'll be getting back to Dark Harbor. The State Police will be waiting for him there. I'll want to tell him what happened. I'll be back later."

Derek got to his feet. "Thank you, Constable."

"Your missus can thank old Zachary Miller. He's the one who saw through it all."

The constable left and Derek told his mother and adopted

sister, "There's no need to remain here. I can get along well enough until the doctor comes."

Regina Mills sniffed. "Well, if that's all the thanks we get for our trying to help we might as well go. Come along, Mona." And the two strode out of the living room and up the stairs.

When they were alone Joyce smiled up at her handsome husband, "That's the first time I've ever really heard you put them in their place."

Derek sat by her again and took her hand in his. "You would be likely to hear a lot more of it if we continued living here. But I have something else in mind. There's a fine new house for sale on Monastery Road."

She raised herself on an elbow. "Then you're not thinking of leaving the island. I'm glad!"

His eyes showed a twinkle in them. "I thought you hated Pirate Island and Dark Harbor and everything about them."

"That was before," she said, her face glowing with her new happiness. "Now I know it is going to be different!" And she reached out for him to take her in his arms.